The
Redward Edward Papers

The
Redward Edward Papers

AVRAM DAVIDSON

DOUBLEDAY & COMPANY, INC.
GARDEN CITY, NEW YORK
1978

"Sacheverell," *Fantasy & Science Fiction,* March 1964. Copyright © 1964 by Mercury Press, Inc.

"Lord of Central Park," *Ellery Queen Mystery Magazine,* October 1970 as "Manhattan Night's Entertainment." Copyright © 1970 by Avram Davidson

"The Grantha Sighting," *Fantasy & Science Fiction,* April 1958. Copyright © 1958 by Fantasy House, Inc.

"Singular Events. . . ." *Fantasy & Science Fiction,* February 1962. Copyright © 1962 by Mercury Press, Inc.

"Dagon," *Fantasy & Science Fiction,* October 1959. Copyright © 1959 by Mercury Press, Inc.

"The Redward Edward Papers" and all additional material copyright © 1978 by Avram Davidson

ISBN: 0-385-02058-9
Library of Congress Catalog Card Number 74-27578
Foreword and Introduction copyright © 1978 by
Doubleday & Company, Inc.
Copyright © 1978 by Avram Davidson
All Rights Reserved
Printed in the United States of America
First Edition

Contents

Foreword

by MICHAEL KURLAND

Some of you who read this collection are venturing into
the arcane, erudite world of Avram Davidson for the first
time. Probability theory insists that, despite the acres of
trees cut down to provide the wood pulp, the scores of
dragons killed and bled to provide the ink, some of you
will not have read any of the earlier published works of
Don Avram. For that few I issue the following warning:
breathe steadily through the nose, if possible, proceed
slowly, and examine the foliage. Do not search for mean-
ings, as they are scattered like empty oyster shells around
the Walrus.

How to describe Avram's writing? Well, nothing ventured . . . An Avram Davidson story, if you are that sort
of born librarian who must categorize it, will probably lie
somewhat on one side of *Scaramouche* and *Portrait of the
Artist as a Young Man,* but still on the other side of
Topper and *The Idiot.* I hope that helps. The prose itself
will be purely and indisputably Davidson. It is rumored
that a team of irredentist publishers in the Southwest are
attempting, with the aid of a warlock, an experimental
computer, and the faculty of a small nondenominational
college, to duplicate the rich mosaic that is Davidson
prose. They are doomed to ignominious failure, I am

proud to say (proud because I've always wanted to use "ignominious" in a sentence [and now I've managed to use it twice in the same one]).

Avram Davidson is the master of the parenthetical phrase. Many's the time I've seen a parenthetical phrase groveling before Avram's stern hand, begging for mercy. But he takes them and twists them to his will, making them do much more than the pale grammarians who invented them would ever have believed them capable. In the spirit of the true explorer, Avram is ever pushing and prodding at the bounds of language, and discovering new and previously uncharted uses for words, phrases, and other tools of the trade.

To call Avram Davidson a writer's writer would be redundant. Or, at least, prone to misunderstanding. Is a dentist's dentist one who trains other dentists? Or one who only works on the teeth of other dentists? Or one who only takes patients referred by other dentists? And who will shave the barber? Heal the physician? But it is true that if you are sensitive to the sounds of language and take a joy from its nuances, you will delight in the printed words of Avram Davidson. Or, indeed, if you are ever so fortunate, from his spoken words. And if you read, or listen to, the words of Avram Davidson, this will increase your sensitivity to, and your joy in, the sounds and nuances of language.

Avram was born in the first half of this century in Yonkers, New York, a town that keeps stridently trying to maintain its identity despite the looming presence of New York City, the center of town being a mere fifteen miles north of Manhattan. If I were Avram I would now insert, parenthetically, that the land was purchased from the Indians by the Dutch East India Company in 1639, granted in 1646 to "Jonkheer" Van der Donck, and was later a part of Philipse Manor, not becoming incorporated as the

Village of Yonkers until 1855. I would. As a youth Avram
went to sea. We were at war at the time, and Navy Hospital Corpsman Davidson served with the Marines in the
South Pacific. He ventured as far into northern China as
Peiping, whereupon the Chinese immediately changed
the name to Peking and closed the country to all foreigners for twenty-five years.

Except for a stint as editor of *The Magazine of Fantasy
& Science Fiction,* during which he picked up the curious idea that other writers should buy him drinks, Avram
has been a full-time Creator of Myth since he emerged
only slightly scathed from the Great War To End All
Wars (part 2). His writings have been awarded the *Hugo*
for science fiction, the *Edgar* and the Queen's Award for
mystery fiction, and most recently the *Howard* for fantasy. He holds these awards in the proper disdain, does
not allow them to affect his writing, and only carries them
about with him on Tuesdays.

Avram lives in or about Berkeley, California, according
to his whim—and he has a whim of iron. He holds a ninth-
degree black belt in idiosyncrasy, being the originator of
several of the more complex modern moves. He is not an-
tagonistic toward all mechanical devices; he is quite fond
of the water wheel and maintains a strict neutrality toward the spinning jenny.

The nineteenth-century term "well-read" has gone out
of fashion today, probably because so few of us are. In
the course of my life I have met many people who are ex-
tremely learned in one or two, or perhaps half a dozen,
different fields, but only two, Avram Davidson and Willy
Ley, who were really well-read. Within his field of interest, which was wide, Willy had encyclopedic knowledge
at his mental fingertips and a knack for that minutia of
detail that makes an obscure subject sparkle in the telling.
Avram has the same ability and the same knack, although

his interests center on history and the humanities, while Willy's were focused on science and technology.

Now a word about the stories in this volume and how they were chosen: I picked them because I liked them. They are not of a type, they illustrate no premise, they define no parameter, they were not picked to show anything about Avram Davidson's writing except its consistant quality and enjoyability. They have been arranged not chronologically, nor alphabetically, nor in ascending or descending order of length, but merely in the order that I think the reader will find the most pleasing.

Thank you for your attention. Enjoy the book.

Introduction to
Avram Davidson

by

RANDALL GARRETT

After knowing a man like Avram for damn near a quarter of a century, it is difficult to write a *short* introduction to Avram Davidson. The man has too many facets, too many wrinkles in his brain, too many varied abilities. Even I, brilliant though I am, find it impossible to tell all about Avram Davidson.

I'm not talking about his biography, the story of his life, his past history. I'm not talking about the stories he has written over that same quarter of a century, nor the impact he has had on many fields of fiction writing during his career. I am talking about the man himself.

Physically, he's easy enough to describe, but like all such descriptions, it sounds like a police report, and I cannot imagine anybody wanting to report Avram to the police. Unless he is a hell of a lot more subtle than I think he is, he has never even violated a parking regulation. He doesn't drive a car, for one thing. He is of average height and has a magnificent salt-and-pepper beard. He has a face which is highly expressive in spite of the hirsute adornment. Like myself and Isaac Asimov, he used to be

fat but is now merely stout. (All three of us have had
sense enough to see that fat gets you nowhere.)

You would like Avram Davidson. You might think him
a little odd, but I have yet to meet the science-fiction/fan-
tasy author who wasn't a little odd. At _least_.

Avram reminds me in many ways of the late, marvelous
Anthony Boucher; he is a widely read, subtle, and humorous man who has no enemies. The fact that, like Tony, he
was once editor of _The Magazine of Fantasy & Science
Fiction_, is merely fortuitous; we are talking about personality, not editorial ability.

Humorous? Subtle? Aye, lads and lassies. One of my
most delicious memories is that of a Milford Writers' Con-
ference back in the days when it was actually held in Milford, Pennsylvania. The brochure that year emphasized
the swimming facilities, so Avram, who can take swimming or leave it alone, toddled off to one of the big cos-
tume-rental establishments in New York and rented a
two-piece, turn-of-the-century, gentleman's bathing suit.
The trousers came down almost to the knees; the top
looked something like a modern T-shirt. And it was
striped. Wide, two-and-a-half-inch, horizontal, red-and-
white stripes. It did absolutely nothing to de-emphasize
his girth.

Atop this ensemble, he wore a stiff straw "boater" hat,
of the kind seldom seen nowadays except at political con-
ventions.

While everyone else exhausted themselves swimming
or frying themselves sick in the sun, Avram Davidson
relaxed in a canvas chair, under a large beach umbrella,
smoking thin cigars and sipping Bourbon and branch.

Came time for the evening session, and Avram was the
only one there who was not dying of either fatigue or
heat exhaustion or both. (The booze factor can be ig-

nored; it was a constant for each subject of the experiment.)

That evening, a well-known writer was delivering forth on characterization in the short-story form. Quoth he: "Your character must come alive in the first sentence! If that character is not alive by the end of the first paragraph, your story is a total failure."

From the back of the room, in a sepulchral voice, Avram intoned the first sentence of Dickens' immortal *A Christmas Carol:* "'Marley was dead: to begin with.'"

Along with everyone else, the speaker collapsed in laughter and gave up.

Avram is a compassionate man and a good friend. Once, when I was ill, he walked eighteen blocks, most of it uphill, just to bring me good cheer in the tripartite form of hot chicken soup in a vacuum jug, a half-pint of brandy, and, most important of all, himself.

Because his thoughts are often elsewhere, he is notoriously absent-minded. Only a few weeks ago as I write this, he decided to give a special party on a particularly solemn but happy occasion. His planning was meticulous: decorations, setting, comestibles, and liquid refreshments were of the finest. And, up until almost the last minute, he forgot to invite anybody.

But he always has his friends in mind; he never forgets them. He reads a newspaper and sees an article that will particularly interest *you;* he clips it and sends it. If it is from a book or magazine that he cannot clip, he will type it out and send it. If he is browsing through a bookstore and comes across a book he knows *you* will like, you will get it in the mail forthwith. He pays little or no attention to the traditional gift-giving times—Christmas, Chanuka, birthdays, anniversaries, and the like. I more than half suspect he doesn't remember his own birthday unless some officious government agency asks him. He feels no pressure to send a gift or even a card on such occasions. But if he sees something that he feels is specifically *yours* —you'll get it. Every day of the year is a gift-day to Avram Davidson.

If all the above makes Avram sound like a goody-goody milquetoast, I'm sorry to have misled you. I have never seen him punch anybody out with his fists, but when he becomes angry, you almost wish he *had* punched you out. If you goof, you will hear about it in no uncertain terms, and you will retire from the scene with your coccyx curled into your crotch. His anger is not only righteous, but *right*. I have never seen him *unjustly* angry.

And I have never seen him angry for long.

Prejudices? Yes. Not against race, color, creed, nationality, or previous condition of aptitude. But he cannot stand the stupid. I do not mean the ignorant; he does not pride himself on his admittedly great learning. I do not mean the mentally handicapped; he has the greatest compassion for such folk. But the person who has a good education and a reasonably good brain *and doesn't use them* is stupid. And if they are intractably stupid, they are not of Avram's company.

As I said earlier, I have not intended to say anything about Avram's writing; that's what the *rest* of this book is all about. Personally, I think he's great as a writer, and perhaps even greater as a human being. A saint? Theologically and strictly speaking, no. For one thing, he is not, *Deo gratias*, dead yet. But as far as being a good and decent and awesomely gifted and wonderful person, lo! ben David's name leads all the rest.

—December 1976
Castro Valley, California

The
Redward Edward Papers

sort of click. The voice resumed, wavering at first, "Coko and Moko? No—I'm very sorry, I really can't invite them, they're very stupid, they don't know how to behave and they can't even talk . . ."

The man on the stained mattress woke in a convulsive movement that brought him sitting up with a cry. He threw his head to the right and left and grimaced and struck at the air.

"Did you have a bad *dream*, George?" the voice asked, uncertainly.

George said, "*Uhn!*" thrusting at his eyes with the cushions of his palms. He dropped his hands, cleared his throat and spat, thickly. Then he reached out and grabbed the slack of a chain lying on the floor, one end fastened to a tableleg, and began to pull it in. The chain resisted, he tugged, something fell and squeaked, and George, continuing to pull, hauled in his prize and seized it.

"Sacheverell—"

"I hope you didn't have a bad *dream*, George—"

"Sacheverell—was anybody here? You lie to me and—"

"No, George, honest! Nobody was here, George!"

"You lie to me and I'll kill you!"

"I wouldn't lie to you, George. I know it's wicked to lie."

George glared at him out of his reddened eyes, took a firmer grip with both hands, and squeezed. Sacheverell cried out, thrust his face at George's wrist. His teeth clicked on air, George released him, abruptly, and he scuttled away. George smeared at his trouser-leg with his sleeve, made a noise of disgust. "Look what you done, you filthy little ape!" he shouted.

Sacheverell whimpered in the shadows. "I can't help it, George. I haven't got any sphincter muscle, and you *scared* me, you *hurt* me . . ."

Sacheverell

The front windows of the room were boarded up, and inside it was dark and cold and smelled very bad. There was a stained mattress on which a man wrapped in a blanket lay snoring, a chair with no back, a table which held the remains of a bag of hamburgers, several punched beer cans, and a penny candle which cast shadows all around.

There was a scuffling sound in the shadows, then a tiny rattling chattering noise, then a thin and tiny voice said, tentatively, "You must be very *cold*, George . . ." No reply. "Because I know *I'm* very cold . . ." the voice faded out. After a moment it said, "He's still asleep. A man needs his rest. It's very *hard* . . ." The voice seemed to be listening for something, seemed not to hear it; after an instant, in a different tone, said, "All right."

"*Hmm?*" it asked the silence. The chattering broke out again for just a second, then the voice said, "Good afternoon, Princess. Good afternoon, Madame. And General—how very nice to see *you*. I wish to invite you to a tea-party. We will use the best set of doll dishes and if anyone wishes to partake of something *strong*er, I believe the Professor—" the voice faltered, continued, "—has a drop of the oh-be-joyful in a bottle on the sideboard. And now pray take seats."

The wind sounded outside; when it died away, leaving the candleflame dancing, there was a humming noise which rose and fell like a moan, then ended abruptly on a

George groaned, huddled in under his blanket. "A million dollars on the end of this chain," he said; "and Om living in this hole, here. Like a wino, like a smokey, like a *bum!*" He struck the floor with his fist. "It don't make sense!" he cried, shifting around till he was on all fours, then pushing himself erect. Wrapping the blanket around his shoulders, he shambled quickly to the door, checked the bolt, then examined in turn the boarded-up front windows and the catch on the barred and frost-rimmed back window. Then he did something in a corner, cursing and sighing.

Under the table Sacheverell tugged on his chain ineffectually. "I don't *like* it here, George," he said. "It's cold and it's dirty and *I'm* dirty and cold, too, and I'm hungry. It's all dark here and nobody ever comes here and I don't like it, George, I don't like it here one bit. I wish I was back with the Professor again. I was very *happy* then. The Professor was nice to me and so was the Princess and Madame Opal and the General. They were the only ones in on the secret, until *you* found out."

George swung around and looked at him. One eye sparked in the candle-light.

"We used to have tea-parties and Madame Opal always brought chocolates when she came, even when she came alone, and she read love stories to me out of a magazine book with pictures and they were all true. Why can't I be back with the Professor again?"

George swallowed, and opened his mouth with a little smacking sound. "Professor Whitman died of a heart-attack," he said.

Sacheverell looked at him, head cocked. "An attack . . ."

"So he's *dead!* So forget about him!" the words tore out of the man's mouth. He padded across the room. Sacheverell retreated to the end of his chain.

"I don't know what the hell Om gunna *do* . . . In a few weeks now, they'll tear this rotten building down. Maybe," he said, slyly, putting his foot down on the chain, "I'll sell you to a zoo. Where you belong." He bent, grunting, and picked up the chain.

Sacheverell's teeth began to chatter. "I *don't!*" he shrilled. "I *don't* belong in a zoo! The little people they have there are *stu*pid—they don't know how to be*have,* and they can't even *talk!*"

George closed one eye, nodded; slowly, very slowly, drew in the chain. "Come on," he said. "Level with me. Professor Whitman had a nice little act, there. How come he quit and took off and came here?" Slowly he drew in the chain. Sacheverell trembled, but did not resist.

"We were going to go to a laboratory in a college," he said. "He told me. It was a waste to keep me doing silly tricks with Coko and Moko, when I was so smart. He should have done it before, he said."

George's mouth turned up on one side, creasing the stubble. "Naa, Sacheverell," he said. "That don't make sense. You know what they do to monkeys in them labs? They cut 'em up. That's all. I *know.* I went to one and I asked. They pay about fifteen bucks and then they cut 'em up." He made a scissors out of his fingers and went *k'khkhkhkh* . . . Sacheverell shuddered. George set his foot on the chain again and took hold of him by the neck. He poked him in the stomach with his finger, stiff. It had grown colder, the man's breath shown misty in the tainted air. He poked again. Sacheverell made a sick noise, struggled. "Come on," George said. "Level with me. There's a million dollars inside of you, you dirty little ape. There's *gotta* be. Only I don't know *how.* So you tell me."

Sacheverell whimpered. "I don't *know,* George. I don't *know.*"

The man scowled, then grinned slyly. "That's what *you* say. I'm not so sure. You think I don't know that if They found out, They'd take you away from me? Sure. A million bucks . . . how come I'm being followed, if They don't know? First a guy with a beard, then a kid in a red snow-suit. *I* seen them together. Listen, you frigging little jocko, you better *think*, I'm telling you—you better think hard!" He poked again with his stiff and dirty finger. And again. "I always knew, see, I always *knew* that there was a million bucks waiting for me somewhere, if I only kept my eyes open. What the hell is a guy like me doing unloading crates in the fruit market, when I got plans for a million? And then—" His voice sank and his eyes narrowed. "—this Professor Whitman come along and put up at the Eagle Hotel. I caught his act in the sticks once, I been around. *First* I thought he was practicing ventriloquism, *then* I found out about *you—you* was the other voice in his room! And that's when I—"

Abruptly he stopped. The outside door opened with a rusty squeal and footfalls sounded in the hall. Someone knocked. Someone tried the knob. Someone said, "Sacheverell? Sacheverell?" and George clamped his hairy, filthy hand over the captive's mouth. Sacheverell jerked and twitched and rolled his eyes. The voice made a disappointed noise, the footfalls moved uncertainly, started to retreat. And then Sacheverell kicked out at George's crotch. The man grunted, cursed, lost his grip—

"*Help!*" Sacheverell cried. "*Help! Help! Save me!*"

Fists beat on the door, the glass in the back window crashed and fell to the floor, a wizened old-man's face peered through the opening, withdrew. George ran to the door, then turned to chase Sacheverell, who fled, shrieking hysterically. A tiny figure in a red snow-suit squeezed through the bars of the back window and ran to pull the bolt on the door. Someone in boots and a plaid jacket and a woolen watch-cap burst in, melting snow glittering on a big black beard.

"Save me!" Sacheverell screamed, dashing from side to side. "He attacked Professor Whitman and knocked him down *and he didn't get up again—*"

George stooped, picking up the chair, but the red snow-suit got between his legs and he stumbled. The chair was jerked from his hands, he came up with his fists clenched and the bearded person struck down with the chair. It caught him across the bridge of the nose with a crunching noise, he fell, turned over, stayed down. Silence.

Sacheverell hiccupped. Then he said, "Why are you wearing *men's* clothing, Princess Zaga?"

"A bearded *man* attracts quite enough attention, thank you," the Princess said, disengaging the chain. "No need to advertise . . . Let's get out of here." She picked him up and the three of them went out into the black, deserted street, boarded-shut windows staring blindly. The snow fell thickly, drifting into the ravaged hall and into the room where George's blood, in a small pool, had already begun to freeze.

"There's our car, Sacheverell," said the man in the red snow-suit, thrusting a cigar into his child-size, jaded old face. "What a time—"

"I assume you are still with the carnival, General Pinkey?"

"No, kiddy. The new owners wouldn't reckernize the union, so we quit and retired on Social Security in Sarasota. You'll like it there. Not that the unions are much better, mind you: Bismarkian devices to dissuade the working classes from industrial government on a truly Marxian, Socialist-Labor basis. We got a television set, kiddy."

"And look who's waiting for you—" Princess Zaga

opened the station wagon and handed Sacheverell inside. There, in the back seat, was the hugest, the vastest, the fattest woman in the world.

"Princess Opal!" Sacheverell cried, leaping into her arms—and was buried in the wide expanse of her bosom and bathed in her warm Gothick tears. She called him her Precious and her Little Boy and her very own Peter Pan.

"It was Madame Opal who planned this all," Princess Zaga remarked, starting the car and driving off. General Pinkey lit his cigar and opened a copy of *The Weekly People*.

"Yes, I did, yes, I did," Mme. Opal murmured, kissing and hugging Sacheverell. "Oh, how neglected you are! Oh, how thin! We'll have a tea-party, just like we used to, the very best doll dishes; we'll see you eat nice and we'll wash you and comb you and put ribbons around your neck."

Sacheverell began to weep. "Oh, it was *awful* with George," he said.

"Never mind, never mind, he didn't know any better," Mme. Opal said, soothingly.

"The hell he didn't!" snapped Princess Zaga.

"Predatory capitalism," General Pinkey began.

"Never mind, never mind, forget about it, darling, it was only a bad dream . . ."

Sacheverell dried his tears on Mme. Opal's enormous spangled-velvet bosom. "George was very *mean* to me," he said. "He treated me *very* mean. But worst of all, you know, Madame Opal, he *lied* to me—he lied to me all the time, and I almost believed him—that was the most horrible part of all: I almost believed that I was a monkey."

Afterword for Sacheverell

Well, *I* am rather fond of this small story, be it addressed to the human (and/or inhuman) condition, or what. Despite the fact that it has somehow failed to attract the same attention once devoted to De Maupassant's *The Piece of String*. What are its origins? Scholars may point to James Otis's *Toby Tyler, or Ten Weeks with a Circus:* let them. (Not that I mean to put down one of the earlier in-depth studies of child labor as obtaining in a nonindustrialized enclave of a rapidly industrializing society, shwew.) (I shed *buckets* of tears when Mr. Stubbs, Toby's beloved monkey, died of pneumonia.) The fact is that I do not *know* what prompted me to write this story —besides, of course, a pure and disinterested desire for money. *The New Yorker* magazine probably had something to do with it, as it had printed articles on those massive wounds euphemistically termed Urban Renewal, as well as a profile about a bearded lady. Joseph Mitchell wrote that one; he was a good writer. And it was about that time too, I think, that The Greatest Show on Earth (Ringling Brothers, Barnum and Bailey), partly due to labor troubles, eschewed forever its performances under the Big Top, as the immense canvas tent was called: henceforth performing only in places like Madison Square Garden. Thus ended an era, indeed. I myself inclined to think that the ascerbic circus midget, General Pinkey, an ideologically convinced member of the Socialist Labor Party (possibly apocryphal boast, "The Socialist Labor Party stands right where it stood in 1896!"), was a nice touch. I have received no reactions whatsoever from the Socialist Labor Party on this, which will perhaps explain why it has never gotten anywhere.

One other point—the *name*. It is in our day best known

via Sir Sacheverell Sitwell, who has written so richly and copiously on art, particularly Baroque art. It will also recall to some the Anglican Bishop Sacheverell, whose trial during the reign of Queen Anne was a landmark in the history of freedom of speech. (I hope. Conceive my embarrassment if it turns out that the prelate had instead been accused of pinching the fanny of a lady-in-waiting.) No put-down of either bishop or baronet was intended by the choice of name: it merely seemed, somehow, the *right* name. And, as to how it is pronounced—if you find out, let me know.

The Lord of Central Park

This all took place a while back. . . .

It was a crisp evening in middle April.

Cornelius Goodeycoonce, the river pirate, headed his plunder-laden boat straight at an apparently solid wall of pilings, steering with the calm of a ferryboat captain nearing a slip, and cut his motor.

Up in Central Park, where he was kipped out in a secluded cave, Arthur Marmaduke Roderick Lodowicke William Rufus de Powisse-Plunkert, 11th Marquess of Grue and Groole in the Peerage of England, 22nd Baron Bogle in the Peerage of Scotland, 6th Earl of Ballypatcoogen in the Peerage of Ireland, Viscount Penhokey in the Peerage of the United Kingdom, Laird of Muckle Greet, Master of Snee, and Hereditary Lord High Keeper of the Queen's Bears, heard a familiar beat of wings in the night and held out a slice of bread just in time to catch a medium-rare charcoal-broiled steak.

Not a mile away the Grand Master of the Mafia, Don Alexander Borjia, admired for the ten-thousandth time the eternally enigmatic smile on the lips of the *original* Mona Lisa, which hung, as it had for 50 years, on the wall of the Chamber of the order's Grand Council.

A certain foreign visitor, who called himself Tosci, came down the gangway ladder on the side of the yacht which in daylight flew the flag of the landlocked nation whose citizenship he claimed, and got gingerly into the launch which was to bear him to shore.

Daisy Smith, in her trim and tiny bachelor-girl apartment, prepared herself a tuna-fish sandwich without enthusiasm, and reflected how much more—how very much more—she would rather be preparing, say, roast beef and potatoes for a young man, if only she knew a young man she considered worth preparing roast beef and potatoes for.

And across the North River, on the Jersey shore, a thin line of green still hugged the outline of the cliffs; and over that, a thin line of blue. And then the night rolled all the way down, and the lines of light were lost. . . .

The momentum of Cornelius' boat carried it swiftly toward the bulkhead. A crash seemed inevitable. Then Cornelius picked up an oar and prodded one certain timber well below the waterline. Instantly a section of the pilings swung open, just wide enough and just high enough for the boat to pass through; then it swung shut once more.

The boat proceeded onward in gathering darkness as the light from the river dimmed behind it. Gauging the precise instant when the momentum would cease to propel his boat against the mild current of Coenties' Kill—walled in and walled over these 150 years—the man lowered his oar and began to pole. The eyes of an alligator flashed briefly, then submerged.

Presently a light showed itself some distance off, then vanished, reappeared, vanished once more in the windings of the sluggish creek, and finally revealed itself, hissing whitely, as a Coleman lamp. It sat on the stone lip of what had been a fairly well-frequented landing in the days when De Witt Clinton was Mayor and Jacob Hays was High Constable of the City of New York. Cheap as labor had been in those days—and fill even cheaper—it had been less expensive to vault up rather than bury the Kill when the needs of the growing metropolis demanded the space. Experience had proved that to be the case when other Manhattan "kills" or streams, refusing meekly to submit to burial, had flooded cellars and streets.

The Goodeycoonce-the-river-pirate of that time had noted, marked, mapped, and made the private excavations. They were an old, old family, loath to change what was even then an old family trade.

"Well, now, let's see—" said the present-day Cornelius. He tied up. He unloaded his cargo onto a pushcart, placed the lamp in a bracket, and slowly trundled the cart over the stone paving of the narrow street, which had echoed to no other traffic since it lost the light of the sun so long ago.

At the head of the incline the path passed under an archway of later construction. The Goodeycoonce-of-*that*-time, trusting no alien hand, had learned the mason's trade himself, breaking in onto a lovely, dry, smooth tunnel made and abandoned forever by others—the first, last, and short-lived horse-car subway. The wheels of the pushcart fitted perfectly into the tracks, and the grade was level.

Granny Goodeycoonce was reading her old Dutch family Bible in the snug apartment behind her second-hand store. That is, not exactly *reading* it; it had been generations since any member of the family could actually read Dutch; she was looking at the pictures. Her attention was diverted from a copperplate engraving of the she-bear devouring the striplings who had so uncouthly mocked the Prophet Elisha with the words, *Go up, baldhead* ("Serve them right!" she declared. "Bunch of juvenile delinquents!"), by a thumping from below.

She closed the Book and descended to the cellar, where her only grandchild was hauling his plunder up through the trap door.

"Put out that *lamp*, Neely!" she said sharply. "Gasoline costs *money!*"

"Yes, Granny," the river pirate said obediently.

Denny the Dip stared in stupefaction at the sudden appearance of a steak sandwich's most important ingredient. Then he stared at the winged visitor which had appeared a second after the steak. The winged visitor stared back— or, perhaps "glared" would be the *mot juste*—out of burning yellow eyes. "Cheest!" said Denny the Dip.

There had been a time when, so skillful was The Dip, that he had picked the pocket of a Police Commissioner while the latter was in the very act of greeting a Queen. (He had returned the wallet later, of course, via the mails, out of courtesy, and, of course, minus the money.) But Time with her wingéd Flight, and all that—age and its concomitant infirmities, much aggravated by a devotion to whatever Celtic demigod presides over the demijohn—had long rendered The Dip unfit for such professional gestures.

For some years now he had been the bane of the Mendicant Squad. His method was to approach lone ladies with the pitch that he was a leper, that they were not to come any nearer, but were to drop some money on the sidewalk for him. This, with squeaks of dismay, they usually did. But on one particular evening—this one, in fact— the lone lady he had approached turned out to be a retired medical missionary; she delivered a lecture on the relative merits of chaulmoogra oil and the sulfonamides in the treatment of Hansen's Disease ("—not contagious in New York, and never was—"), expressed her doubts that The Dip suffered from anything worse than, say, ichthyosis; and the paper she gave him was neither Silver Certificate nor Federal Reserve Note, but the address of a dermatologist.

Her speech had lasted a good quarter of an hour, and was followed by some remarks on Justification Through Faith, the whole experience leaving Denny weak and shaken. He had just managed to totter to one of those benches which a benevolent municipality disposes at intervals along Central Park West, and sink down, when he was espied by the 22nd Baron and 11th Marquess aforesaid, Arthur Marmaduke et cetera, who was walking his dog, Guido.

The dog gave Denny a perfunctory sniff, and growled condescendingly. Denny, semisubliminally, identified it as a whippet, reidentified it as an Italian greyhound, looked up suddenly and whimpered, "Lord *Grey* and Gore?"

"Grue and Groole," the dog's master corrected him. "Who the juice are you?" The dog was small and whipcord-thin and marked with many scars. So was his master. The latter was wearing a threadbare but neat bush-jacket, jodhpurs, veldt-schoen, a monocle, and a quasi-caracul cap of the sort which are sold three-for-two-rupees in the Thieves' Bazaar at Peshawar. He scowled, peered through his monocled eye, which was keen and narrow, the other being wide and glassy.

"Cor flog the flaming crows!" he exclaimed. "Dennis! Haven't seen you since I fingered that fat fool for you aboard the *Leviathan* in '26. Or was it '27? Demned parvenu must have had at least a thousand quid in his wallet, which you were supposed to divide with me fifty-fifty, but didn't; eh?"

"Sixty-forty in my favor was the agreement," Denny said feebly. "Have you got the price of a meal or a drink on yez, perchance?"

"Never spend money on food *or* drink," said the Marquess primly. "Against my principles. Come along, come along," he said, prodding The Dip with his swagger stick, "and I'll supply you with scoff *and* wallop, you miserable swine."

The Dip, noting the direction they were taking, expressed his doubt that he could make it through the Park.

"I don't live *through* the Park, I live *in* the Park, mind your fat head, you bloody fool!" They had left the path and were proceeding—master and hound as smoothly as snakes, Denny rather less so—behind trees, up rocks, between bushes, under low-hanging boughs. And so came at last to the cave. "Liberty Hall!" said the Marquess. "After you, you miserable bog-oaf."

A charcoal fire glowed in a tiny stove made from stones, mud, and three automobile license plates. A kettle hummed on it, a teapot sat beside it, in one corner was a bed of evergreen sprigs covered with a rather good Tientsin rug woven in the archaic two blues and a buff, and a Tibetan butter-lamp burned on a ledge. There was something else in the cave, something which lunged at Denny and made fierce noises.

"Cheest!" he cried. "A baby eagle!" And fell back.

"Don't be a damned fool," his host exclaimed pettishly. "It's a fully grown falcon, by name Sauncepeur . . . There, my precious, there, my lovely. A comfit for you." And he drew from one of his pockets what was either a large mouse or a small rat and offered it to the falcon. Sauncepeur swallowed it whole. "Just enough to whet your appetite, not enough to spoil the hunt. Come, my dearie. Come up, sweetheart, come up."

The Marquess had donned a leather gauntlet and unleashed the bird from the perch. Sauncepeur mounted his wrist. Together they withdrew from the cave; the man muttered, the bird muttered back, a wrist was thrown up and out, there was a beating of wings, and the falconer returned alone, stripping off his gauntlet.

"Now for some whiskey. . . . Hot water? Cold? Pity

I've no melted yak butter to go with—one grew rather used to it after a bit in Tibet; cow butter is no good—got no body. What, straight? As you please."

Over the drink the 11th Marquess of Grue and Groole filled in his visitor on his career since '25—or was it '26? "Poached rhino in Kenya, but that's all over now, y'know. What with the Blacks, the Arabs, and the East Injians, white man hasn't got a prayer in that show—poaching, I mean. Ran the biggest fantan game in Macao for a while, but with the price opium's got to, hardly worthwhile.

"Signed a contract to go find the Abominable Snowman, demned Sherpas deserted only thirty days out, said the air was too thin for their lungs that high up, if you please, la-de-da—left me short on supplies, so that when I finally found the blasted *yeti*, I had to eat it. No good without curry, you know, no good a-tall.

"Lost m'right eye about that time, or shortly after. Altercation with a Sikh in Amritsar. Got a glass one. Lid won't close, muscle wonky, y'know. Natives in Portuguese East used to call me Bwana-Who-Sleeps-With-One-Eye-Waking; wouldn't come within a hundred yards after I'd kipped down for the night."

He paused to thrust a Sobranie black-and-gold into a malachite cigarette holder and lit it at the fire. With the dull red glow reflected in his monocle and glass eye, smoke suddenly jutting forth from both nostrils, and the (presumably) monkey skull he held in one hand for an ashtray as he sat cross-legged in the cave, the wicked Marquess looked very devilish indeed to the poor Dip, who shivered a bit, and surreptitiously took another peg of whiskey from the flask.

"No, no," the Marquess went on, "to anyone used to concealing himself in Mau Mau, Pathan, and EOKA country, avoiding the attention of the police in Central Park is child's play. Pity about the poor old Fakir of Ipi, but then, his heart always was a bit dicky. Still, they've let Jomo out of jail. As for Colonel Dighenes—"

And it was brought to the attention of the bewildered Dip that the Marquess had fought *for*, and not against, the Mau Maus, Pathans, EOKAs, et cetera. The nearest he came to explaining this was, "Always admired your Simon Girty chap, y'know. Pity people don't scalp any more—here, give over that flask, you pig, before you drink it all. It's a point of honor with me never to steal more than one day's rations at a time.

"Travel light, live off the country. I was one of only two White men in my graduating class at Ah Chu's College of Thieves in Canton. Took my graduate work at Kaffir Ali's, Cairo. I suppose you little know, miserable fellow that you are, that *I was the last man to be tried by a jury of his peers before the House of Lords!* True, I did take the Dowager's Daimler, and, true, I sold it—lost the money at baccarat—never trust an Azerbaijanian at cards, but—"

He stopped, harkened to some sound in the outer darkness. "I fancy I hear my saucy Sauncepeur returning. 'What gat ye for supper, Lord Randall, my son?'—eh? Chops, steak, Cornish rock hen, what? Curious custom you Americans have—charcoal grills on your balconies. Though, mind, I'm not complaining. Bread ready? *Ahhh*, my pretty!"

The steak was just fine, as far as Denny the Dip was concerned, though Lord Grue and Groole complained there was a shade too much garlic. "Mustn't grumble, however—the taste of the Middle Classes is constantly improving."

The man who called himself Tosci rose to his feet.
"Don Alexander Borgia, I presume?" he inquired.
"No, no, excuse me—Borjia—with a 'j'," the Grand

Master corrected him. The Grand Master was a tall, dark, handsome man, with a head of silvery-gray hair. "The Grand Council is waiting," he said, "to hear your proposition. This way."

"I had no idea," Tosci murmured, impressed, "that the headquarters of the Mafia were quite so—quite so—" He waved his hand, indicating an inability to find the *mot juste* to fit the high-toned luxury and exquisite good taste of the surroundings.

"This is merely the Chamber of the Grand Council," said Don Alexander. "The actual headquarters, which we are required by our charter to maintain, is in back of a candy store on Mulberry Street. The dead weight of tradition, huh? Well, pretty soon that time will come of which the political philosophers have predicted, when the State shall wither away. 'No more Tradition's chains will bind us,' yeah? After you." Don Alexander took his seat at the head of the table and gestured the visitor to begin.

The latter gazed at the assembled Masters of the Mafia, who gazed back, unwinking, unblinking, but not—he was quite sure—unthinking.

After a moment he began, "*Signori*—" and paused; "then, *Fratelli*—"

—and was interrupted by Grand Master Borjia.

"Excuse me, Hare Tosci, or Monsoon Tosci, or however you say in your country, but evidently you have fallen victim to the false delusion that the Mafia is a strictly Eyetalian organization, which I have no hesitation in saying it is a nerroneous concept and a misinformation disseminated by the conscript press, see? I would like it clearly understood that you should get it through your head we of the sorely misconstrued and much maligned Mafia do not discriminate in any way, shape, or form, against race, creed, color, national or'gin, or, uh, what the hell is the other thing which we don't discriminate against in any way, shape, or form, somebody?"

"Previous kahn-dition of soivitood," said a stocky Grand Councilor, wearing a Brooks Brothers suit, two cauliflower ears, and an eyepatch.

"Yeah. Thanks very much, Don Lefty McGonigle."

"Nat a-tall," said Don Lefty, with a slight blush, as he bent his slightly broken nose toward the orchid in his buttonhole—one of three flown up for him daily from Bahía. "'Rank is but d'guinea stamp, an' a man's a man for all dat,'" he added. "A quotation from d' poet Boyns; no offensive ettnic connotations intended."

"Exactly," said the Grand Master, a slight scowl vanishing from his distinguished features. "Our Grand Council is a veritable microcosm of American opportunity, as witness, besides myself, Don Lefty McGonigle, Don Shazzam X—formerly Rastus Washington—Don Gesú-María Gomez, Don Leverret Lowell Cabot, Don Swede Swanson, Don Tex Thompson, Don Morris Caplan, and Don Wong Hua-Fu, which he's the Temporary Member of the Permanent Representation of the Honorable Ten Tongs—in a word, a confraternity of American business and professional men devoted to the study of the Confucian classics, the Buddhist Scriptures, and the art of horticulture as it might be exemplified by the peaceful cultivation of the *ah-peen* poppy."

He paused and drew breath. "The Mafia," he continued, "despite the innumerable slanders and aspersions cast upon it by scoffers, cynics, and the ever-present envious, is no more than a group of humble citizens of the world, determined to provide, besides certain commercial services, a forum wherein or whereby to arbitrate those differences which the lack of communication—alas, all too prevalent in our society—might otherwise terminate untowardly; as to its supposed origins in romantic Sicily, who, indeed, can say? What's on your mind, Tosci?" he concluded abruptly.

Mr. (or Herr, or Monsieur, or whatever way they say in his country) Tosci blinked. Then he smiled a small noncommittal smile, appropriate to the citizen of a neutral nation.

"As you are aware, my country is landlocked," he began. "Despite, or perhaps because of this situation, the question of providing a merchant marine of our own arises from time to time. It has arisen lately. My company, the *Societé Anonyme de la Banque de la Commerce et de l'Industrie et pour les Droites des Oeuvriers et des Paysans*, known popularly and for convenience as *Paybanque*, is currently interested in the possibilities of such a project.

"It is those 'certain commercial services' of the Mafia, of which you spoke, that we propose to engage. Our merchant marine headquarters in the New World would naturally be located in the New York City port area. Although at the present time the North River, or such New Jersey areas as Hoboken or Bayonne are most heavily favored by shipping, it was not always so. It is our opinion that excellent possibilities exist along the East River side of Manhattan, particularly the lower East River.

"It is our desire therefore that you provide us with a land, sea, and air survey, largely but not exclusively photographic in nature, engaging for the duration of the survey more or less centrally located quarters on the waterfront area in this locale. Something in the neighborhood of the Williamsburg Bridge would be ideal. Our representatives would participate with you, though the home office, so to speak, would remain aboard my yacht.

"This portfolio," he went on, placing it on the table and opening it, "contains a more detailed description of our proposal, as well as the eleven million dollars in United States Treasury Notes which your Northern European contact informed us would be your fee for considering the proposal. If you are agreeable to undertake the work, we can discuss further terms."

He ceased to speak. After a moment the Grand Master said, "Okay. We will leave you know." After Tosci had departed, Don Alexander asked, "Well, what do you think."

"An Albanian Trotskyite posing as a Swiss Stalinist. If you ask me, I think he wants to blow up the Brooklyn Navy Yard," Don Morris Caplan said.

"Of *course* he wants to blow up the Brooklyn Navy Yard," Borjia snapped. "That was obvious right from the beginning—I can spot them Albanian deviationists a mile away. Now the point is: Do we *want* the Brooklyn Navy Yard blown up? It is to this question, my esteemed fellow colleagues, which we must now divert our attention."

Events went their traditional way in the Goodeycoonce household. Granny had dressed herself up as though for a masquerade, the principal articles of costume consisting of a tasseled cap, a linen blouse with wide sleeves, a pair of even wider breeches, and wooden shoes; all these articles were very, very old. She next picked up a pipe of equally antique design, with a long cherrywood stem and a hand-painted porcelain bowl, and this she proceeded to charge with genuine Indian Leaf tobacco which she had shredded herself in her chopping bowl. The tobacco was purchased at regular intervals from the last of the Manahatta Indians—that is, he was one-eighth Last-of-the-Manahatta-Indians, on his mother's side—who operated the New Orleans Candle and Incense Shop on Lexington Avenue. ("*I* don't know what them crazy White folks want with that stuff," he often said; "they could buy *grass* for the same price.") Granny struck a kitchen match, held it flat across the top of the pipe bowl, and began to puff.

Neely seated himself and took up a spiral notebook and a ballpoint pen. A scowl, or rather a pout, settled on his usually good-natured countenance.

First Granny coughed. Then she gagged. Then she inhaled with a harsh, gasping breath. Then she turned white, then green, then a bright red which might have startled and even alarmed Neely, had he not seen it all happen so often before. Presently she removed the pipe. Her face had taken on an almost masculine appearance. She rolled up one hand into a somewhat loose fist, then the other, then she placed one in alignment with the other and lifted them to her eyes and peered through her simulated telescope.

Neely, in a tone of voice obviously intended as mockery, or at least mimicry, said, "'To arms, to arms! Blow der drums and beat der trumpet! De dumdam Engels ships ben gesailing up de River!'"

The eye which was not looking through the "telescope" now looked at him, and there was something cold and cruel in it. Neely's own eyes fell. After a moment he mumbled, "Sorry, Oude Piet. I mean Oom Piet. I mean, *darn* it, Heer—um—Governor—ah—Your Highness."

The eye glared at him, then the "telescope" shifted. After a while a heavily accented and guttural voice, quite unlike his grandmother's usual tones, came from her throat and announced, in a businesslike drone, "Shloop by der vharf in Communipaw. Beaver pelts—"

Neely clicked his tongue in annoyance. "You're in the wrong century, darn it, now!" he cried. Again, the cold old eye glared at him. But he stood his ground. "Come on, now," he said. "A promise is a promise. What would the *Co*mpany say?"

The "telescope" shifted again. The drone recommenced. "Pier Dvendy-Zeven—Durkish Zigarettes—Zipahi brand—vhatchman gedding dronk—"

Neely's ballpoint scribbled rapidly. "*That's* the ticket!" he declared.

Daisy Smith finished the tuna-fish sandwich (no mayonnaise—a girl has to watch those calories every single *minute*) and washed the dish. For dessert she had half a pear. Then the question could no longer be postponed—what was she going to *do* that evening? It had all seemed so simple, back in Piney Woods, New Jersey: she would take her own savings, all $80, plus the $500 or so, most of it in old-fashioned long bills, but including the $100 Liberty Bond, which had been found in the much-mended worsted stocking under Uncle Dynus' mattress after his funeral (the note found with it—thise is four *Dasi*—seemed to make traffic with the Surrogate's Court unnecessary), and come to New York. There she would find, in the order named, an apartment, a job, and Someone-To-Go-Out-With.

She had found the first two without much trouble, but the third, which she had thought would proceed from the second, did not materialize. Her employer, Mr. Katachatourian, was the nicest old man in the world, but, though a widower, he was *old;* somehow the importing of St. John's bread—his business—didn't seem to attract *young* men. And if, from time to time, with trepidation, he took a flyer on a consignment of sesame seeds, or pistachio nuts, it helped Daisy's prospects not at all. The jobbing of sesame seeds, or pistachio nuts, attracted exactly the same sort of gentlemen as did the jobbing of St. John's bread— either middle-aged and married, or elderly.

Once, to be sure, and once only, Daisy had made a social contact from her job. Mr. Imamoglu, one of the largest *ex*porters of St. John's bread on the eastern Aegean littoral, had come to New York on business, had dropped in to see his good customer, The Katachatourian Trading Company, and had immediately fallen in love with Daisy. With true Oriental opulence he took her out every night for a week. He took her to the opera, to the St. Regis, to the Horse Show at Madison Square Garden, to Jack Dempsey's restaurant, to a Near Eastern night club on Ninth Avenue, to Hamburger Heaven, to a performance of *Phèdre* in the original French, to the Bowery Follies, and to a triple-feature movie house on 42nd Street which specialized in technicolor Westerns, of which Mr. Imamoglu was inordinately fond.

Then he proposed marriage.

Well, the prospect of living in a strawberry-ice-cream-pink-villa in the fashionable suburb of Karsiyaka across the picturesque Bay from the romantic port of Izmir, where she would be waited on, hand and foot, by multitudes of servants, *did* appeal to Daisy. But although Mr. Imamoglu assured her that both polygamy and the harem were things of the past in Turkey, that, in fact, neither veil nor *yashmak* could be procured for love or money in all his country, still, you know, *after all*. And furthermore, Mr. Imamoglu was somewhat on in years; he must have been in his thirties.

And besides, she didn't love him.

So Daisy said No.

The departure of the semidisconsolate exporter left Daisy's evenings emptier than before. Go to church? Why, bless you, of course she went to church, every single Sunday, sometimes twice, and met a number of young men who played the organ or were in the choir or conducted a Sunday-school class. Most of them lived in the YMCA and were careful to explain to Daisy that it would be many, many years before they could even begin to *think* of marriage; and their ideas of a social evening were

quite different from Mr. Imamoglu's; they would arrange
to meet her somewhere after supper and then go to a free
illustrated lecture on the Greenland missions; followed by
a cup of coffee or a coke, followed by a chaste farewell at
the subway kiosk.

Sometimes a girl thought she might just as well be back
in Piney Woods, New Jersey.

What, then, to do tonight? Wash her hair? Watch TV?
Catch up on her letters? Mending? Solo visit to a movie?
She decided to take a walk.

A few blocks from her apartment she saw a familiar trio
leaning in familiar stances against a wall. They nudged
one another as they saw Daisy coming, as they had the
first time and as they did every time. By now she knew
there would be no wolf whistles, no rude proposals.

"Good evening, miss."

"G' evening, miss."

"Evening, miss."

"Good evening," Daisy said, pausing. "Oh, look at your
new hats!" she exclaimed. "White fedoras. My goodness.
Aren't they nice!"

The three men beamed and smirked, and readjusted
their brims. "All the big fellows wear white fedoras," said
the leader of the trio, whose name was Forrance.

"The big fellows?"

"Sure. Like on that, now, TV show, *The Unthinkables*.
Al–Lucky–Baby Face–*you* know."

As Forrance mentioned these people his two associates
pursed lips and nodded soberly. One was quite small and
suffered from nosebleeds. ("Must be a low pressure rarea
comin' down from Canada," he would mumble; "I c'n
alwees tell: Omma reggella human brommeter.") He was
known, quite simply, as Blood.

His companion, as if in compensation, was obese in the
extreme. ("A glanjalla condition," was his explanation; he

indignantly denied gluttony. Taxed with overeating, he pleaded a tapeworm. ("It's not f' *me*," was his indignant cry, over a third helping of breaded pork chops and French fries; "*it's f' the woim!*") Not unexpectedly he was called Guts. Now and then he pretended that it was an acknowledgement of personal courage.

"Al?" Daisy repeated. "Lucky? Baby Face? White fedoras? *The Unthinkables?* But *you're* not *gangsters?*" she burst out. "*Are* you?" For, as often as she had seen them, she had never thought to ask their trade.

Forrance drew himself up. Blood slouched. Guts loomed. A look of pleased importance underlay the grim look they assumed at the question. "Listen," Forrance began, out of the side of his mouth, an effect instantly spoiled by his adding, "miss."

"Listen, miss, you ever hear of—" he paused, glanced around, drew nearer—"the Nafia?" He thrust his right hand into his coat pocket. So did his two lieutenants. Daisy said, No, she never did; and at once the three were cast down. Was it, she asked helpfully, anything like the Mafia? Forrance brightened, Blood brightened, Guts brightened.

"*Sump*thing like the Mafia," said Forrance. "Om really very surprised you never—but you're from outatown, aintcha?"

"But what do you *do?*" Daisy demanded, mildly thrilled, but somehow not in the least frightened.

"We control," said Forrance impressively, "*all the gumball and Indian nut machines south of Vesey Street!*"

"My goodness," said Daisy. "Uh—are there many?"

"We are now awaiting delivery of the first of our new fleet of trucks," said Forrance formally.

"*Well*," said Daisy, "lots of luck. I've got to go now. Good night."

"Good night, miss."

"G' night, miss."

"Night, miss."

The crisp air was so stimulating that Daisy walked a considerable distance past her usual turning-around point, and then decided to come home by a different route, window shopping on the way. And in one window she noted many good buys in linoleum and tarpaulins, ships' chandlery, bar-and-grill supplies, and various other commodities; but somehow nothing she really *needed* just at the moment.

Then the flowered organdy caught her eye, but the bolt of blue rayon next to it was just as adorable. She looked up at the sign. THE ALMOST ANYTHING SECOND-HAND GOODS AND OUTLET STORE, it said. Wondering slightly, Daisy opened the door and went in. A bell tinkled. After a moment another door opened and a tall vigorous-looking woman, whose brown hair was turning gray, came in from the back. She smiled politely on seeing Daisy.

"I thought I might get some of that organdy in the window, the one with the flowers, enough for a dress."

"Yes, isn't it lovely? I'll get it for you right away. Was there anything else in the window you liked, while I'm there? Leather goods, outboard motors, canned crab-meat?"

"No, just—"

"Seasoned mahogany, yerba maté, manila hemp? Turkish cigarettes—Sipahi brand?"

"No, just the organdy, and, oh, maybe that blue rayon?"

"That's lovely, too. You have very good taste."

While the lady was reaching into the window, the door at the back opened again and a voice said, "Granny," and then stopped. Daisy turned around. She saw a well-made young man with a healthy open countenance and light brown hair which needed combing. He wore a peacoat, corduroy trousers, and a woolen cap. He stared at Daisy. Then he smiled. Then he blushed. Then he took off his cap.

Daisy instantly decided to buy, not just enough material for a dress, but both entire bolts, plus so large an amount of leather goods, outboard motors, canned crabmeat, seasoned Honduras mahogany, yerba maté, manila hemp, and Turkish Sipahi cigarettes as would leave the proprietor no choice but to say, "Well, you can never carry all that by yourself; my grandson will help you take it home,"—or words to that effect.

What actually happened was quite different. The lady emerged from the window with the bolts of cloth and said, "I really don't know which is the lovelier," then noticed the young man and said, "Yes, Neely?"

"I finished the, uh, *you*-know," said the young man. He continued smiling at Daisy, who was now smiling back.

"Then start stacking the Polish hams," his grandmother directed crisply. "Smash up all those old crates, pile the raw rubber up against the north wall, but not too near the Turkish cigarettes because of the smell. Go on, now."

"Uh—" said Neely, still looking at the new young customer.

"And when you're finished with *that*," his grandmother said, "I want all the cork fenders cleaned, and the copper cable unwound from the big reel onto the little ones."

"Uh—"

"Now, never mind. *Uh*—you go and do as I say, or we'll be up all night . . . *Neely!*"

For a moment the young man hesitated. Then his eyes left Daisy and caught his grandmother's glance. He looked down, swallowed, scraped his boots. *"Well?"* Neely threw Daisy a single quick glance of helplessness, wistfulness, and embarrassment. He said, "Yes, Granny," turned and went out the door.

Daisy, her purchase under her arm, walked home full of indignation. "There are no young men any more!" she told herself vexedly. "If they're *men*, they're not *young*, and if they're *young*, they're just not *men*. 'Yes, Granny!' How do you like *that*? Oh, I'd 'Yes, Granny' him!" she declared. "I'd show *him* who was boss!" she thought, somewhat inconsistently.

"Milksop!" she concluded. She was surprised to realize that, in her annoyance, she had bought only the flowered organdy. There was really no help for it; much as she despised the grandmother and grandson, if she wanted that blue rayon she would have to revisit THE ALMOST ANYTHING SECOND-HAND GOODS AND OUTLET STORE a second time. Too bad, but it wasn't really *her* fault, was it?

The man called Tosci stepped from the yacht's launch onto the gangway ladder and was steadied by a stubble-faced man in dungarees. "Thank you, boatswain," he said.

"Did you enjoy your visit ashore, M. Tosci?" the bosun asked.

"Ah, New York is such a stimulating city," said Tosci, going up the ladder. "One simply cannot absorb it on a single visit."

He handed his hat to the man, who followed him to his cabin, where he tossed the hat aside, and turned on a device which not only blanked out the sound of their actual conversation against any electronic eavesdropping, but supplied a taped innocuous conversation to be picked up by such devices instead.

"Well?" the "boatswain" demanded.

Tosci shrugged. "Well, Comrade Project Supervisor," he said, "they took the Treasury Notes and said they would let us know. One really could not expect more at the moment."

"I suppose not," the Project Supervisor said gloomily. "Do you think they will '*take the contract*,' as I believe the phrase goes?"

"Why should they not, Comrade Project Supervisor? How could they resist the temptation? We are, after all, prepared to go as high as a *hundred* and eleven million dollars. It would take them a long time to collect a hundred and eleven million dollars from their, how do they call it, 'numbers racket'."

"About a week and a half; not more. Well, well, we shall see. Meanwhile, I am hungry. You took your time coming back."

"I am sorry, Comrade Project Supervisor, but—"

"No excuses. Bring me my supper now. And see that the cabbage in the borsht is not soggy as it was last night, and that there are no flies in the yogurt. Do you hear?"

"Yes, Comrade Project Supervisor," said Tosci.

Don Sylvester FitzPatrick, Second Vice-President of the Mafia (Lower Manhattan Branch) and son-in-law of Don Lefty McGonigle, sat brooding in his tiny office in the wholesale foodstuffs district. Despite his title he was a mere petty don in the hierarchy; well did he know that it was rumored he owed even this to nepotism, and these circumstances rankled (as he put it) in his bosom. "A man of my attainments, which they should put him in the front ranks of enterprise," he muttered, "and what am I doing? I'm in charge of the artichoke rake-off at the Washington Market!" Don Sylvester laughed bitterly; Don Sylvester sulked.

Meanwhile, in the Grand Chamber Council, discussion among the senior dons went on apace.

"Blowing up the Brooklyn Navy Yard," said Don Tex Thompson reflectively, "might be just the thing the national economy is in need of. Unemployment among skilled laborers went up seven point-oh-nine percent in the last fortnightly period, and among unskilled laborers the figure scores an even higher percentile. The Mafia," he said, "cannot remain indifferent to the plight of the workingman."

"Not if it is to retain that position of esteem and pre-eminence to which it is rightly entitled," said Don Morris Caplan.

"To say nothing of the excellent effect upon our National Defenses of clearing out all that obsolete equipment and replacing it with the newest devices obtainable through modern science," Don Shazzam X (formerly Rastus Washington) declared. "The Congress could scarcely refuse appropriations in such circumstances."

Don Wong Hua-Fu pursed his thin lips and put the tips of his six-inch fingernails together in church-steeple fashion. "The Honorable Ten Tongs do include sound common stocks in the various heavy-metals industries in their portfolio. Still," he said, "we must consider the great burdens already borne by the widows and orphans who constitute the majority of American taxpayers."

And Don Leverret Lowell Cabot pointed out another possible objection. "We cannot neglect our own heavy commitments in the Brooklyn Navy Yard area," he said. "As part of our responsibility to the men who man our country's ships we have, need I remind the Grand Council, leading interests in the bars, restaurants, night clubs, strip-joints, clip-joints, and gambling hells of the area—to say nothing of the hotels used for both permanent and temporary residence by the many charming ladies who lighten the burdens of the sea-weary sailors."

"It's a problem, believe *me*," sighed Don Gesú-María Gomez. "Little does the public know of our problems."

"Decisions, decisions, decisions!" Don Swede Swanson echoed the sigh.

"Gen-tle-men, gen-tle-men," said Don Lefty McGonigle, a note of mild protest in his hoarse voice. "Aren't we being a lit-tul pre-ma-chua? *We* are not being asked to blow up duh Brooklyn Navy Yahd dis minute. *We* are not even being asked to de*cide* if fit should be blown up dis minute. All we are being asked to do, gen-tle-men, is to decide if we are going to make a soyvey of de Iowa East Trivva estuary from d' point of view of its amen-i-ties as a pos-si-ble headquarters faw moychant marine offices. I yap-peal to you, Grand Master, am I creckt?"

Don Alexander Borjia tore his eyes away from the Mona Lisa on the wall. The lineaments of La Gioconda never ceased to entrance him, and there was the added fillip to his pleasure that the rest of the world naively thought the original still hung in the Louvre, little realizing that this last was a mere copy, painted, true, by Leonardo, but by Leonardo in his ancient age. The switcheroo had been arranged by Don Alexander's father, the late Grand Master Don César Borjia, before the First World War. Copies of masterworks of art, stolen at various times from museums and private collectors around the world, adorned the other walls. But Don Alexander Borjia's favorite remained the Mona Lisa.

"Don Lefty McGonigle is correct," he said. "Take the contract for the survey, charge them eighty-seven million dollars for it, and when it comes time for a decision on the *big* question, so we'll leave them know further. All in favor say *Aye*. Opposed, *Nay*. The Ayes got it."

There was a silence.

"A foyda question," said Don Lefty finally. He fingered the cabochon emerald which nestled in his watered-silk four-in-hand, and fiddled with his eyepatch.

"Speak."

"Whom is to be ap-poin-ted to take over d' soyvey?"

"Whom did you have in mind?"

"A young man which he oughta be given more responsibility than he's being given, to wit, my son-in-law, the Second Vice-President of the Mafia, Lower Manhattan Branch. Woddaya say, gen-tle-men?"

The pause which followed this suggestion seemed faintly embarrassed. Then Don Swede Swanson was heard to express the opinion that Don Sylvester FitzPatrick couldn't find the seat of his pants in the dark with both hands.

Don Lefty turned to him and pressed both his hands to his chest. "You wound me!" he exclaimed, his voice deep with suppressed emotion. "Night afta night I come home an' my liddle Philomena is eating huh haht out. 'Daddy, Daddy, Daddy,' she asks, weeping, 'what has everybody got against poor Sylvester? Din't he soyve his apprenticeship the same as everybody else? Is-int he loyal? Trustwoythy? Coyteous? Kind? So why, afta twelve years, is he still only in chahge of ahtichokes at Wahshington Mahket?'

"An' ya know what? *I* don't know what ta *say* ta huh! *If* fit was a matta of money, so I'd buy him a sand-and-gravel company, or a broory. But it's a matta of tra-*di*-tion, gen-tle-men! All of youse got sons. I ain't got no son! All I got is my liddle Philomena. A bee-uty in thuh Hollywood sense a thuh woid she may not be, but she yiz the yimage of huh sainted mother, rest her soul, an' huh husband is like a son ta me, so when ya spit on *him*, gen-tlemen, it's like ya spitting on *me!*"

Throats were cleared, eyes wiped, noses blown. Don Alexander essayed to speak, but was prevented by emotion. At last the silence was broken by Don Swede Swanson. "So let it be Sylvester," he said huskily. There was a chorus of nods.

"Of course, there is one hazard of the chase involved in my sweet Sauncepeur's snaffling hot broils off these out-

door grills," Lord Grue and Groole observed. "It—shall I
sweeten the air in here a bit? I've a packet of frankin-
cense that my friend, Osman Ali the Somali, sent me not
long ago; I wouldn't *buy* incense, of course," he said,
sprinkling the pale yellow grains on the glowing embers.
A pungent odor filled the cave. •

Denny the Dip coughed. The Marquess donned his
gauntlet and examined the falcon's talons, particularly
about the pads. "It makes the poor creature's petti-toes
sore. I've experimented with various nostra and it's my
considered opinion that Pinaud's Moustache Wax is
above all things the best. Is there anything more left in
the flask? Shall we kill it, as you say over here? Ah, good
show."

With a gesture he motioned to Denny to take the bed;
he himself reclined on a tiger skin which was stored during the day in a dry niche. Thus settled, he grew expan-
sive. "Ah, it's not what I've been accustomed to, me that
used to have my own shooting lodge in the grouse season,
waited on, hand and foot, by a dozen Baloochi servants;
well, and now here I am, like a bloody eremite, living on
me wits and the $5.60 I get from home each week."

Denny lifted his head. "You're a remittance man?" he
inquired.

"Sort of remittance man, you might say, yes. Me
nevew, Piers Plunkert, pays me two quid a week, not so
much to stay away as to stay alive. 'Avoid alcohol, Uncle,'
he writes, 'and mind you wear your wooly muffler when
the north wind blows.' It's not filial piety, mind, or avuncular piety, or anything like it. You see, if I pop off, *he* becomes the twelfth Marquess of Grue and Groole, and all
the rest of that clobber—the mere thought of it makes his
blood run cold. No, he's not a Labour M.P.; his fix is
worse than that. He's one of the *Angry Young Men!*

"Struth! Lives in a filthy little room in South Stepney,
and composes very bad, very blank verse damning The

Establishment, under the pseudonym of 'Alf Huggins.' Well, now, I ask you—would *you* pay any attention to an Angry Young Man named Lord Grue and Groole? No, of course you wouldn't. And neither would anyone else.

"Once a year I threaten suicide. 'It doesn't matter about me, my boy,' I write. '*You* will carry on the name and title.' My word, what a flap that puts him in! *Always* good for ten quid pronto via cablegram."

A sound, so dim and distant that it failed to reach the ear of Denny the Dip, caused the peerless peer to break off discourse and raise his head. "Bogey," he announced. "Policeman, to you. Weighs about a hundred and sixty and has trouble with his left arch. Neglects his tum, too— hear it rumble!"

Denny strained, could hear nothing but the traffic passing through the park, its sound rising and falling with the wind, like surf. He murmured, "What a talent you got, Grooley! What a team we'd make!"

"A team we certainly will *not* make!" the peer snorted. "But, as to your playing squire to my knight, hmm, well, we'll consider it. I plan to take a brisk walk in the morning, down to the Battery and vicinage. We'll see if you can stand the pace—no sinecure being gunbearer, as it were, to the man who outwalked The Man-Eater of Mysore. And another thing—" He thwacked The Dip across the feet with his swagger stick. "No more of this 'Grooley!' Call me Sahib, Bwana, Kyrios, or M'lord."

"Hmm," murmured Lord Grue and Groole, pausing and looking in the shop window. "I find that curious. Don't *you* find that curious, Denny?"

Denny, panting and aching from the long trek down from Central Park, was finding nothing curious but his inability to break away and sink to rest. "Wuzzat, Gr—I mean Bwana?" he moaned. He was bearing, in lieu of gun, the Marquess' swagger stick.

"Use your *eyes*, man! There, in the window. What do you see?"

The Dip wiped the sweat out of his eyes. "Leather goods?" he inquired. "Outboard motors? Canned crab-meat?" the Marquess clicked his tongue, and swore rap-idly in Swahili (Up-Country dialect). "Seasoned Hon-duras mahogany?" The Dip continued hastily. "Flowered organdy? Blue rayon? Manila hemp?"

"*Ahah!* Just so, a great lovely coil of Manila hempen rope. Notice anything odd about it? *No?* You were pull-ing the wrong mendicant dodge, you should've used a tin cup. You really don't see that scarlet thread running through it, so cleverly and closely intertwined that it can-not be picked out without spoiling the rope? You *do* see it; good. No use to ask if you know what it means; you don't, so I'll tell you. It means that rope was made by and for the Royal Navy. It is *never* sold, so it must have been stolen. No one would dare fence it in Blighty, so they've shipped it over here. Clever, I call that. Must look into this."

He entered the shop, followed by Denny, who sank at once into a chair. The dog Guido, looking as cool and fresh as his master, stood motionless. Mrs. Goodeycoonce emerged from the back.

"Afternoon, ma'am," said Lord Grue and Groole, touching the brim of his quasi-caracul cap, and giving her no chance to speak. "My name is Arthur Powisse, of the Powisse Exterminating Company. Allow me to offer you my card—dear me, I seem to have given the last one away; ah, well, it doesn't signify. This is my chief assist-ant, Mr. Dennis, and the animal is one of our pack of trained Tyrolean Rat Hounds. We have just finished a rush job at one of the neighborhood warehouses, and, happening to pass by and being entranced by your very attractive window display, thought we would drop in and offer you an estimate on de-ratting your premises."

Mrs. Goodeycoonce opened her mouth, but the Marquess swept on. "I anticipate your next comment, ma'am. You are about to say, 'But I keep a clean house'—and so you do, so you obviously do. But do your *neighbors?* Aye, there's the rub; they don't, alas. Around the corner is an establishment of the type known as, if you will pardon the expression, a common flophouse—the sort of place where they throw fishbones in the corner and never sweep up. Three doors down is the manufactory of Gorman's Glossy Glue Cakes, a purely animal product, on which *ratus ratus* thrives, ma'am, simply *thrives!*"

Something flickered in Granny Goodeycoonce's eyes which seemed to indicate she had long been aware of the proximity of Gorman's Glossy Glue Cakes, particularly on very warm days, and found in it no refreshment of soul whatsoever.

"How often at night," Lord Grue and Groole waxed almost lyrical, "when all should be quiet, must you not have heard Noises, eh?—and attributed them to the settling of the timbers, the expansion and contraction of the joists and beams. Not a bit of it! *Rats!*" His voice sank to a whisper. "Oh, the horror of it! First one gray shadow, then another—"

He took a step forward, she took one backward, he advanced, she retreated. "Then great grisly waves of them, first in the foundations, then in the cellar, then—does this door lead to the cellar? I had better examine it."

Later that evening found the Marquess and his bearer deep in the shadowy doorway of an empty warehouse. "It was the advent of that offensively wholesome-looking young chap, her grandson, that broke the spell," the Mar-

quess mused. "Said she'd consider it. No matter. I saw the
cellar. Those crates and crates of Polish hams! Those
bales of raw rubber! Turkish Sipahi Cigarettes! That
infinite variety of portable, seaborne merchandise!

"It can only mean one thing: the people are pukka
river pirates. I know the signs—seen them on the Thames,
the Nile, Hoogli, Brahmapootra, Whampoa, Pei-Ho—*eheu
fugaces*. Nice set-up she's got there—snug shop, tidy
house, fine figger, and a widow woman, I'm sure—no sign
of a husband and anyone can see she's not the divorcing
type. Hmm, well, question is: How does the lad get the
stuff there? How do river pirates *usually* get the stuff
there? Just so."

And they had walked along the waterfront, the Marquess examining the water as intently as one of the inhabitants of the Sunda Straits peering for *bêche-de-mer*, The
Dip plodding along to the rear of Guido, as sunken beneath the weight of the swagger stick as if it had been an
elephant gun. He reflected on the day he might have
spent, conning old ladies out of coins, and on a certain
bat-cave he knew of, where an ounce and a quarter of
Old Cordwainer retailed for the ridiculous sum of 31
cents. But there was that about the Marquess which said
Hither to me, caitiff, and therein fail not, at your peril;
therefore Denny plodded meekly.

"Ho," said His Lordship, stopping, and pointing at the
filthy waters of the East River, which, in a happier time,
lined with forests and grassy meads, were thick with sal-
mon, shad, cod, alewives, herring, sturgeon, and all fruits
of the sea; now the waters were merely thick. "Observe,"
said His Lordship. "You see how—there—the oil slick, orange peel, bad bananas, and other rubbish floats down
with the tide. Whereas the flotsam rides more or less
straight out from under us and joins the current at a right
angle. The *main* current, that is. Let's have a dekko," he

declared, and shinnied down the side of the wharf timbers almost to the water's edge.

His enthusiasm, as he clambered up, almost com-
municated itself to The Dip. "Whuddaya see, Sahib?" he
asked, craning.

"Enough. Tonight, when the eyes of the Blessed
Houris in Paradise, yclept 'stars' in our rude Saxon Tongue,
shine as clearly as this filthy air will allow them to, we
shall follow young Mr. Goodeycoonce. Here are rupees, or
whatever the juice they call them—'quarters'? Just so. Go
thou and eat, and return within the hour. As for me, a
strip of biltong will do, and fortunately I took care to
refill the flask. They make good whiskey in Belfast, I must
say, cursed Orangemen though they be." He raised his
drink and waved it across a trickle in the gutter. "To the
King over the water"—and drank. His glass eye glittered
defiance to all the House of Hanover.

All was quiet in the kitchen behind THE ALMOST ANY-
THING SECOND-HAND GOODS AND OUTLET STORE. Granny
Goodeycoonce was pasting in her scrapbook the latest letter she had received in reply to a message of congrat-
ulations sent on the birthday of one of the Princesses of
the Netherlands. It read, as did all the others in the scrapbook: *The Queen has read your letter with interest and
directs me to thank you for your good wishes.* And it was
signed, as nearly as could be made out, Squiggle Van
Squiggle, Secretary.

"Gee," said Neely, looking up from a trade journal he
was reading, "here's a bait business for sale on Long Island, on the North Shore." There was no answer. He tried
again. "And a boat basin in Connecticut. 'Must be sold at
once,' the ad says, 'to settle estate.' Gee."

His grandmother capped the tube of library paste. "I
suppose Princess Beatrix will be getting engaged pretty

soon," she observed. "I wonder who to. How old is the Crown Prince of Greece? No, that wouldn't do, I suppose; he'll be *King* of Greece some day, and she'll be Queen of Holland. Hmm." She knit her brows, deep in the problems of dynasty.

"They could be combined," Neely suggested.

Granny Goodeycoonce looked up, amazed. "What, Greece and *Holland*?"

"No, I mean a bait business and a boatyard. People," he explained enthusiastically, "would buy *bait* to fish with from their *boats*. And—"

She clicked her tongue. "The idea! A Goodeycoonce becoming a fishmonger!"

"Better than being a river pirate," he mumbled.

"Never let me hear you use that word again!" she snapped. "The very idea! Have you *no* respect for the traditions of the family? Why, it makes my blood boil! And don't you forget for one minute, young man, that I am a Goodeycoonce by descent as well as by marriage; don't you forget *that!*"

"Fat chance," Neely muttered.

His grandmother opened her mouth to release a thunderbolt, but at that moment there came a thud from the cellar, followed by a clatter.

"Oh, my land," Granny whispered, a hand at her throat. "Rats! I should've listened to that Limey. Is the door to the cellar locked?"

Answer was superfluous, for at that moment the door swung open and in stepped the Limey himself, more properly described as Arthur Marmaduke Roderick Lodowicke William Rufus de Powisse-Plunkert, Baron Bogle, Earl of Ballypatcoogan, Viscount Penhokey, Laird of Muckle Greet, Master of Snee, 11th Marquess of Grue and Groole in the Peerage of England, and Hereditary

Lord High Keeper of the Queen's Bears. "Good evening, all," he said.

Neely went pale. "I knew it!" he cried. "I knew we couldn't go on getting away with it forever, not after almost three hundred years! That exterminator story was just a dodge—he must be from the Harbor Patrol, or the Coast Guard!"

The Marquess took his swagger stick from the quivering Denny (who had made the underground voyage with his head under his coat, for fear of bats), and smacked it gently into the palm of his hand. "You know, I resent that very much," he said, a touch of petulance in his voice. "I will have you know that I am no copper's nark, common informer, or fink. I—"

"You get out of my house," said Granny Goodeycoonce, "or I'll—"

"Call the police? Oh, I doubt that, my good woman; I doubt that entirely. How would you explain all those cork fenders in the cellar? The copper cable, raw rubber, Turkish Sipahi Cigarettes, Polish hams? To say nothing of enough sailcloth to supply a regatta, a ton of tinned caviar, five hundred *oka* of Syrian arrack, twenty canisters of ambergris, several score pods of prime Nepauli musk, and, oh, simply ever so many more goodies—all of which, I have no hesitation in declaring, are the fruits of, I say not 'theft,' but of, shall I say, impermissive acquisition. Eh?"

Granny Goodeycoonce, during the partial inventory, had recovered her aplomb. "Well, you simply couldn't be more wrong," she said, a smile of haughty amusement on her lips. "'Impermissive'? Poo. We have the best permission anyone could ever want. Neely, show this foreign person our permission."

Still pale, and muttering phrases like *I'll be an old man when I get out*, Neely unlocked an antique cabinet in one corner of the room and removed a flat steel case, which he handed to his grandmother. She opened it with a key of her own, and reverently extracted a parchment document festooned with seals, which she displayed to the Marquess with the words: "Look, but don't touch."

He fixed his monocle firmly in his good eye and bent over. After a while he straightened up. "Mph. Well, I must confess that my knowledge of Seventeenth Century Dutch orthography is rather limited. But I *can* make out the name of Van Goedikoentse, as well as that of Petrus Stuyvesant. Perhaps you would be good enough to explain?"

Nothing could have pleased Granny more. "*This*," she said in tones both hushed and haughty, "is a Patent from the Dutch West India Company, granting to my great-great-great-great-great-great-great-grandfather, Nicolaes Jacobus Van Goedikoentse, *and* 'to his heirs forever,' the right of collecting customs in the harbor port of Nieuw Amsterdam. It was granted in return for Myn Heer Van Geodikoentse's valiant help in resisting the insolent British demand for surrender in 1662. Governor Stuyvesant promised he would never forget."

For a moment no word broke the reverent silence. Then, slowly, Lord Grue and Groole removed his cap. "And naturally," he said, "your family has never recognized that surrender. Madam, as an unreconstructed Jacobite, I honor them for it, in your person." He gravely bowed. Equally gravely, Mrs. Goodeycoonce made a slight curtsy. "Under no circumstances," he went on, "would I dream of betraying your confidence. As a small effort to amend for the sins of my country's past I offer you my collaboration—my very, very *experienced* collaboration, if I do say so."

Three hundred years (almost) of going it alone struggled in Mrs. Goodeycoonce's bosom to say No. At the

same time she was plainly impressed with Lord Grue and
Groole's offer—to say nothing of his manner. It took her a
while to reply. "Well," she said finally, "we'll see."

Don Sylvester FitzPatrick, Second Vice-President of
the Mafia (Lower Manhattan Branch), was nervous. The
survey was almost finished, and the Grand Council still
hadn't made up its mind about blowing up the Brooklyn
Navy Yard. In fact, it was even now debating the project
in their Chamber, at the window of the anteroom to
which Don Sylvester now sat. Elation at being at long last
removed from the artichoke detail had gradually given
way to uneasiness. Suppose they *did* decide to blow it up?
Would the United States Government take the same
broad view of this as the Dons did? Visions of being
hanged from the yardarm of, say, the USS *Missouri*,
danced like sugar plums in Sylvester's head.

A flutter from the crates at his foot distracted his attention. In one was a black pigeon, in one was a white. Very
soon the mysterious Mr. Tosci would appear with
$87,000,000 in plain, sealed wrappers, and be told the
Grand Council's decision. Even now the Mafiosi bomb
squads were standing by at the ready in Brooklyn. Informed only that morning that police had put the traditional, semiannual wire tap on the Mafiosi phones, the
Mafiosi had brought out the traditional, semiannual pigeon post.

"Now, remember," Don Lefty McGonigle had instructed his son-in-law, "d' black boid has d' message
Bombs Away awready in d' cap-sool fastened to its foot.
And d' white boid's got d' message *Everyt'ing Off* in-
scribed on d' paper in d' cap-sool on *its* foot. Ya got dat?"

"Yeah, Papa," said Don Sylvester, wiping his face.

"So when ya get d' woid, *Yes*, ya leddout d' *black* pigeon. But if ya get d' woid, *No*, den ya leddout d' *white*
pigeon. An' nats all dere's to it. Okay?"

"Okay, Papa."

"Om depending on you. Philomena is depending on you. So don't chew be noivous."

"No, Papa," said Don Sylvester.

When Forrance told Daisy that the "Nafia" was awaiting delivery of the first of its new fleet of trucks he was speaking optimistically. The new truck was "new" only in the sense that it was newer than the one it replaced, a 1924 Star, which had to be thawed out with boiling water in cold weather and cranked by hand before it would start, in all weather. The Nafia treasury had suffered a terrible blow when the Cherry Street Mob, in the mid-fifties, took over the distribution of birch beer south of Vesey Street—during the course of which epic struggle Guts had his ears boxed and Blood suffered a sympathetic nasal hemorrhage; as a result, the treasury could only afford to have the single word NAFIA painted on the side panels. Still it was *something*.

"Rides like a dream, don't it," Forrance said, as they headed along South Street one bright afternoon.

"No, it don't," said Blood. "It liss."

"Whaddaya mean, 'it liss'?"

"I mean, like it liss ta one side. Look—"

Guts said, "He's right, boss. It *does* liss. Them new gumball machines ain't equally distribitted. They all slide to one side."

Forrance halted the truck with a grinding of gears. "All right," he said resignedly; "then let's take'm all out and put'm back in again, but *evenly* this time."

So the smallest criminal organization in New York got out of its fleet of trucks to unload and reload its gumball machines.

Tosci paused on the deck of the yacht to receive his superior's final instructions. "I have counted the money," he said. "Eighty-six million in negotiable bearer bonds, and one million in cash."

"Very well. Perhaps they will have time to spend it all before we Take Over; perhaps not. I have instructed the Chief Engineer to test the engines in order that we can leave as soon as the decision is made. They *say* the bombs are set for four hours, but who knows if we can believe them?"

As if to confirm his fears, the Chief Engineer at this moment rushed on deck, grease and dismay, in equal parts, showing on his face.

"The engines won't start!" he cried.

"They *must* start!" snapped the Project Supervisor. "Go below and see to it!" The Chief, with a shrug, obeyed. The Project Supervisor scowled. "An odd coincidence—if it is a coincidence," he said. "Personally, I have never trusted sailors since the Kronstadt Mutiny." To conceal his nervousness he lifted his binoculars to his eyes, ordering Tosci not to leave the ship for the time being. Scarcely had he looked through the glasses when an exclamation broke through his clenched lips.

"There is a truck on the waterfront," he cried, "with the Mafia's name on it! And three men are lifting something from it. Here—" he thrust the glasses at Tosci—"see what you can make of it."

Tosci gazed in bewilderment. "Those machines," he said. "I've never seen anything like them. I don't understand—why should the Mafia be unloading such strange devices so near our ship?"

Suspicion, never far below the surface of the Project Supervisor's mind, and usually right on top of it, burst into flames. "They must be electronic devices to keep our engines from functioning!" he cried. "They think to leave us stuck here in the direct path of the explosions, thus destroying alien witnesses! Clever, even admirable—but we cannot allow it. Come—" he seized Tosci by the arm holding the portfolio in which the bonds and money were—"to the launch! We must see about this!" Together they rushed down the gangway ladder into the boat.

"White pigeon if it's No," Don Sylvester mumbled. "Black pigeon if it's Yes. White, No. Black, Yes. I got it." But he was still nervous. Suppose he fumbled his responsibilities at the crucial moment—*suppose he bungled the job?* For the hundredth time his fingers examined the catches on the cage, lifted one up a fraction of an inch, closed it, then lifted the other—and there was a sudden sound from the cage.

Don Sylvester's startled fingers flew to his mouth. The catch snapped up. The black pigeon hopped out, fluttered to the window sill, cooed again, and—as Sylvester made a frantic lunge for it—spread its wings and flew out. It soared up, up, up, circled once, circled twice, then flew off toward Brooklyn.

Sylvester stared at the air in wordless horror. Then he stared at the door of the Grand Council Chamber. Any moment now, it might open. He tiptoed over and listened.

"I say *no!*" a voice declared.

"And I say *yes!*" declared a second voice.

Helplessly, his eyes roamed the anteroom, fell at length on the telephone. Regardless of possible wiretaps, he quickly and fearfully dialed a number. "Hello?" he whispered hoarsely. "Hello, Philomena? Listen, Philomena—"

The black pigeon flapped its way toward Brooklyn with leisurely strokes, thinking deep pigeonic thoughts. Now and then it caught an updraft and coasted effortlessly. It was in no hurry. But, of course, it really was not very far to Brooklyn, as a pigeon flies. . . .

"Easy does it—watch my toes, ya dope—down, down."

"Good afternoon, boys," said Daisy. "I just came out to

mail a letter to Turkey. Did you know that airmail is ten cents cheaper to the west bank of the Hellespont, because it's in Europe? Oooh—gumballs! Let me see if I have a penny—"

"No, let me see if *I* got one, Miss—no, lem*me* see, Forry —aa, c'*mon*, I gotta have one—"

While the three Nafiosi were plunging in their pockets, the yacht's launch drew up to the pier. Out of it came Tosci, the Project Supervisor, and three crewmen. "What are you up to?" Tosci shouted.

"What's it to you?" Forrance countered.

"I order you to remove those machines from this area at once!"

Instantly truculent, Forrance thrust out his jaw. "Nobody orders the Nafia what to do with its machines," he said. "Anyways, not south of Vesey Street," he amended.

"Put them on the truck and see that they are driven away," Tosci instructed a crewman, who began to obey, but was prevented by Blood. The crewman swung, Blood's nose, ever sensitive, began to bleed, and Daisy, aroused, cried, "You let him alone!" and wielded her pocketbook with a will. The crewman staggered. Guts, gauging his distance to a nicety, swung his ponderous belly around and knocked him down.

"Take the girl," shouted the Project Supervisor, in his own language. "She is undoubtedly their 'moll.' We will keep her aboard as a hostage." And while he, Tosci, and one of their men engaged the tiny syndicate in combat, the other two sailors hustled Daisy into the launch, muffling her cries for help.

Mrs. Goodeycoonce, Neely, Denny, Guido, and Lord Grue and Groole were out for a walk. No decision had yet been made on the noble lord's proposal, but nevertheless everyone seemed to be growing somewhat closer. The

Marquess was telling about the time that he rescued the Dowager Begum of Oont from the horrid captivity in which she had been placed by her dissolute nephew, the Oonti Ghook. All listened in fascination, except the dog Guido, who had heard the story before.

So taken up in his account was the Marquess that he absent-mindedly abstracted from his pocket a particularly foul pipe (which respect for the lady had normally prevented his smoking in her presence), and proceeded to charge it with the notoriously rank tobacco swept up for sale to the inhabitants of the lower-income quarters of Quetta; and struck a match to it. At the first unconsidered whiff Mrs. Goodeycoonce coughed. Then she gagged, then she inhaled with a harsh, gasping breath. And next she turned white, green, and bright red.

Neely was the first to notice. "Granny!" he said. "Granny?" Then, "It must be your pipe—"

The Marquess was overcome with confusion and remorse. "Terribly sorry," he declared. "I'd knock the dottle out, except that's all it *is*, you know—dottle, I mean. I say, Mrs. Goodeycoonce—oh, I *say*."

But Mrs. Goodeycoonce's face had taken on an almost masculine appearance. She rolled up first one fist, loosely, and then the other, placed them in alignment, lifted them to her eyes, and peered out upon the River. And in a gutturally accented and heavy voice quite unlike her usual tones she declared, "Zound der alarm! Beat to qvarters! *Zo, zo, wat den duyvel!*"

The Marquess' eagle-keen eyes followed her glance and immediately observed something very much amiss upon the waters.

"Stap my vitals, if I don't believe a gel is being forced aboard that vessel over there," he said. "Bad show, that. What?"

Instantly the possessing spirit of Peter Stuyvesant

vanished and was replaced by that of Mrs. Goodey-coonce. She uttered a cry. "White slavery, that's what it must be! And in broad daylight, too. Oh, the brazen things! What should we *do?*"

Neely hauled an old-fashioned but quite authentic and brass-bound telescope from his pocket and swung it around. As he focused in and recognized Daisy, struggling desperately while being taken up the gangway, he uttered a hoarse shout of rage.

"'Do'?" he yelled. "We've got to save her! Come on! My boat! Let's *go!*"

The black pigeon passed over City Hall, dallied for a few moments in the currents around the Woolworth Building, and then pressed on in the general direction of Sand Street. . . .

As Neely's boat zoomed under the bow of the yacht, the Marquess kicked off his shoes, seized the anchor chain, and swarmed up like a monkey. Neely and Denny were met at the foot of the gangway ladder by two crewmen, who shouted, gesticulated, and menaced them with boathooks. But in a moment the boatmen's attention was diverted by a tumult from above. Part of this was caused by Lord Grue and Groole who, darting from one place of concealment to another, called out (in different voices) battle cries in Pathan, Kikuyu, and Demotic Greek; and part of it was caused by the alarm of the crew at being boarded—so they thought—by a host of foes.

While their opponents' attention was thus distracted, Denny and Neely gained the deck where Neely at once knocked down the first sailor he saw. Denny's contribution was more circumspect. Noting an oily rag in a corner he took out a match. In a moment clouds of black smoke arose.

"Fire!" cried the Dip. "Fire! *Fire!*"

Part of the crew promptly swarmed down the ladder into Neely's boat and cast off. The rest jumped over the side and commenced swimming briskly toward the nearer shore.

"Hello!" Neely shouted, stumbling along the passageways, opening doors. "Hello, hello! Where are you?"

A muffled voice called, he burst in, and there was Daisy, gagged and bound, struggling in a chair. Neely cut her loose, removed the gag, and—after only a very slight hesitation, perhaps natural in a shy young man of good family—kissed her repeatedly.

"*Well*," said Daisy tremulously, as he paused for breath, and then to herself, "I guess he's not such a milksop after all."

On deck Denny the Dip and the Marquess stomped out the smoldering rag, though not, however, in time to avoid having attracted two police boats, a Coast Guard cutter, the Governor's Island ferry, a Hudson River Dayliner, and the New York City Fireboat, *Zophar Mills*, all of which converged on the yacht.

"Thank you, thank you," called out the Marquess, between cupped hands. "We don't require any assistance, the fire is out. You will observe, however, that officers and crew have abandoned the ship, which means that she is now, under maritime law, by right of salvage, the property of myself and my associates, both *in personam* and *in rem*."

The failure of the engines to start, it was ascertained after a careful scrutiny, was owing to the intrusion of a large waterbug into one of the oil liners; this was soon set right. An attempt of a floating delegate of the Masters, Mates, and Pilots Union to question the Marquess' right to take the helm of the salvaged vessel was quickly terminated by the revelation that he possessed a first-class nav-

igation certificate in the Siamese Merchant Marine. The
delegate addressed him henceforth as "Captain," and on
departing, offered him the use of all the amenities of the
Union Hall.

It was while seeing this personage off that Lord Grue
and Groole observed a familiar shadow on the deck of the
yacht, and, taking off his quasi-caracul and waving it,
lured Sauncepeur down from what the poet Pope once so
prettily described as "the azure Realms of Air."

"She has clutched a quarry," he observed. "Well-
footed, my pretty, well-trussed. Let me have pelt, dearie—
nay, don't mantle it—there. Good. You shall have new
bewits, with bells, and silver varvels to your jesses, with
my crest upon them. Hel-lo, *hel*-lo, what have you *done*,
you demned vulture? You've taken a carrier pigeon!" He
opened the message capsule. *"Bombs Away,"* he read.
"Rum, very rum. Doubtless the name of a horse, and
some poor booby of a bookmaker has taken this means of
evading the puritanical Yankee laws dealing with the dis-
semination of racing intelligence. Hmm, well, not my pid-
jin. Haw, haw!" he chuckled at the pun. "Denny!" he
called.

"Yes, M'Lord?"

The Marquess tossed him the bird. "A pigeon for the
pot. See that Sauncepeur gets the head and the humbles;
afterwards she's to have a nice little piece of beefsteak,
and a bone to break."

That, in a way, concludes the story. The epilogue is
brief. Don Lefty McGonigle, though heartbroken at the
abrupt and (to him mysterious) disappearance of his son-
in-law and daughter, takes some comfort in the frequent
picture postcards that Philomena sends him from such
places as Tahiti, Puntas Arenas, Bulawayo, and other lo-
cales where the Mafia's writ (fearsomely hard on de-

serters) runneth not. The Nafia (originally organized in 1880 under the full name of the National Federation of Independent Artisans, a "Wide Awake" or Chowder and Marching Society, as part of the presidential campaign of General Winfield Scott Hancock, whose famous declaration that "the tariff is a local issue" insured his defeat by General J. Abram Garfield)—the Nafia still controls all the gumball and Indian nut machines south of Vesey Street; and revels in the publicity resultant from its members' brief incarceration, along with Tosci, the Project Supervisor, and the three crewmen. The Cherry Street Mob would now not *dream* of muscling in on a syndicate whose pictures were in all the papers in connection with a portfolio containing $87,000,000; it is the Mob's belief that the fight was caused by the Nafia's attempting to hijack this sum.

Cornelius ("Neely") and Daisy Goodeycoonce have purchased, out of their share of the salvage money, one of the most up-and-coming bait-and-boatyard businesses on Long Island Sound. Granny Goodeycoonce at first was reluctant, but on learning that Daisy's mother was a Van Dyne, of the (originally) Bergen-op-Zoom, Holland, Van Dynes, she extended her blessings. It remains her view, however, that the family profession of nocturnal customs collecting is merely in abeyance, and will be kept in trust, as it were, for the children.

Granny is, in fact, for the first time in her life, no longer a Goodeycoonce, but Mistress of Snee, Lady of Muckle Greet, Baroness Bogle, Countess Ballypatcoogen, Viscountess Penhokey, Marchioness of Grue and Groole— and, presumably, Lord High Keeperess of the Queen's Bears—although on this last point Debrett's is inclined to be dubious. The fact that the older couple has chosen to go on a prolonged honeymoon with their yacht to the general vicinage of the Sulu Sea where, those in the know report, the opportunities for untaxed commerce (coarsely called "smuggling" by some) between the Philippines, Indonesia, and British North Borneo are simply splendid, is doubtless purely coincidental.

One thread (or at most two) in the gorgeous tapestry we have woven for the instruction of our readers remains as yet untied. This is the question of what happened to Tosci and his Project Supervisor after their release from brief confinement on unpressed charges of assault.

It is unquestionably true that their pictures were in all the papers. It is equally true, and equally unquestionable, that the Mafia frowns on publicity for those connected with its far-flung operations. Rumors that the two men were fitted for concrete spaceshoes and subsequently invited to participate in skindiving operations south of Ambrose Light, no matter how persistent, cannot be confirmed.

A Mr. Alexander Borjia, businessman and art connoisseur, questioned by a Congressional investigating committee, said (or at any rate, read from a prepared statement): "My only information about the so-called Mafia comes from having heard that it is sometimes mentioned in the Sunday supplements of sensation-seeking newspapers. I do not read these myself, being unable to approve of the desecration of the Lord's Day which their publication and distribution necessarily involve. Nor can I subscribe to the emphasis such journals place upon crime and similar sordid subjects, which cannot but have an unfortunate effect upon our basically clean-living American youth."

It was at or about this point that Senator S. Robert E. Lee ("Sourbelly Sam") Sorby (D., Old Catawba), chose to light up his famous double-bowl corncob pipe, of which it has been said that the voters of his native state sent him to Washington because they could not stand the smell of it at home. Mr. Borjia (evidently as unimpressed as the Old Catawba voters by Senator Sorby's statement that the mixture was made according to a formula invented by the Indians after whom the State was named)— Mr. Borjia coughed, gagged, gasped, turned white, green, red; and after leveling an imaginary telescope consisting of his own loosely rolled fists, proceeded (in a strange, guttural, and heavily accented voice quite unlike his own) to describe what was even then going on in the secret chambers of the Mafia in such wealth of detail as to make it abundantly clear to the Executive, the Judicial, and the Legislative branches of the Government (as well as to himself, when with bulging eyes he subsequently read the transcripts of his own "confession") that he must never be allowed outside any of the several Federal caravanserais in which he has subsequently and successively been entertained.

And there let us leave him.

Afterword for The Lord of Central Park

I have been told (by whom?—who knows by whom?— you think I have time to ask the ID of every nut who comes down the pike?) (ans.: No.) I have been told that Plato, somewhere, says in effect that when a carpenter makes a table he is merely copying, in wood, a table (a prototable?) which already exists in his mind. Which already exists in his mind as a sort of mental reflection of a sort of celestial table. As it were. If Plato did not call this latter an archetype of a table, it was because Plato had not read Jung. Although of course, if Plato *did* call it an archetype, does this mean that Plato *had* read Jung? If history is, as some Greek philosophers said it is, cyclical, perhaps Plato had indeed read Jung. (This, by the way is called "metaphysics." If you had a brother, would he love noodles?) What is all this leading up to? Why are you so suspicious? The archetype or it may be the prototype of this story is a book by Robert Nathan. Chap who had lost his home during the Depression, and all his goods save for a four-poster bed, had moved the bed to a cave in Central Park. What's the matter? Shakespeare didn't steal from Holinshed? I wrote this story a long time ago, and on reading the as-yet-untitled ms., Lorna Moore, then wife to Ward Moore, said, "I know just the title for it: *The Lord of Central Park.*" And I thought she was right. And I still think so. But somewhere along the line came an editor who thought he had a better one. And so it goes. (It *does* go so.)

Now. Was there an actual prototype for the Lord of Central Park himself? Well . . . In a way it is a composite of all the magnificent loonies which used to flourish in the days of the Ever-victorious British Raj. And in a way it is based slightly upon an actual (nonroyal) duke who *was* actually the last man to be tried by the House of Lords as "a jury of his peers." The House of Lords has relinquished this right. And is Britain visibly better off? However. Not my pidgin. The duke is dead now. So never mind which one. *Fe dux* does not, after all, imply the duke was gay.

And as for the Manhattan exemplified in this tale of things odd and curious, there are those who say that it is not the real Manhattan. To which *I* say, It is *a* real Manhattan: I have walked its streets. And if much has been destroyed in the Manhattan of others, none of it has been destroyed in the Manhattan of my mind. The archetype remains, for archetypes do not suffer themselves to be destroyed.

(*Note:* Augustus Van Horne Stuyvesant has died, at a great age, after this story was written. He was the last living male descendant of Peter Stuyvesant, last Dutch Governor of New York, then New Amsterdam, New Netherlands.)

The Grantha Sighting

There were visitors, of course—there were visitors pretty nearly every night nowadays. The side road had never had such traffic. Emma Towns threw the door open and welcomed them, beaming. Walt was there behind her, smiling in his usual shy way.

"Hello there, Emma," Joe Trobridge said. "Won't let me call her 'Mrs. Towns,' you know," he explained to his friends. They went into the warm kitchen of the farmhouse. "This is Si Haffner, this is Miss Anderson, this is Lou DelBello—all members of the Unexplained Aerial Phenomena Coordinators, too. And *this* gentleman," he added, when the other three had finished shaking hands, "is Mr. Tom Knuble."

"Just call me Long Tom," said Long Tom.

Emma said, "Oh, not the radio man? *Really?* Well, my goodness!"

"Tom would like to make some tape recordings from here," Joe explained. "To replay on his program. If you don't mind, that is?"

Why of *course* they didn't mind. And they made the visitors sit right down and they put hot coffee on the table, and tea and home-baked bread and some of Emma's preserves and some of Walt's scuppernong wine, and sandwiches, because they were sure their visitors must be tired and hungry after that long drive.

"This is mighty nice of you," Long Tom said. "*And*

very tasty." The Townses beamed, and urged him to take more. Joe cleared his throat.

"This must be at least the fifth or sixth time *I've* been up here," he said. "As well as people I've told they could come up——"

"Any time——" said Emma.

"Any friends——" said Walt.

Joe half-smiled, half-chuckled. A slight trace of what might have been embarrassment was in the sound. "Well, from what I hear, you always put out a spread like this no matter who comes, and I . . . we . . . well . . ."

Miss Anderson came to his rescue. "We talked it over coming up," she said. "And we feel and we are agreed that you are so helpful and accommodating and in every way," she floundered.

"So we want to pay for the refreshments which is the least we can do," Lou DelBello intervened. The visitors nodded and said, Absolutely. Only Right.

Walt and Emma looked at each other. Either the idea had never occurred to them or they were excellent actors. "Oh, *no!*" said Walt. "Oh, we wouldn't *think* of it," said Emma.

They were glad to, she said. It was their privilege. And nothing could induce them to take a cent.

Long Tom put down his cup. "I understand that you wouldn't take any payment for newspaper stories or posing for photographs, either," he said. The Townses shook their heads. "In short—wait a minute, let's get these tapes rolling. . . .

"Now, Mr. and Mrs. Walter F. Towns up here in Paviour's Bridge, New York," he continued after a moment, having started the recording machine, "I understand that you have both refused to commercialize in any way your experiences on the third of October, is that right? Never taken any money—AP, UP, *Life* magazine, *Journal-*

American—wouldn't accept payment, is that right, Mr. and Mrs. Walter F. Towns up here in Paviour's Bridge, New York?"

Emma and Walt urged each other with nods of the head to speak first into the whizzing-rolling device, wound up saying together, "That's *No we* right *didn't.*"

"I would just like to say—— Oh excuse me, Tom——" Lou began.

"No, go right ahead——"

"I would just like——"

"This is Lou DelBello, you folks out there on the party line: Lou. Del. Bello. Who is up here in Paviour's Bridge, New York, at the Walter F. Townses', along with Miss Jo Anderson, Si Haffner, and Joe Trobridge—as well as myself, Long Tom—all members of that interesting organization you've heard of before on our five-hour conversations over Station WRO, sometimes called familiarly the Flying Saucer Club, but known officially as the Unexplained Aërial Phenomena Coördinating Corps. *Well.* Quite a mouthful. And we are up here accepting the very gracious hospitality of Walt and Emma, who are going to tell us, in their own words, just exactly. what. it was. that happened on the famous night of October third, known as the October Third Sighting or the Grantha Incident; go right ahead, Lou DelBello."

Still dogged and game, Lou went ahead. "I would just like to say that in speaking of that very gracious hospitality that Walt and Emma have refused to take one red cent for so much as a sandwich or a cup of coffee. To all the visitors up here, I mean. So that certainly should take care of in advance of any charges or even the mention of, ah, com*mer*cialism."

Long Tom paused with a piece of home-baked bread and apple butter halfway into his mouth and gestured to Joe Trobridge.

"Yes, Lou," Joe leaped into the breach, "the same people who didn't believe Columbus and are now so scornful of all the various and innumerable U.A.P. sightings, well, the same *type* people, I mean—some certain individuals who shall be nameless who have been suggesting that the Grantha Incident is just a *trick*, or maybe the Townses and myself are in business together——"

Miss Anderson said, "The Cloth-Like Substance, you mean, Joe?"

Long Tom swallowed, wiped his mouth. "Well, I didn't know they *made* apple butter like that any more, Emma," he said. "Yessir folks out there on the party line, the Townses up here in Paviour's Bridge, New York, are poultry farmers by profession but any time Emma wants to go into the preserves business she can sure count on me to——"

Joe interrupted. "I'd just like to clear up one point, Tom——"

"Why sure, Joe, go right ahead. This is the Long Tom Show, you folks out there on the party line. Five hours of talk and music on Station WRO . . ."

Si Haffner for the first time spoke up:

"I understand this Cloth-Like Substance is still refusing or rather I should say *defying* analysis in the laboratories; is that right, Joe?"

Joe said it certainly was. This Cloth-Like Substance, he reminded the listeners-to-be, was left behind at the Townses' after the October Third Sighting. It was soft, it was absorbent, it was non-inflammable; and it resembled nothing known to our terrestrial science. He had tried to analyze it in his own lab, but, failing to do so, he had turned it over to the General Chemical Company. So far even *they*, with their vastly superior facilities, were unable to say just what it was. And while in a way he was *flattered* that some people thought well maybe he was in cahoots with an outfit like GenChem, well——

"Yessir," said Long Tom; "just let me tell you folks out there on the party line that there is *noth*ing like this chicken-salad samwich that Mrs. Emma F. Towns puts up out here in Paviour's Bridge, New York. *Won*derful. But I would like you to tell us in your own words, Emma, just what exactly *did* happen that certain night of October third, known to some as the Grantha Incident. Tell us in your own words."

Emma said, "Well."

"Tell us what kind of a day it was. What was the first thing you did?"

Emma said, "Well . . ."

The first thing she did was to get up and heat the mash for the chicks. Not that she minded getting up that early. Some people who'd lived in the city and talked of settling down on a little poultry farm, when it actually came *to* it, they found they didn't care for it too much. But not Emma. No; it wasn't the hours she minded.

And it wasn't the work. She *liked* work. The house was well built, it was easy to keep warm, it had a lovely view. But it was so far away from everybody. Even the mailman left his deliveries way down at the bottom of the hill. There was the radio, there was the television, but—when you came right down to it—who came to the house? The man who delivered the feed. The man who collected the eggs. And that was all.

The day passed like every other day. Scatter cracked corn. Regular feeding. Scatter sawdust. Clean out from under the wiring. Mix the oats and the clarified buttermilk. Sardine oil. Collect the eggs. Wash them. Pack them. And, of course, while the chickens had to eat, so did the Townses.

No, there was nothing unusual about the day. Until about——

"—about five o'clock, I think it was," Emma said.

"*Noth*ing unusual had happened previous to this?" Long Tom asked. "You had *no* warning?"

Emma said No, none.

"I would just like to say——" Joe Trobridge began.

"Well, now just a min——" Tom cut in.

"I just want to clear up one point," Joe said. "Now, prior to the time I arrived at your doorstep that night, had you ever seen or heard of me before, Emma?"

"No, never."

"That's all I wanted to say. I just wanted to clear up that point."

"You got that, did you, all you folks out there on the party line?" inquired Long Tom. "They. had. never. seen, *or* heard. of each other. before. And then, Emma, you were about to say, about five o'clock?"

About five o'clock, when the dark was falling, Emma first noticed the cloud. She called it to Walt's attention. It was a funny-looking cloud. For a long time it didn't move, although the other clouds did. And then—as the bright reds of the sunset turned maroon, magenta, purple—the cloud slowly came down from the sky and hovered about ten feet over the Townses' front yard.

"Walt, there is something *very* funny about that cloud," said Emma.

"I don't believe it's no cloud," Walt declared. "Listen to that noise, would you." It came from the . . . cloud—thing—whatever it was: a rattling muffled sort of noise, and an angry barking sort of noise. The air grew very dark.

"Do you think we should put on the lights?" Emma

said. Walt grunted. And the—whatever it was—came down with a lurching motion and hit the sod with a clonk. It was suddenly lit up by a ring of lights, which went out again almost at once, went on, went out. Then there was a long silence.

A clatter. A rattle. And again, the barking sound.

"Sounds like someone's cussing, almost. Somehow," Walt said.

"*I* am going to put on the *light*," said Emma. And she did. The noise stopped. Emma put on her sweater. "Come out on the porch with me," she said. They opened the door and stepped out on the porch. They looked over at the . . . thing. It sat on the ground about fifty feet away.

"Is anything *wrong?*" Emma called. "Yoo-hoo! Anything wrong?"

There was a slither and a clatter. The lights went on again in the thing and there was now an opening in it and two figures in the opening. One of them started forward, the other reached out a—was that an *arm?*—but the first figure barked angrily and it drew back. And there was another sound now, a sort of yelping noise, as the first figure walked toward the house and the second figure followed it.

"A man and his wife," said Emma. Walt observed they were dressed light, considering the time of year.

"That's really nothing but what you might call, well, bloomers, that they got on, though they *are* long and they *do* reach up high."

"Sssshh! Hello, there. My name is Mrs. Towns and this is my husband, Mr. Towns. You folks in any trouble?"

The folks halted some distance away. Even at that distance it was possible to see that they were much shorter and broader than the Townses.

"Why, you'll catch your *death* out there with no coats

on!" Emma exclaimed. "You're all *blue!*" Actually, it was a sort of blue-*green*, but she didn't want to embarrass them. "Come in, come on in," she gestured. They came on in. The yelping noise began again. "There. Now isn't it warmer?" Emma closed the door.

From the crook of her—*was* it an arm? It couldn't be anything else—one of the figures lifted up the source of the yelping. Emma peered at it.

"Well, my *goodness!*" Emma said. She and Walt exchanged glances. "Isn't it just the picture of its father!" she said. An expression which might have been a smile passed over the faces of the two figures.

The first figure reached into its garment and produced an oval container, offered it, withdrew it as a petulant yelp was heard. The figure looked at Emma, barked diffidently.

"Why, don't you *know* what she's saying, Walt?" Emma asked.

Walt squirmed. "It seems like I do, but I know I couldn't, hardly," he said.

Emma was half-indignant. "Why, you can, too. She's saying: 'The car broke down and I wonder if I might warm the baby's bottle?' *That's* what she's saying.—Of *course* you may. You just come along into the kitchen."

Walt scratched his ear, looked at the second figure. It looked at him.

"Why, I guess I'd better go along back with you," Walt said, "and take a look at your engine. That was a bad rattle you got there."

It was perhaps half an hour later that they returned. "Got it fixed all right now," Walt said. "Loose umpus on the hootenanny . . . Baby OK?"

"Sshh . . . it's asleep. All it wanted was a warm bottle and a clean diaper."

There was a silence. Then everyone was talking (or barking) at once—of course, in low tones. "Oh, glad to do it, glad to be of help," said Emma. "Any time . . . and whenever you happen to be around this way, why just you drop in and see us. Sorry you can't stay."

"Sure thing," Walt seconded. "That's right."

Emma said, "It's so lonely up here. We hardly ever have any visitors at all. . . . Goodby! Goodby, now!" And finally the visitors closed the opening in their vehicle.

"Hope the umpus stays fixed in the hootenanny . . ." There was a burst of pyrotechnic colors, a rattling noise, and a volley of muffled barks. "It didn't," Walt said. "*Hear* him cussing!" The rattling ceased, the colors faded into a white mist. "Got it now . . . look at those lights go round and round . . . there they go. Wherever it is they're going," he concluded, uncertainly. They closed the door. Emma sighed.

"It *was* nice having someone to visit with," she said. "Heaven only knows how long it will be before anyone else comes here."

It was exactly three hours and five minutes. Two automobiles came tearing up the road and screamed to a stop. People got out, ran pounding up the path, knocked at the door. Walt answered.

At first they all talked at once, then all fell silent. Finally, one man said, "I'm Joe Trobridge of the U.A.P.C.C. —the Unexplained Aërial—— Listen, a *sighting* was reported in this vicinity! Did you see it? A flying saucer? Huh?"

Walt nodded slowly. "So *that's* what it was," he said. "I thought it was some kind of a airship."

Trobridge's face lit up. Everyone began to babble again. Then Trobridge said, "You *saw* it? Was it close?

What? SHUT UP, EVERYBODY! On your front lawn? What'd they look like? What——?"

Walt pursed his mouth. "I'll tell ya," he began. "They were blue."

"*Blue?!*" exclaimed Trobridge.

"Well . . ." Walt's tone was that of a man willing to stretch a point. "Maybe it was green."

"*Green!?*"

"Well, which was it?" someone demanded. "Blue or green?"

Walt said, in the same live-and-let-live tone, "Bluish-green." Joe Trobridge opened his mouth. "Or, greenish-blue," Walt continued, cutting him off. The visitors milled around, noisily.

"How were they dressed?"

Walt pursed his mouth. "I'll tell ya," he said. "They were wearing what ya might call like bloomers . . ."

"*Bloomers!?*"

Emma glanced around nervously. The visitors didn't seem to like what Walt was telling them. Not at all.

Joe Trobridge pressed close. "Did they say what their purpose was, in visiting the Earth?" he asked, eagerness restored somewhat—but only somewhat.

Walt nodded. "Oh, sure. Told us right away. Come to see if they could warm the baby's bottle." Someone in the crowd made a scornful noise. "That was it, y'see. . . ." His voice trailed off uncertainly.

The man named Joe Trobridge looked at him, his mouth twisted. "Now, *wait* a minute," he said. "Just wait a *mi*nute. . . ."

Emma took in the scene at a glance. No one would believe them. They'd all go away and never come back and no one would ever visit them again—except the man who delivered the feed and the man who collected the eggs.

She looked at the disappointed faces around her, some beginning to show anger, and she got up.

"My husband is joking," she said, loudly and clearly. "Of *course* it wasn't like that."

Joe turned to her. "Did you see it, too, lady? What happened, then? I mean, *really* happened? Tell us in your own words. What did they look like?"

Emma considered for a moment. "They were very tall," she said. "And they had on spacesuits. And their leader spoke to us. He looked just like us, only maybe his head was a bit bigger. He didn't have no hair. He didn't really speak English—it was more like tleppathy——"

The people gathered around her closely, their eyes aglow, their faces eager. "Go on," they said; "go on——"

"His name was . . . Grantha——"

"*Grantha*," the people breathed.

"And he said we shouldn't be afraid, because he came in peace. 'Earth people,' he said, 'we have observed you for a long time and now we feel the time has come to make ourselves known to you. . . .'"

Long Tom nodded. "So that's the way it was."

"That's the way it was," she said. "More coffee, anybody?"

"You brew a mighty fine cup of coffee, Mrs. Emma Towns up here in Paviour's Bridge, New York, let me tell the folks on the party line," Long Tom said. "No sugar, thanks, just cream. . . . Well, say, about this piece of Cloth-Like Substance. It's absorbent—it's soft—it doesn't burn—and it can't be analyzed. Now, about how big is this wonderful item which Grantha and his people left behind as a sample of their superior technicology and peaceful intentions and which continues to baffle scientists? About how big is it? Just tell us in your own words. . . ."

Emma considered. Joe pursed his lips.

Lou DelBello smiled. "Well, I've had the good fortune to see it," he said, "and—speaking as the father of three—the, uh, best comparison of its size which I could give you, I'd say it's just about as big as a diaper!"

He guffawed. Joe burst out laughing, as did Si Haffner. Miss Anderson giggled. Long Tom chuckled. Emma and Walt looked nervously at each other, looked anxiously at their oh, so very welcome guests—but only for a moment. Then, reassured, they leaned back and joined in the merriment.

Afterword for The Grantha Sighting

If even Herman Melville got story ideas from other stories written by other people—including, and I kid you not, not merely the idea for *Moby Dick*, but even eppis the title (*Mocha Dick, or the White Whale of the Pacific* . . . would you believe? You'd better. Symbol? *What* symbol? Melville didn't know a symbol from a cistern. He wrote the book because he needed some publication to establish himself as a writer in order to get a job in the Customs House: standard operational procedure for the day—look at Hawthorne—and as soon as he *got* the job, he didn't bother trying for publication any more. Calmly spent his time writing down things like *ad valorem duty on six cases of corset stays at 2 per cent*, and periodically calling to the messenger, "Louie, another pitcher of rum cocktail, and tell them, for Christ's sake, not to run the whole goddamn East River into it this time!"), why, then, so why can't I? And I can. Ha-*hem*.

The precise story which gave me the idea for this one was Bill Brown's very funny "The Star Ducks," printed in *The Magazine of Fantasy and Science Fiction* some-

time in the early fifties. Look it up and read it. And the
other fructifying influence was of course the Long John
radio show out of Station WOR from about midnight to
cockcrow. Every kook in the country used to creep forth
and enunciate on it; plus some lulus from the provinces
outre mer. What has since become commonplace as Sau-
cerology was the burden of much of these revelations—I
hesitate to say ravings. Long John Knebel, the moderator,
had as much faith in flying saucers as he had in, shall we
say, talking Tootsie Rolls: but business was business.
Bridie Murphy came and went, but the saucers flew on
forever.

There is only one little oddity which remains in my
mind after all these weary years—in connection with this
story, I mean. I wanted to have an appearance made in
the story of a group of people who were organized to try
and track down reported "sightings." And I did not want
to use the words "Flying Saucers." I did not believe in
Flying Saucers. I did believe (and still do) that after
every explanation to explain things was syphoned off,
there still remained a certain residuum of things seen but
not explained. And so I decided to call them "Unexplained Aërial Phenomena." So far as I can strainingly
remember, *I had never heard those words before. . . .*
Since then a generation has gone by. And I have on nu-
merous occasions both heard *and seen* them. Did someone
rip off my sonorous phrases? and not give me credit?
Shame! Oh, for shame! Did someone invent them inde-
pendently of me? (You mean, Columbus *wasn't* the first
honky who—?) Or—and here is a thought to chill one's
blood—did someone, or someTHING, for reasons un-
known to me/us/our mundane earthly sciences so-called,
plant these words in my mind?

If so, and after interplanetary trade is established as a
result, the least they can do, then, is give me a job in the
Customs House.

The Singular Events. . . .

In 1961, the year when the dragons were so bad, a young
man named George Laine, an industrial alchemist by profession, attended the coronation of the new president in
Washington. The guilds were in high favor with the presi-
dent-select, John V (the first of that name since John IV
C. Coolidge), who sent to each and every of their delega-
tion, as a mark of his esteem, garments of vertue worthy
of the occasion, viz. a silken hat, a pair of galoshes with
silvern buckles, a great-coat with a collar of black samite,
cuff-links enchased in gold, and a pen-and-pencil set of
malachite and electrum which it were guaranteed to
write under water and over butter: both, as it happened,
essential to the practice of industrial alchemy.

The ceremonies proceeded without any untowardness.
The Supreme Justice of the Chief Court placed on the
President's head the sacred beaver with the star-spangled
band and declared that "Regardless of rape, crude,
choler, or national ore or gin, any resemblance is purely
coincidental." The Chairman of the Board of Augurs of
the Federal Reserve System pronounced a curse in weirdmane and in womrath on anyone who should presume to
send gold o'er the white-waved seas. The new Veep,
wearing the ritual ten-gallon hat, and mounted on a palo-
mino, cantered up and down before the Selectoral College, and uttered the prescribed challenge: "Whosoever
doth deny that the Honorable John V Fitz-Kenneth is the
rightful Chief Executive of Thiscountry lies, and is an

S.O.B." The out-going Jester raised the liturgical *hwyl* of *We want Wilkie,* and was smitten twice with a slapstick and thrice with a bladder, both wielded by his successor. The Fall River Chamber of Commerce and Horror presented the ceremonial breakfast of cold mutton soup, sliced bananas, and an axe: it was ceremoniously refused. A Boston Brahmin, clad in cutaway, *dhoti,* and sacred thread, offered a salver bearing two curried codfish balls; the new President ate both whilst the Brahmin intoned,

> Eat it up, wear it out,
> Make it do, or do without;

after which he, the B.B., hurried to wash himself in sacred 6% Charles water to remove the impurity of feeding with a lower caste.

George Laine and his fellows of the alchemists and other guilds were not forgotten even afterwards; for Prex Jax (as the newsguild had already termed him *in parvo*) sent them out great smoking helpings of buffalo hump, bear paws, caponized peacocks, pemmican, ptarmigan, succotash, and syllabub, from the high table where he was dining with his notables, including Surgeon-General Doctor Caligari, who had just been raised to Cabinet rank.

It was during these moments of revelry and mirth that George choked on a quartern of orange in an Old Fashioned Cocktail, all went black before his face, and, on awakening to find himself bound with silken cords in a hovel on an alley off of Eye Street, knew that he had been ensorceled.

There was a bim looking bemused at him with a bodkin in her bosom, and he wotted well it were for lack of wit anent her that he bode bound: for who was she but Yancey-Courtney Belleregarde, a Drum Majorette, 1/c, who had been sitting in his lap that time he raised the dram-glass to his lips.

"I say, that bodkin must hurt something dreadful," he said (not having attended the N.Y. High School of Gallanterie Trades in vain); "untie me and I'll have it out for you in a trice: there's a good gel, do."

The bim smiled scornfully. Her lips were as red as the chassis of a new-model Jaguar of the first enameling. "Not on your tin-type, Cully," she said. "Rats. Nit." She spoke in the Archaic tongue of the bim-folk, which is akin to elf-talk, and cognate with 23 Skiddoo (unlawful for a man to know until he has passed his finals in The Deep School, and been awarded the right to wear the Navel Plug, with two Pips).

"Nix on the soft-soap, Charlie," she said; "I only keep the bodkin there because these, now, sorcelsacquets don't have any pockets in them, as if you didn't know. Oh you kid!" she concluded, archly. And with this she withdrew the bodkin, dipped its prickle into a pot labelled *Poyson Moste Foule*, and approached the supine young industrial alchemist with the tip of her tongue held between her teeth.

"Slip me the Formula for the Transmutation of Borax Without the Use of Cockatrice-egg," she said (speaking with some difficulty, her tongue, as we have already noted, you clod, being between her teeth), "and we'll be back in the Grand Ballroom of the Mayflower in lots of time to see Ed Finnegan made a K.T.V.; afterwards we can tiptoe up to any of the thirty-odd double rooms which my Company keeps rented at all times, and you may have your wicked will o' me without fearing the House-Dick, because I'll put a Cheese-it spell on the door, see, which it's proof against Force, Force-Fields, Stealth, Mort-Main, Nigromancy, Mopery, and Gawk: so give, Cully, give."

A cold sneer crossed George's hot lips. "I say, what an absolutely rotten proposal!" he exclaimed. "You know perfectly well that I have sworn by the most frightful oaths to remain true in mind and deed to Alchymy, Ltd., of Canada, and to keep myself physically clean, mentally straight, and morally square! I suppose you're one of these simply awful party girls which one hears that General Semantics, Inc., of Delaware, keeps on their payrolls to entrap, ensorcel, enviegal, enchaunt, enduce, endive, and endamage clean-living young chaps into betraying secrets. Well, I shan't, do you hear? Better I should die. So there!"

But the bim, far from being one whit abashed by this manly defiance, laughed as coarsely as the position of her tongue would permit. "Well, if that don't take the cake," she snickered. "Gee, what a simp!" and made feint as though she would withdraw George's Plug, two Pips or no two Pips.

"No, really, don't touch me, do you hear?" George said, stoutly, trying to roll over on his stomach, "I'm really most frightflie ticklish, and besides, without the Plug I should swell up with lint in simply no time; funny thing about me, I'm very susceptible to navel lint, always was, from a child."

But the silken cords held him fast.

"The Formula for the Transmutation of Borax Without the Use of Cockatrice-egg," she said, inexorably, making little jabs at him with the bodkin dip't in Venom.

George mimicked her: "'—Uthe of Cockatwithe-egg'!"

Unguardedly she laughed, releasing the tip of her tongue from between her teeth, and thus . . . Those who are Cupboard Certified Auditors of The Deep School will understand *thus*, and those who are *not* needn't imagine for one minute that we are going to reveal for free, secrets for which others have paid good money, no siree. Suffice it, then, to say that in a trice George had leapt out of his bonds, flung the bodkin from the bim's hands with such force that it pierced the door and hung quivering. This produced a startled cry from behind the door, which George flung open, revealing a man, a tape-recorder, and a flash-camera. The man first cringed, then assumed an expression combining both defiance and a falsely hearty air of good will.

"Weh-hell, Laine," he burbled.

"What," demanded George, sternly, "is the Assistant Director of Research for the Middle Atlantic States Division of Alchymy, Ltd., of Canada, doing cowering behind the door of a hovel on an alley off of Eye Street, with a tape-recorder and a flash-camera; what?"—a question which, put like that, might make any man pause before answering.

Mr. Marcantonio Paracelcus (for such was his name), paused before answering. He swallowed. "It was a Test, you see, George."

"I fail to see."

"Well, it was a *test*. The Company is considering you for an important new job. In order to find out how you would shape up under pressure, we have tested you. I am, um, happy to say that you have passed the Test."

George said, "Oh, good. Then I get the job. *What* job?"

Mr. Marcantonio Paracelcus seemed to find some difficulty in answering this question. Whilst he stood, there came a buzz and a clatter, and that which George had hithertofore considered to be merely a tallboy-sized TV set opened up, revealing itself to be an Observation Armoire containing a microphone, *two* tape-recorders, an automatic closed-circuit television camera, and Dr. Roger Bacon Buxbaum, Chief Director of Research for the Middle Atlantic States Division of Alchymy, Ltd., of Canada.

Marcantonio Paracelcus, on perceiving his superior, turned ashen, livid, and pale, in that order.

"The job in question, George," said Dr. Buxbaum, "is that which until a moment ago was held by the gentleman you now see cowering behind the door; but which is no longer so held. On realizing that you were being considered for his position, he determined on this unworthy method of discrediting you: hence, the tape-recorder, on which he hoped to capture the sound of your voice as you revealed the Formula for the Transmutation of Borax Without the Use of Cockatrice-egg; hence the flash-camera with which he hoped to capture the sight of you in a," and here the benign, balding Buxbaum blushed a bit, "compromising position with this young female person here. Little did he know," the urbane researcher winked, and placed his right forefinger by the right side of his nose, "that we were onto his jazz from the word Go . . .

"And to think that he would sully the semi-sacred season of the Coronation by his meretricious machinations; fie, sir, do you call yourself a Thiscountrean? But I forebear harshness; modern science has taught us that such a one as you is really sick, and needs help. Come along now —George! Expect to see you for lunch, day after tomorrow, at the Alembic, one sharp!"

George went pink with pleasure, for what was the Alembic but the most expensive eatery favored by the upper echelons of the M.A.S.D. of Alchymy, Ltd. (Canada); and this invite betokened his full acceptance into the post previously held by his unfortunate predecessor, who even now, sniveling miserably, was being firmly guided out by the elbow. George's feelings of sorrow, which did him credit, were tempered by the reflection that, after suitable treatment at the Company's Rehabilitation Farm in North Baffin Land, the man might still prove capable of many years of devoted service; though, of course, in a minor capacity.

For a moment all was silent in the hovel on the alley off of Eye Street. George eyed the bim. The bim eyed the floor. After a while she spoke. "I suppose you hate me," she said.

"No, I—"

"I suppose you think I'm miserable and treacherous."

"No, I—"

"I suppose you think I would really have stuck you with a poysoned bodkin, don't you? Well, the jar only contained a Sophronia Finkelstein preparation for the treatment of tired skin and subcutaneous tissues; so there."

George said, "No, I fully realize that as a bim, and as a sorceress under contract to General Semantics, Inc., of Delaware, you were only carrying out your duty. And now, if you don't mind, I wonder if I might use your phone to call a taxi?"

Fancy his astonishment when she burst into tears.

"We have no phone," she wept. "I'm not a bim. I never worked for General Semantics. My parents couldn't afford to send me to Sorcery School. How I put you under that spell and brought you here, my old Auntie Eglantine was a white witch and I picked up some little piddly old spells from her, is all. I am really just a Drum Majorette, 1/c. Oh, I wish I were dead! A hoo, hoo, hoo!"

George, at first with awkwardness, then with growing appreciation for the task, patted her hands, her shoulders, and the general area of the small of her back. "To tell you the truth, Miss Yancey-Courtney," he said, "I would just purely hate it if you were to be a bim. I mean, like, those hairy *feet?* And their toe-nails *glow* in the dark? Why, a man couldn't hardly relish his victuals, let alone keep his mind on his Transmutations. . . . Of course, I'm just speaking speculatively, I mean; having always kept myself physically clean, mentally straight, and morally square, according to the terms of my Triune Oath to the Company, which I have never regretted," he said, regretfully.

"Of course," she murmured, wiping her eyes on his shirttail.

"Listen," she said, "do you know when it was that I first felt a revulsion I was barely able to conquer at the infamous Marcantonio Paracelcus's proposal? It was when the Veep rode in. When he gave out the Challenge I could see you clench your fists until your knuckles went what I mean *white;* as if you were just *daring* any old Recounter to challenge the Selection!"

"Hm," said George, grimly.

"I'll bet you must be awfully strong."

George, modestly, said, well, shoving all that lead and gold around, *you* know. She said that she could well imagine. There was a pause. Then he asked what time it was. She said it was 7:45, why? He said that if they hurried, they could still get to see Ed Finnegan dubbed a K.T.V. She said, yes, they could, couldn't they? She asked if he was very fond of Ed Finnegan. There was a pause. He said that as a matter of fact he couldn't stand Ed Finnegan.

"Neither can I!"

"All those trained wombats!"

"And that incessant, hearty laugh!"

There was another pause. Then, "My, those are handsome galoshes!" she said.

"Gift of the President."

"Pipe the silvern buckles, will yuh?"

"Mmm."

"But don't you think you'd be more comfortable if you took them off?"

"The buckles?"

"Oh you silly! The ga*loshes!*"

"I might at that."

And he did. And he was.

Outside, the Northern Lights hissed and crackled (or, again, it might have been the dragons, which were so bad that year); outside, the noise of revelry continually rose and fell in the streets; but inside, all was quiet in the hovel on the alley off of Eye Street.

Afterword for The Singular Events. . . .

It must have been evident that this small tale was written during the latter days of John Fitzgerald Kennedy, President of the United States. If it had not been written before he was murdered, I should not ever have had the heart to write it afterwards. If the murder of a magistrate is no more than the murder of any other man, surely it is no less. And, surely, enough time has passed for us to remember that there was a spirit in the land then, felt by too many of us to have been a mere myth, which is not with us now: and in that time, when in the now too-much-polluted air there were still little flecks of gold, a certain spirit of joy and humor plucked me by the sleeve and sat me down. And I have written what you have just read.

Dagon

*Then the Lords of the Philistines gathered together
to rejoice before Dagon their god, and behold, the
image of Dagon was fallen upon its face to the
ground, with both his face and his hands broken off,
and only the fishy part of Dagon was left to
him. . . .*

The old Chinese, half-magician, half-beggar, who made
the bowl of goldfish vanish and appear again, this old
man made me think of the Aztecs and the wheel. Or gunpowder. Gunpowder appeared in Western Europe and
Western Europe conquered the world with it. Gunpowder had long ago been known in China and the Chinese
made firecrackers with it. (They have since learned better.) When I was free, I heard men say more than once
that the American Indians did not know the use of the
wheel until Europeans introduced it. But I have seen a
toy, pre-Conquest, fashioned from clay, which showed
that the Aztecs knew the use of the wheel. They made
toys of it. Firecrackers. Vanishing goldfish.

Noise.

Light and darkness.

The bright lotos blossoms in the dark mire. Lotos. Plu-
ral, lotoi? Loti? That is a coincidence. On October 12,
1900, Pierre Loti left at Taku the French naval vessel
which had brought him to China, and proceeded to Peking. Part of that city was still smoking, Boxers and their
victims were still lying in the ruins. On October 12, 1945,

I left the American naval vessel which had brought me
and my fellow officers to China, and proceeded to Peking
—Peiping, as they called it then. I was not alone, the
whole regiment came; the people turned out and hailed
and glorified us. China, our friend and partner in the late
great struggle. The traffic in women, narcotics, stolen
goods, female children? Merely the nation's peculiar insti-
tution. Great is China, for there I was made manifest.

Old, old, old . . . crumbling temples, closed-off palaces,
abandoned yamens. Mud-colored walls with plaster crumbling off them reached a few feet over a man's head and
lined the alleys so that if a gate was closed all that could
be seen was the rooftop of a one-story building or the
upper lineage of a tree, and if a gate was open, a tall
screen directly in front of it blocked the view except for
tiny glimpses of flagstone-paved courtyards and plants in
huge glazed pots. Rich and poor and in between and
shabby genteel lived side by side, and there was no way
of knowing if the old man in dun-colored rags who squatted by a piece of matting spread with tiny paper squares
holding tinier heaps of tea or groups of four peanuts or
ten watermelon seeds was as poor as he and his trade
seemed, or had heaps of silver taels buried underneath
the fourth tile from the corner near the stove. Things
were seldom what they seemed. People feared to tempt
powers spiritual or temporal or illegal by displays of well
being, and the brick screens blocked both the gaze of the
curious and the path of demons—demons can travel only
in straight lines; it is the sons of men whose ways are de-
vious.

Through these backways and byways I used to roam
each day. I had certain hopes and expectations based on
romantic tales read in adolescence, and was bound that
the Cathayans should not disappoint. When these alleys
led into commercial streets, as they did sooner or later, I

sought what I sought there as well. It is not too difficult to gain a command of spoken Mandarin, which is the dialect of Peking. The throaty sound which distinguishes, for example, between *lee-dza*, peaches, and *lee'dza*, chestnuts, is soon mastered. The more southerly dialects have eleven or nineteen or some such fantastic number of inflections, but Pekingese has only four. Moreover, in the south it is hot and steamy and the women have flat noses.

In one of my wanderings I came to the ponds where the carp had been raised for the Imperial table in days gone by. Strange, it was, to realize that some of the great fish slowly passing up and down among the lily pads must have been fed from the bejeweled hands of Old Buddha herself—and that others, in all likelihood (huge they were, and vast), not only outdated the Dowager but may well have seen—like some strange, billowing shadow above the watersky—Ch'ien Lung the Great: he who deigned to "accept tribute" from Catherine of Russia—scattering rice cake like manna.

I mused upon the mystery of fish, their strange and mindless beauty, how—innocently evil—they prey upon each other, devouring the weaker and smaller without rage or shout or change of countenance. There, in the realm of water, which is also earth and air to them, the great fish passed up and down, growing old without aging and enjoying eternal growth without the softness of obesity. It was a world without morality, a world without choices, a world of eating and spawning and growing great. I envied the great fish, and (in other, smaller ponds) the lesser fish, darting and flashing and sparkling gold.

They speak of "the beast in man," and of "the law of the jungle." Might they not (so I reflected, strolling underneath a sky of clouds as blue and as white as the tiles and marble of the Altar of Heaven), might they not better

speak of "the fish in man?" And of "the law of the sea?"
The sea, from which they say we came. . . ?

Sometimes, but only out of sociability, I accompanied
the other officers to the singsong houses. A man is a fool
who cannot accommodate himself to his fellows enough
to avoid discomfort. But my own tastes did not run to
spilled beer and puddles of inferior tea and drink-
thickened voices telling tales of prowess, nor to grinning
lackeys in dirty robes or short sessions in rabbit warren
rooms with bodies which moved and made sounds and
asked for money but showed no other signs of sentient
life.

Once, but once only, we visited the last of the Imperial
barber-eunuchs, who had attended to the toilet of the
Dowager's unfortunate nephew; a tall old man, this cas-
trate, living alone with his poverty, he did for us what he
would for any others who came with a few coins and a
monstrous curiosity.

I mingled, also, officially and otherwise, with the European colony, none of whom had seen Europe for years,
many of whom had been born in China. Such jolly Ger-
mans! Such cultured Italians! Such pleasant spoken, *çi-
devant* Vichy, Frenchmen! How well dressed and well
kept their women were, how anxious, even eager, to
please, to prove their devotion to the now victorious
cause—and to the young and potent and reasonably per-
sonable officers who represent it.

After many an afternoon so well spent, I would arise
and take a ricksha to one of the city gates to be there at
the sunset closing, and would observe how, when half the
massy portal was swung shut, the traffic would increase
and thicken and the sound of cries come from far down
the road which led outside the city and a swollen stream
pour and rush faster and faster—men and women on foot
and clutching bundles, and carriers with sedan chairs,

and families leading heavily laden ox-carts and horses, children with hair like manes, trotting women swollen in pregnancy, old women staggering on tiny-bound feet, infants clinging to their bent backs. The caravans alone did not increase their pace at this time. Slow, severe, and solemn, woolly, double-humped, padfooted, blunt, their long necks shaking strings of huge blue beads and bronze bells crudely cast at some distant forge in the Gobi or at the shore of Lop Nor, the camels came. By their sides were skullcapped Turkomen, or Buryat-Mongols with their hair in thick queues.

My eyes scanned every face and every form in all this, but I did not find what I looked for.

Then I would go and eat, while the gates swung shut and the loungers dispersed, murmuring and muttering of the *Bah Loo,* the said to be approaching slowly but steadily and as yet undefeated *Bah Loo,* the Communist Eighth Route Army; and the air grew dark and cold.

One afternoon I chose to visit some of the temples—not the well-frequented ones such as those of Heaven, Agriculture, Confucius, and the Lamas—the ones not on the tourist lists, not remarkable for historical monuments, not preserved (in a manner of speaking) by any of the governments which had held Peking since the days of "the great" Dr. Sun. In these places the progress of decay had gone on absolutely unchecked and the monks had long ago sold everything they could and the last fleck of paint had peeled from the idols. Here the clergy earned corn meal (rice in North China was a delicacy, not a staple) by renting out the courtyards for monthly fairs and charging stud fees for the services of their Pekingese dogs. Worshipers were few and elderly. Such, I imagine, must have been the temples in the last days of Rome while the Vandal and Goth equivalents of the Eighth Route Army made plans to invest the city at their leisure.

These ancients were pleased to see me and brought bowls of thin tea and offered to sell me dog-eared copies of pornographic works, poorly illustrated, which I declined.

Later, outside, in the street, there was an altercation between a huge and pock-marked ricksha "boy" and a Marine. I stepped up to restore order—could not have avoided it, since the crowd had already seen me—and met the Man in Black.

I do not mean a foreign priest.

The coolie was cuffed and sent his way by the Man in Black, and the Marine told to go elsewhere by me. The Man in Black seemed quite happy at my having come along—the incident could have gotten out of hand—and he stuck to me and walked with me and spoke to me loudly in poor English and I suffered it because of the face he would gain by having been seen with me. Of course, I knew what he was, and he must have known that I knew. I did not relish the idea of yet another pot of thin tea, but he all but elbowed me into his home.

Where my search ended.

The civil police in Peking were nothing, nothing at all. The Japanese Army had not left much for them to do, nor now did the Chinese Nationalist Army nor the U. S. Forces, MPs and SPs. So the Peking police force directed traffic and cuffed recalcitrant ricksha coolies and collected the pittance which inflation made nothing of.

Black is not a good color for uniforms, nor does it go well with a sallow skin.

She was not sallow.

I drank cup after cup of that vile, unsugared tea, just to see her pour it.

Her nose was not flat.

When he asked her to go and borrow money to buy some cakes, not knowing that I could understand, I man-

aged to slip him money beneath the table: he was startled
and embarrassed as this was well. After that, the advantage was even more mine.

She caught my glance and the color deepened in her
cheeks. She went for the cakes.

He told me his account of woes, how his father (a
street mountebank of some sort) had starved himself for
years in order to buy him an appointment on the police
force and how it had come to nothing at all, salary worth
nothing, cumshaw little more. How he admired the
Americans—which was more than I did myself. Gradually,
with many diversions, circumlocutions, and euphuisms,
he inquired about the chances of our doing some business.

Of course, I agreed.

She returned.

I stayed long; she lighted the peanut oil lamps and in
the stove made a small fire of briquettes fashioned from
coal dust and—I should judge, by a faint but definite odor
—dung.

After that I came often, and we made plans; I named
sums of money which caused his mouth to open—a sight
to sell dentifrice, indeed. Then, when his impatience was
becoming irritating, I told him the whole thing was off—
military vigilance redoubled at the warehouses, so on. I
made a convincing story. He almost wept. He had debts,
he had borrowed money (on his hopes) to pay them.

No one could have been more sympathetic than I.

I convinced him that I wished only to help him.

Then, over several dinner tables I told him that I was
planning to take a concubine shortly. My schedule, naturally, would leave less time for these pleasant conversations and equally pleasant dinners. The woman was not
selected yet, but this should not take long.

Finally, the suggestion came from *him*, as I had hoped

it would, and I let him convince me. This was the only amusing part of the conversation.

I suppose he must have convinced *her*.

I paid him well enough.

There was the apartment to furnish, and other expenses, clothes for her, what have you. Expenses. So I was obliged to some business after all. But not, of course, with *him*. The sulfa deal was dull enough, even at the price I got per tablet, but the thought of having sold the blood plasma as an elixir for aging Chinese vitality (masculine) was droll beyond words.

So my life began, my real life, for which the rest had been mere waiting and anticipation, and I feel the same was true of her. What had she known of living? He had bought her as I had bought her, but my teeth were not decayed, nor did I have to borrow money if I wanted cakes for tea.

In the end he became importunate and it was necessary to take steps to dispense with him. Each state has the sovereign right, indeed the duty, to protect its own existence; thus, if bishops plot against the Red governments or policemen against the Kuomintang government, the results are inevitable.

He had plotted against *me*.

The curious thing is that she seemed genuinely sorry to hear that he'd been shot, and as she seemed more beautiful in sorrow, I encouraged her. When she seemed disinclined to regard this as the right moment for love, I humbled her. In the end she came to accept this as she did to accept everything I did, as proper, simply because it was I who had done it.

I.

She was a world which I had created, and behold, it was very good.

My fellow officers continued, some of them, their joint

excursions to the stews of Ch'ien Men. Others engaged in
equally absurd projects, sponsoring impecunious students
at the Protestant university, or underwriting the care of
orphans at the local convent schools. I even accompanied
my immediate superior to tea one afternoon and gravely
heard the Anglican bishop discuss the moral regeneration
of mankind, after which he told some capital stories
which he had read in *Punch* several generations ago.
With equal gravity I made a contribution to the old man's
Worthy Cause of the moment. Afterwards she and I went
out in my jeep and had the chief lama show us the image
of a jinni said to be the superior of rhinoceros horn in the
amorous pharmacopoeia, if one only indulged him in a
rather high priced votive lamp which burned butter. The
old Tibetan, in his sales talk, pointed out to us the "Pas-
sion Buddha's" four arms, with two of which he held the
female figure, while feeding her with the other two; but
neither this, nor the third thing he was doing, interested
me as much as his head. It was a bull's head, huge, brutal,
insensate, glaring. . . .

If I am to be a god, I will be such a god as this, I
thought; part man and part . . . bull? No—but what? Part
man and——

I took her home, that she might worship Me.

Afterwards, she burned the brass butter lamps before
Me, and the sticks of incense.

I believe it was the following day that we saw the old
Chinese. We were dining in a White Russian restaurant,
and from the unusual excellence of the food and the way
the others looked at Me I could sense that awareness of My
true Nature, and Its approaching epiphany, was beginning to be felt.

The persimmons of Peking are not like the American
persimmons; they are larger and flattened at each end. In
order for the flavor to be at its best, the fruits must have

begun to rot. The top is removed and cream is put on, heavy cream which has begun to turn sour. This is food fit for a god and I was the only one present who was eating it. The Russians thought that persimmons were only for the Chinese, and the Chinese did not eat cream.

There was an American at the next table, in the guise of an interfering angel, talking about famine relief. The fool did not realize that famine is itself a relief, better even than war, more selective in weeding out the unfit and reducing the surfeit of people from which swarming areas such as China and India are always suffering. I smiled as I heard him, and savored the contrast between the sweet and the sour on My spoon, and I heard her draw in her breath and I looked down and there was the old Chinese, in his smutty robe and with some object wrapped in grimed cloth next to him as he squatted on the floor. I heard her murmur something to him in Chinese; she greeted him, called him *lau-yay*—old master or sir—and something else which I knew I knew but could not place. The air was thick with cigarette smoke and cheap scent. The fool at the next table threw the old man some money and gestured him to begin.

His appearance was like that of any beggar, a wrinkled face, two or three brown teeth showing when he smiled in that fawning way. He unwrapped his bundle and it was an empty chinaware bowl and two wooden wands. He covered the bowl with cloth again, rapped it with wands, uncovered it, and there was a goldfish swimming. He covered, he rapped and rapped and whisked away the cloth and the bowl was gone. I darted My foot out to the place where it had been, but there was nothing there.

The American at the next table spread out a newspaper on the floor, the old man rolled his sleeves up his withered, scrannel, pallid-sallow arms; he spread the cloth, struck it with his sticks, and then removed it, showing a much larger bowl with the goldfish, on top of the newspaper. So it had not come from some recess in the floor, nor from his sleeve. I did not like to see anyone else exercising power; I spoke roughly to the old man, and he giggled nervously and gathered his things together. The fools opposite began to protest, I looked at them and their voices died away. I looked at *her*, to see if she would still presume to call him *old master;* but she was My creation and she laughed aloud at him and this pleased Me.

My powers increased; with drops of ink I could kill and I could make alive. The agents of the men of Yenan came to Me at night and I wrote things for them and they left offerings of money on the table.

Infinitely adaptive, I, polymorphous, porphyrogenitive, creating iniquity, transgression, and sin.

But sometimes at night, when they had left and we had gone to bed and I pretended to sleep as others, sometimes there was a noise of a faint rattling and I saw something in the room turning and flashing, like a flash of gold, and the shadows loomed like the shadow of an old man. And once it came to Me—the meaning of the Chinese words she had used once. They meant *father-in-law,* but I could not remember when she had used them, though distantly I knew she had no more husband. I awoke her and made her worship Me and I was infinitely godlike.

When was this? Long ago, perhaps. It seems that I do not remember as well as formerly. There is so little to remember of present life. I have withdrawn from the world. I do not really know where I now am. There is a wall of some sort, it extends everywhere I turn, it is white, often I press my lips against it. I have lips. I do not know if I have hands and feet, but I do not need them. The light, too, has an odd quality here. Sometimes I seem to be in a small place and at other times it seems larger. And in between these times something passes overhead and all goes dark and there is a noise like the beating of heavy staves and then it is as if I am nothing . . . no place . . . But then all is as before and there is light once more and I can move freely through the light, up and down; I can turn, and when I turn swiftly I can see a flashing of gold, of something gold, of something gold, and this pleases and diverts Me.

But when I am still I cannot see it at all.

Afterword for Dagon

As for this story, what can I indeed tell you? Only this: I was there. And I saw it.

The Redward Edward Papers

I WEEP, I CRY, I GLORIFY

—*The Autobiography
of Alice B. Toklas*

To a certain extent our story will deal with witches and warlocks and things, but unlike many another such, it is laid right here in the good old U.S.A. We don't point morals or force the fire signs, let Smokey the Bear who bathes not in Ocean's stream do that, we just tell the story. We will make you smell the sunset fires in the great camel caravanserai of Carmel-by-the-Sea, make you see the glitter and the flash of the flotillaw of junks and caravels riding at anchor off the tiny but rich-rich orifice which opens into the port of Fort Bragg: and *mind* the rocks, the rocks, the rocks, lest they gore your sides like the horns of an angry bull. Edward minded them, as he did so many more things; and he told it to us, he told it to us over handsel and housel of home-baked bread, spiced coffee, and plain-baked beans in our cabin by Pickerel Creek, where the Mountains of Morne come down to the Sea. No connection with the Irish hills of the same name, which lie under the protection of the Holy Trinity, which ours do not, at least we don't think so. We have never noticed it. Still, many a thing does take place without our ever noticing it. We never noticed, for instance, that "Both Mexico and France are under the protection of the

Blessed Virgin Mary," till Big Charley told us so, what time he spoke to something like a million spectators (only three quarters of them being civil servants given the afternoon off) at Chapultepec. Also there, and continuing The Work of the Revolution, was Presidente Licenciado Diaz Ordaz. He said *France*. De Gaulle said *Mexico*. They kissed each other on the chops and they and others said a lot of other things, but, Christ have mercy on us, you can bet your ass that nobody said *Maximilian*.

Certainly not Edward.

Redward Edward.

Red Ed.

"I started out from the old Greyhound Station on La Cienega, back in Hollywood," he said, said Ed. "And seated next to me was an old blind Colored Man with weak kidneys; we made every men's room between Ellay and Chula Vista. 'Just lead me to the stall,' he would say. 'I can do the rest by myself.' He said that he was going into 'Old Mexico' as they call it by the Border, where he had lots of friends, he said that he was entitled to many benefits of Mexican citizenship inasmuch as he was the father of seven children born under the Eagle, Serpent, and Nopal: and that under the terms of the Laws, The Unity of the Family Must Never Be Destroyed. All the other Ashanti aboard were scared shitless of him, which was how I happened to draw the coveted position of Captain of the Head, regardless of."

Nevertheless the Old One vanished whilst using it in Chula Vista.

"Enna bodda with me," he said, "nevva have to put his hann in his pocket while he in Mexico. Evva bodda in Mexico know *me*. 'Bline Juanito,' whut they caw me, see; that mean Bline John. I use to be barber faw Poncho Pilato, lass ole-time President of Mexico, cose that befaw

I lose muh sight. Spanish man with big hannel bah type
mus tash. Don Poncho Pilato."

Edward's foxfire face gleamed as he spooned up the
beans onto a strip of breakfast beef. I tried to imagine
what he had altogether looked like without the rufous
beard. Pretty much the same, I had to suppose, though
beardless and face-smooth and lighter as to weight. But
the sharp humorous nose must have been the same as
now. Must have been the same the moment they drew the
mucus from nose and mouth and dropped the silver ni-
trate in his eyes and hung the autoclaved witch-bundle
round his little neck. Not so much change, no.

"I said, 'You don't mean Pontius Pilate, you mean
Porfirio Diaz, don't you?'" This was of course before it
was made a capital offense to contradict a coon.

Blind John must have been due for another trip to the
sloughs and was anyway pissed. "Well, I *happen* to know
what I'm *talk*ing about," he snapped. "You What Boy,
ain't you?" Edward admitted it. Old man grunted. "Well
I gun do you favor," he said. "Coawze you hep me. Aine
none a them Black muthafuckas boawd this V-hickle dun
hep me, they thenk I doe know, but I know, so I gun do
you favor. You doe know *enna* theng bout History of
Mexico, child. Never less. Now listen." He put his mouth
next to Edward's russet ear, which he found without
groping. "Sposen you see Spanish-type Colored Person,
Vera Cruz or Porto Rico, Tlaloc, oaw any of them. You
say like, 'Dinga?' And if he *nod*, then *you* say like, 'Man-
dinga.'"

"And then," said Edward, "will he take me to his
sister?"

Blind John moved restlessly in his seat. "Maybe," he
said. "Trouble with them type oppress people, they
mostly what we calls analfabeticos. Very ignorant. *Very*
unreliable. Don Poncho Pilato, he say to me, 'Juanito,

them people is not yet ready for parliamentary democ-
racy.' And as of the present day, I cline to thenk he
maybe right. But I exempts from them strictures the
Nuestra Señora de Guadelupe. She *nev*-er let you down."

Never apologize never explain. Onward. Edward is still
very young and has just run away from home while there
was still something to steal from his stepfather, "Earl,"
who had been depleting Edward's paternal estate as
though it were an oil allowance: a liar and a rum-dum. So
Edward had told him a story about several kilos of fine
Afghan hash for sale at bargain rates blibbledey blibbledey, and the old man, who knew about dope strictly what
he read in the *Reader's Digest* (the daily paper got only a
skip and a toss, but the *Reader's Digest* was kept faith-
fully in the head and read religiously whilst "Dad" tried
to avoid hitting hemorrhoids), "Earl" at once leapt to
the conclusion that here was the chance of a lifetime,
huge profits, *much* better than diddling your orphaned
stepson or even raising giant frogs in your basement. Eh
la-bas. So out came what was left of Edward's patrimony,
though not so identified by "Dad"; and, thus financed,
Edward left home, having prudently packed and stashed
a suitcase elsewhere.

It was on another voyage, northward-bound this time,
and far from the legend-haunted Vales of Anahuac, that
an old wizard said to him—this was not long before he
met the mermaid in the lagoon near the State Park,
sheest, talk about having to have eyes in the back of your
head, trying to avoid both the Vice Squad *and* the Game
Warden, well, whose fault was it? Did the mermaids have
the clap before the White Man gave it to them?—the wizard said to him, "Never apologize, never explain, but
pause in your questing, kid. Take it easy, relax a while, let
down your hair (Edward had his auburn autumn locks

tied in a queue and fastened up into a headband, and
this, in fact, although it prevented the hair from flying,
wind-blown, into his eyes, truth to tell it did give him a
slight headache), whatever you're looking for, the philosopher's stone, the lost Dutchman mine, or the secret of success and sweetness of breath, it'll wait fr ya if it's there
a-tall. Bide a bit, me bonny boy, and we'll smoke a little
rope together."

He let his sun-washed blue eyes crinkle in their nest of
wrinkle.

"Are you sure that you don't just want to bugger me?"
Edward asked, cautiously, feeling for the smooth rock:
hankey-wrapped in his pocketses.

"No, oh no, I'm too old for that now, lad," said the wizard ruefully; "and when your pencil's empty, your heart
is pure. Being a wizard isn't the twenty-hour-a-day job it
used to be, them foreigners having played hell with the
business: their goddamn cheap-labor spells. But I made
my pile, got my see-cure little home here by the emerald-
green the wine-dark the dolphin-torn the dong-tormented
sea, free and clear with a chemical toilet and a salaman-
der laid on to provide hot water in any quantity on demand, day or night. I just like a little company, is all. I
mean, *I* can talk to my familiar but my familiar can't talk
to *me*. In fact, considering our respective ages and
strenths, wouldn't you say that it's me who's running the
risks, not you?"

So Edward stayed the night there. The house was
builded largely out of flotsam and jetsam and sea-wrack;
the riverine hamlets of Northern California after the big
floods of the past few decades had given much spoil, a lot
of it dating in origin from well *well* before the days when
the construction unions in conspiracy with the mortgage
bankers have made it necessary to build houses out of
smaller and smaller pieces of cardboard: there were pil-

lars and carven porticos and gothick gingerbreads galore, redwood beams and cedar and all good things as that. A green encrusted bronze bell washed from some low-built church hung next to a pair of the big gate lamps which haven't even been *made* since the turn of the century. There were oriental rugs, discolored to be sure, but all still glowing and lovely in the dimlight, as well as Indian blankets and fine pieces of furniture robbed of a certain measure of arrogance by virtue of their having no legs or feet and squatting flat-ass on the floor. And in one corner was a six-sided fireplace which drew like a charm without andirons, and driftwood burned sedately with many a green and blue, a green and red flicker. And old large books and rolled scrolls and suchlike tempting evidence of the wizard's craft or office were in visual testimony here and there.

The venerable warlock knew many surf-casting spells, a several ways of the wrist to cast with cantrips appropriate: in short, Edward stayed three weeks and learned a lot of useful things—might have stayed even longer and learned even more, except that the old man *did* try to bugger him but couldn't get it up, chased Edward round and round the suit of Satsuma armor, weeping and grunting and hoping that contact (could he but make it) and a magic or two would yet win the day. Edward, however, had on the one hand grown too old to willingly submit out of curiosity and thrill and had not by far and again grown old enough to submit out of indifference. So he feinted this way and that way, made a successful dash for his suitcase, and out the door he went, flying down the smooth brown beachways with his grip banging against his legs, until the old weirdmane's wailings and woanings and callings upon unclean demons had receded into the wind-washed distances.

The incident taught Redward Edward a lesson, you

may bet your sweet umbilicus, and as soon as he could, he purchased after much chaffering from a Romany chal in the great early Fall encampment near Mendocino a carrypack with sufficient magic laid into it to run a mile in two-twenty, as long as it was given sufficient encouragement, and just a little love.

So he felt rather set up after he'd transferred his odds and ends into the new pack, and was walking along the streets of "Laredo" when he saw A Cat with fine threads and an E. A. Poe-type pussytickler, or mustachio. The Cat had certainly not rubbed into anything mussy of late and his eyes were so clear that Edward was sure that it would be futile to ask him if he knew if there was any grass around anywhere. So he just smiled and was thoughtlessly going to walk on, when, as they came face to face, The Cat really looked at Edward as though the latter were a beatific vision, and said, "Hey, Jesus digs you, Man!"

Privately, Edward thought to himself, That is all as it may be, only on the other hand, maybe *not*. But aloud he at once snapped to, as it were, sort of sliding his pack forward in front of The Cat's feet, and he said, "Do you know where I can find a place to crash?" And he reached forward to catch The Cat and/or prevent him from going ass over teakettle.

"Oh, wow, thanks, Man," The Cat said, glowing at Edward the Red. "You removed a stumbling-block. I love someone who really lives the parables, or, no, that was a mid-*Rash*, some rabbinical Cat laid it all onto us at the last Ecumenical All Life-Styles Be-In. Yeah, I do know of a place to crash, it's a real *trip*, Man and Brother, the far-out-est place to crash in Laredo." And without a pause he swung one arm around and took hold of Edward's arm and started walking on in a manner which combined good humor and enormous physical strength. So that Edward had a fleeting notion that The Cat might, purely for Edward's own good and in a spirit of Christian Love, *break* his arm if he failed to come on along. The only hesitation, besides not wanting to get his arm broken, that Edward had, lay in The Cat's having called the town *Laredo.*

"'Laredo'?" said Edward.

"'Laredo,'" said The Cat.

"Man told me that this was Mendocino," said Edward, cautiously.

The Cat turned his head and flashed a loving smile. "*Used* to *be!*" he said. "Mendocino used to be here, and Laredo used to be in Texas: but, you know, Man and, and, let me say it: Brother: you know, Brother, there is *noth*ing that profound faith and some good Christian cantrips cannot do, I mean, like *noth*ing: so we, uh, well, we, like, *switch*ed them."

Edward strode along at a fairly good rate, pacing The Cat, who also after all had his gear and stuff. "Well, as you say it, be it so . . . but the fact is, this doesn't *look* like Laredo. . . . It looks like Mendocino."

The Cat stopped so swift and quick that Edward almost slid his rufous locks in the gutter. "I know," said The Cat. "I *know!* That's what makes it so groovy, Man and Brother!" he said, his face shining. "We have absolutely defeated what our Oriental Brothers call om, Maya or Illusion! It *does* still look like Mendocino! But, Brother, we are enabled by the clear-seeing faculty of the Third Eye (which is the Christ) to recognize that behind the illusion it really *is* Laredo! And here we are."

They were in front of the kind of building that used to be so common and taken-for-granted in the days before nice-looking buildings were made illegal, and it was kind of settled down a path on a hillside, slightly squat and rather long and with a steeple on one hand and shingles over everything, and a glassed-in bulletin board out in front. "Looks like a church," said Redward Edward.

The Cat agreed. "There you are again! It *does* look like a church. But it's *not*." And he waved his hand to the bulletin board, the top of which (where the name of the church would have been if it had been a church) had been painted out. Edward couldn't make out the faint letters underneath the paint. The letters on the board now said

THE CHILDREN OF THE BRIDEGROOM
Encounter Groups and Crash Pad
Demonstrations of Christian Thaumaturgy
Thy Servant,
Hughie Pemberton
LOVE IS OUT OF SIGHT, MAN

"Who is Hughie Pemberton?" asked Edward.

"That's *me*, Thy Servant!" The Cat said happily.

"Looks real nice," said Edward. The Cat's grip slightly relaxed. "There's a far-out Gospel Rock group going to be woodshedding here pretty soon," he said. "You're reddish-brown. Stick aroun'."

Inside the building where you might have expected to see rows of benches there were no benches, but there were a lot of posters on the walls and cushions on the floors and one side of the building had been ripped out so as to expose and include the kitchen. There was a lot of garbage lying around, but Edward noticed that it all seemed to be inorganic and didn't smell. The holes in the gas burners on the stoves had joss-sticks stuck in them, and two ugly chicks and a real pretty one were fanning a hibachi.

"Hi," they said, and then everybody kissed everybody else.

"Too bad you weren't here just a little while ago when Thy Servant was demonstrating Organic Christian Thaumaturgy," one of the ugly chicks said. She smelled kind of stale.

Edward was naturally interested, and he asked exactly what his Servant had demonstrated.

"Loaves and fishes . . . Hey Hughie. The Establishment turned off the utilities. We have all these groovy candles that Petals and Tabitha made, I mean, as far as *light* goes, but none of us knows how to bake the loaves over this hibachi."

Hughie said, "Then just grill the fishes, then, then."

She shook her head. "The test kit shows that they're all contaminated with DDT. Could you demonstrate some already-baked loaves and some uncontaminated fish, huh?"

He glowed and snapped his fingers. "Later, Man and Sister," he said. "Like, now, all the virtue has gone out of me. So, later."

The pretty chick came up to Edward and handed him a pamphlet and whispered in his rosy ear, "I'm deep into Witches' Lib., Man, but thanks to this trip on Christian Love, I'm not hostile about it; wait till everybody crashes, and I'll take you into the vestry room and show you my witch mark."

"Groovy!" said Edward. "And I'll show you mine!" He was *very* glad he had met this Cat, Thy Servant Hughie Pemberton, and his friends.

"I think I'll demonstrate a macrobiotic supper when the Spirit is on me again," said Hughie. "The only thing is, you have to fight against the illusion that you're hungry again an hour afterwards."

That was *one* trip.

The old Colored Man had paused with one hand on the

door of the jakes. "Enna budda round here can hear us right this minute?"

But everybody else on the bus had already been tapped and drained long before getting to Chula Vista, once famous as the scene of many a brief Wartime romance: but maybe no longer famous for anything. Nobody in the john, then, but a faggot who'd been homesteading one of the stalls, in one wall of which he had made a shall we say hip-level hole into the next retiring room. To this he had inclined his head and raised his eyebrows and smiled hopefully at Edward, but Edward merely smiled back and indicated with gestures that he was only there to help Blind John, whereupon the homesteader had grimaced and flounced out.

"Nobody here but us chickens."

"Well then listen here," said BJ. "To tell you the truth, now, when I had to give up barbering I study be Conjur Man. Now I ain't gun teh you much right now. Becoawse all I know bout you so far is, you young, you White, but you got kine heart. So I just teh you password, maybe save you life when the Black Men of Asia gun come sweeping over this racist nation, *dee* stroy it. You ready?" Edward nodded, then hastily said, "Ready."

The old man again somehow found Edward's ear, murmured, "The word is, *Mister Buz*-zard *is out in the yard.* And the countersign it, *Mister Rab*-bit *is here with the shit.* You got that now? Oawright. Lemme see they got some paper here. Hmmm. Go awn wait foaw me a ways oawf now, I doe like noboddy too close to me when I ease myself. Oeways was delicate that way. Make it kine a hard oawn me in Mexico." His voice subsided into a mutter. "Good theng I merely bline instead a lose one a my upper limbs. Them Mexican public tawlets smeh sum thin terrible. Cain't no one-arm man use *no* public tawlet in Mexico. . . ."

Edward, looking at his own ruddy face in the mirror to see if he could detect signs of any more hair on the upper lip, observed the brown trousers slide down over the heavy old-fashioned half-lace/half-button high shoes, under the bottom of the stall door. And when he looked again, after a moment, they were gone.

The bus driver muttered, "I was all set to go look'n see if that old jig had knifed and robbed you. They'll do that, you know, some of um. He coming?"

"Some's all right, though. But I seem to have lost him. Somehow."

"I wish ya'd losed them all," the driver muttered. In a louder voice he said, "Okay, if he wants to use his ticket and take the next bus, that's his privilege."

Edward took a step forward into the bus, and met with a broadside of swift, sliding, sullen red-and-yellow-eyed glances. He had a vision of the bus being dry-gulched by camel-borne troops of the Lost-Found Nation. Question: "All right, White Boy, what you do with our Brother?"

"On second thought," he said, "I'll use my ticket and I'll take the next bus, too."

Edward came to the conclusion that this particular stall in the men's room of the Chula Vista Greyhound Station must be a nexus to another level or plane of existence. It didn't sound like something to which Helena Petrovna would have given the time of day, but still. And no doubt the so-called password and countersign had constituted an Opening of the Way. Times change, as Albertus Magnus would have been the first to admit. (Say, do you remember? We called him Al. It was Al all the time.) Edward was tempted to go try it, but the homesteader was watching him like a love-sick, hard-up hawk: so he simply left the station and hopped on a local bus which eventually brought him into downtown San Diego.

Having definitely made a vague decision against head-

ing for Old Mexico in the immediate present and circumjacent future, Edward had to consider another of the
enigmas with which Man's Way is fraught, viz. What
Then? Almost without thinking about it, he drifted slowly
down and into an older part of town, and, such was his
bemusement that he wondered why he wasn't moving
even before he observed that right in front of him was
someone who looked somewhat African and somewhat
Hispanican and somewhat impassive and *ver*-ry large.

Someone, in short, who was waiting for him, Edward,
to make the first move—to, as it were, get away. It seemed
a ratty place to die, here by this block of festering,
boarded-up wooden buildings.

So he said, *"Dinga?"*

The head very slowly, *very* slowly nodded.

"Man-dinga?"

The head gave another minimal nod. The body seemed
to be distending himself, and he slowly began to move his
limbs. Anyway, one of them. An arm. Edward's mind
moved, too. Swiftly. "Mister Buz-*zard* is out in the yard,"
he said.

"And Mister Rab-*bit* is here with the shit," said Sancho
Senegambia. He gave Edward a huge hug and slipped
something into his shirt. "That's half a lid, kid," he said.
"Luego."

"Luego," Edward responded, fairly faintly. A block
later he learned that somebody had after all been witness-
ing what he had feared might have been his ritual dis-
memberment, to wit a young chick in a tie-dyed granny
dress who was leaning out of a first-floor window. "That
spade djinn always has great shit, doesn't he?" she said.

"Like to turn on?" he asked. She nodded, smiling, so
fast her small impish face seemed to vibrate. He tossed
his grip up to her and she caught it and he jumped up
and grabbed the window ledge and pulled himself up and

in. The front door was boarded shut, and why waste time
going around the back? The shit was gold, pure gold, the
chick was Fawn—or was it Faun?—nam port—and she
was, she really was, the first chick that Edward really
balled at length and at leisure and after sharing two sticks
of pure gold, or who had balled *him*, thus or however you
want to put it; the two of them free from every bond of
time, floating as they moved on the top of an ocean of
cream, and every word and sigh and sweet movement
slowly, so slowly, oh, so slowly, slipping away so gently,
gently, and the light so changed and sweet and all. It was
clear to Edward, and to Fawn/Faun who agreed with
him, kissing him here and there where it was nice to be
kissed but where he had never been somehow kissed before (still, he was young) by anyone, as they passed the
third joint from lips to lips on her pad in the front room—
they were clearly agreed that the old man who had called
himself Blind John was really le Baron Samedi, the Vou-
doun Loa.

Neither of them could remember anything about Baron
Samedi's kidneys. But they were satisfied and gratified at
such a working-out of the principle that the karma of the
inherently transmigrant soul can be demonstrated from
start to finish in a space of time within a given individual's lifespan, without prolongation through the whole
cycle of metempsychosis.

Which brings us to the King of Elfland's daughter-in-
law. Generation after generation the Queens of Elfland
had had only daughters. Husbands for them were, tradi-
tionally, obtained by enchanting some swain of the Sons
of Men, and conveying him to Elfland. You all know the
tale: how the unions were always happy . . . for a while
. . . how, at length and at last, the earthly bridegroom
grew to long for his friends and kind of old, and for the
old days before he had come to dwell Under the Hill. Oh,

not un*hap*py with the elfin scene, but wishing to spend at
any rate some short time in The Other Place. . . . And
so one day, awakening as though from a dream, again he
found himself on a familiar grassy sward, the sound of
cowbells in his ear, and seeing the smoke of his native
town adown the dale. How, as happily he raced to trace
the street where lay his home and family, he saw none
but strange or at best not quite familiar faces. How he
found that not mere months or years but generations had
gone by whilst he had daunced the faerie glades. And
how of the shock of this knowledge, and of the knowledge
that there was now no return to his elfin bride, soon he
sickened and soon he died.

Pickerel Creek was not merely a brook which ran
through a state park, it was also Fairyland, a well-known
phenomenon, and because of that it had been arranged
by the late (so-called) Collis P. Huntington, an Adept,
that another one of the Adepts should always serve in the
guise of a State Park Ranger at Pickerel Crickerel. Because, karma-shmarma, it is *al*ways good to be rich. Bound
to the Wheel of Change and Chance, as who *isn't*, it
stands to reason that not every tedious tripper who has
bought a few-dollar sticker for his car window is thence
entitled to go any goddamn where in any state park he
suddenly has an itch to. What, I ask you, would be the result, in the average taxpayer's mind—one, say, who has
finally settled his father's or brother's or even better his
bachelor brother-in-*law's* ("brother-in-law," who said
that one?) estate after the simple bastard, having been
gone missing *spurlos versenkt* for seven years and thus
legally *dead*—what is this citizen going to think if Russel
("Yes, let's call him Russell!" said Edward, struck with the
name. And offers his steaming coffee cup to Susanna for a
sip) if Russel suddenly turns up one day, alive as you and

me, not he dreamed last night, but to*day*: alive! and looking not a day older?

"'You son of a *bitch!* Where the *hell* have you *been*, you *bastard?*'" Because, listen, imagine: seven *years*. And *God* only knows what story they had had to cook up to tell the neighbors, and then the legal expenses, and now at last they can cash in the *bonds* and the in*sur*ance policy . . . and *there he is. Alive.* The *prick.* And says:

"Oh . . . I've been in Fairyland. . . ."

And by Fairyland, he informs them, he does not mean by any means that he was shacked up with two interior decorators and a choreographer of independent means: no sir. *Real* Fairyland. Located in *Pickerel Creek State Park!* Why, "Jesus! quoth the Queen!" It would cause internecine and of course "bloody" political war from here to Sacramento: control of the Board of Equalization would be nothing in comparison.

Argal, the citizenry has to be kept the hell out of the dangerous parts of the aforesaid Park, and that is *my* little shtick: maybe you thought that all I had to do was enforce the *Don't Feed the Bears* signs, and keep them from bathing in Ocean's stream? Well, *well.* Wrong *again.*

"There were these two brothers," Edward recalls, "named Yussel and Mendel. And their families wanted them to become Americanized and get new names. So they compromised and each one changed only one letter. And became Russel and Wendel."

"I know, I know," I said. "And one went to sea and one became vice-president, and neither one was ever heard from again. Boy, times have changed."

"He's got a million of um," Edward said, wiping beans off his beard and clasping Susanna around her lovely waist. Susanna has the kind of beautiful, lovely coloring which hasn't hardly been seen at all since the Protective Tariff of nineteen ought three, and also she has a quiet and dreamy-smiley manner, and also she has an incredibly graceful and light-light-on-her-feet kind of walk: almost I might say "deerlike" except that Susanna is a Fine Figure of a Woman, and not a tinykins by any means. "Antelopean," if there is such a word, and if not, why not? One of the larger antelopes. Not a dikdik. A bongo perhaps. Or an eland.

After Hughie Pemberton's demonstration and in between the encounter groups' sessions, the New Groovers, a Gospel Rock group, played, and things got kind of wild. "Sisters and Brothers," Thy Servant said, "before Adam and Eve sinned they were naked and they were not ashamed and in order to re-assume that pre-sinful state or condition we too have got to get naked and unashamed, don't you see, because that's the old-time religion and it's good enough for me," and so saying he started to strip down, and so did everybody else; the music getting just a bit ragged because of the musicians trying to play with one hand while stripping down with the other. And everybody kissed and embraced everybody else. Then everybody washed everybody else's feet. Some of the newcomers were a little shy about this last part, but Thy Servant pointed out that it helped destroy an Evil Archetype.

You can maybe try to imagine Edward's face when, three days later, walking with buoyant step toward, as he thought, the Pacific Ocean, he saw before him the stone-body'd bed of a river with a runnel of water down the middle, and over it a bridge, and straddling each lane was a structure captioned U. S. CUSTOMS: the signs on the other side were in Spanish. And a light-brown-skinned man, seeing him stop short and not just stare but gape, said to him, friendly, "You going into *Old* Mexico, boy, you better be sure you ain't got nothing *on* you, I minn, with that long hair, you know—"

Edward cried, "Jesus Christ, it *is* Laredo!"

And La Raza said, "Only on this side. The other side, Nuevo Laredo."

For a moment Edward was all set to do an about-turn. But then, not feeling at all sure but what whilst he was turning, The Children of the Bridegroom, led by Thy Servant Hughie Pemberton, might exchange Mendocino for, say, Moscow, and reflecting that old High John the Conqueror and/or associated Bloods had been heading for TJ and not Nuevo Laredo, that Old Mexico—while no Australia—is still wondrous large, leagues and leagues from marge to marge; so he shrugged and thanked his informant (who was, who knows—or, *¿quien sabe?*—Minister of Information in the shadow cabinet of Aztlan) and headed south as he had originally intended to do after having split the scene from his larcenous stepfather ("Earl").

(This, by the way, intends no general invidious reflection on the subject of stepfathers, most of whom are *very nice.*)

However long Edward's auburn hair was and however the Border Service of the United Mexican States might basically feel about *existentialistos*—a word within which they included Beatniks and Hippies and Freaks and Bohemians of all varieties—it was very early in the morning and the night shift was too weary to do more than look at him with tired black eyes, listlessly check his documents, type him up a tourist card, and inform him that he would not be asked to go through customs at that point: leaving unanswered and hanging in the dry, crisp air of when, if ever, Los Estados Unidos Mexicanos would check his pack and pockets and bodily orifices, and perhaps shear and shave his head for good measure. Such exempla of Puritan rectitude, *estilo latino,* do occasionally take hold of officials of various classes in our great and good neigh-

bor to the south in their continual struggle for effective
suffrage and no re-election.

Nuevo Laredo looked rather brown and bare and as
though it had used up a good deal of cement. By and by,
however, Edward did find himself in an older section of
town, and sundry good smells reminded his healthy
young body that it hadn't had breakfast. All the chicks
had been asleep, and he hadn't felt like partaking of the
loaves and fishes left over from the previous evening; Thy
Servant had demonstrated yoga date-and-nut loaves, and,
like every variety of newfangled homey health bread in
the *world*, it had been gray and crumbly, with a faint
taste of mold. So now, on perceiving a tiny eatery with a
frontless storefront, he slid between chair and table and
eased his pack to the floor. There were bullfight posters
on the wall and a photograph which he was to see again
and again in Old Mexico: a man wearing spectacles, an
expression of severe integrity, and a sash of office: also on
the wall was this picture's inevitable accompaniment, another picture, in blue and gold or silver foil, of the Virgin
of Guadalupe. Mexico is a secular republic, otherwise the
two potencies would have been photographed together.

An ancient and tiny little brown bird of a woman
looked up from her work behind the counter and flung
him a toothless smile and a few incomprehensible words.
At the next table was an ageless-looking don slowly and
methodically working his way through a breakfast consisting of an immense cup of steaming-hot coffee and
milk, the ritual wicker basket of napkin-wrapped tortillas,
and an object which Edward could not seem to identify,
although it did bear a remarkable and indeed a both
amusing and grotesque resemblance to something which
he knew could not be.

The señor observed his eye, nodded to him, and, without interrupting his own mastication, sliced a brown

wedge of the object and, neatly unskewering it onto a tortilla, passed it over to him with an expression which said more clearly than words, nearer to one than breathing, and closer than hands and feet: "Would you like to try it? It's good."

"Oh, thanks so much," said Edward. And it *was* good, too.

"*¿Le gusta, joven?*"

"*¡Gusta mucha!*" said Edward, and blushed with pleasure at the other's returning smile; for Edward had had no real occasion to use Spanish since Miss Crouper's class in High School: true, he had attended two supposedly interlingual social sessions at the Amistad Group of the Leo Czolgosz Circle of the League for Peace and Justice; but either the young Chicanos had spoken strictly to each other in a speech too swift for his ears, or they had scowled heavily at him when he seemed to get along just fine in English with any of those little Hispana girls with the cute behinds: but the opportunities for enriching himself in the *idioma* of Cervantes, Ibañez, Borges, and Cantinflas somehow hadn't developed.

"*Otra cabeza,*" said the aged gentleman, Don Señor.

"*Norflusta pusta hee ha,*" or something like that, said the tiny little granny, with a cackle of laughter; and in about *nadie* flat she had flung up the combination shelf and barricade and zipped out with a tray, thus:

(a) An enormous fluted glass of orange juice. "*Todos los norteamericanos gustan jugo de naranja.*"

(b) Another basket of napkin-wrapped tortillas.

(c) The mysterious Object, now clearly revealed to be just exactly what Edward had laughingly assured himself it couldn't, videlicet and to wit, a goat's head roasted with the horns still on.

(d) no d.

"Hew like much the Amexican estyle of break-fast?" asked old Don Señor, beaming.

"Dice, 'Gusta mucha!'" quoth Doña Senora, beaming also.

And Edward, reflecting on a philosophical principle, perhaps not phrased according to the idiom of Leibnitz or Kant, but not without its place in the total scheme of things, that is, "Well, what the fuck?!"—Edward beamed too, and prepared to dig in. The eyes were a bit chewy, but just a little. And then there was a plate of refried beans came along later which were very good. It wasn't Christian Thaumaturgy, but then, it had more variety.

"Khwere do you go now?" asked Don Señor. Edward admitted he didn't know. Don Señor asked, "Pair hops hew would like to make a ray roe treep?" The manner in which he asked this seemed to indicate that the answer was important. So Edward thought about it. Like most of his contemporaries, not only had he never taken a real trip on a railroad, he had never even really considered it. And the more he considered it right that minute, the more he liked the idea. And he smiled, and nodded.

"Ven'," exclaimed Don Señor. He frowned and waved aside Edward's sincere attempt to pay for the meal. Doña Senora twittered contentedly as they left, so it seemed cool. Out in the street, Don Señor asked Edward if he would prefer "the old estacion, or the new one."

Before Redward could answer, the older man said, "I wheel show you both."

If Nuevo Laredo itself had consumed a lot of cement, its new railroad station had consumed *lots* of cement, and the waiting room was enormous . . . perhaps not so goddamn *very* enormous, in terms of Grand Central: but Grand Central is full of marble and posters and smartly dressed gringos . . . and this one was merely full of cement masonry and of poor, poor, very poor Mexicans,

none of them smartly dressed, none of whom were playing guitars or doing anything at all interesting or ethnic:
merely sitting stolidly all around the place, on the
benches and on the floors, looking as though they had all
been expelled by executive decree from the State of
Nuevo León. Edward was not enspirited by the new railroad station.

"Do the trains from here go the same way as the ones
from the old station?" he asked.

"Thee work of thee Revolution," said Don Señor, "continue under Diaz Ordaz." He pointed to a long, long (cement, naturally—say, whatever became of adobe in the
land of its birth? *¿quien sabe?*) wall on the side of which,
commencing and concluding with sundry symbols and
the initials PRI, was painted this: LA OBRA DE LA
REVOLUCION CONTINUA BAJO DIAZ ORDAZ.

"I see," said Edward. And then he pointed and said,
"Wow! Oh, wow!" For as they rounded that wall they
came in sight of an entirely different kind of building
than anything he had so far seen in Nuevo Laredo: true,
it was only one story high, as were the others, but it was
made of brick, red brick, there was nothing in the least
stark or functional in its appearance, and it had evidently
been built long before the Mexicans, for to assert their
cultural independence of the EE UU or Estados Unidos,
had begun to bulldoze their old buildings by the hun-
dreds in order to erect in their place blocks and streets
and in fact entire *colonies* of cement and plastic chicken-
coop apartment and office buildings gleaming, if not with
alabaster, at any rate with glass: certain, of course to attract no end of admiration from foreigners who of course
would never have seen cement or plastic chicken-coop
apartment and office buildings gleaming with glass in either their own or any other country. *Sigh*—The red brick
had angles and ingles and nooks and crannies and cren-

elations and turrets—and in short it was a sort of Semi-early Mexican Colonial Republican Native Gothic *joy* of a building, somehow neglected by the Ministry of Bulldozing Old Buildings. And hanging all over and about it, in all the angles and nooks and crannies and crenelations and windows (not glass walls: *win*dows) were pots and cans of flowering plants, and little wooden cages of brightly colored singing birds. And along the tiled roof ridge a line of little flagpoles sported small Mexican flags all whipping bravely in the wind.

"These ease thee old ray roe estacion. Hew like eet?"

"I like it very much." Some idea struck Edward. "You work here?"

Don Señor beamed. "I om thee Estation Master," he said.

A small boy thrust a cardboard box of colored chewing-gum toward Edward and muttered, "Cheek lays?" Edward gave him a coin, and a plasticwrap pair of gaudy Chiclets were slipped into his hand, and, also, even as he turned his head to continue on his way, a slip of paper. He half-stopped, half-stumbled, paused, then glanced at it.

God the Heart, the Elohim (Emotion)
God the Head, the El-roi (Reason)
God the Third Eye, the Christ (Intuitive Revelation)
"The Children of the Bridegroom Rejoice"
Thy Servant, Hughie Pemberton

Redly Edly turned and looked back and around for the niño with the cheek lays, but he was nowhere in sight. From nearby a train whistle blew its blast both long and shrill, and the distinctive smell of soft-coal smoke drifted past his nose. He remembered going with Thy Servant at his offer into a dim quiet bar adorned with deer horns, Redward not keen about it because of being sure of soon being tossed out for not having ID proving him to be over twenty-one, then ye age of Man's Estate. But the bartender, a withdrawn-looking man with dark eyes and longish hair and a beard, had not asked or even looked odd about Edward's presence.

"Well, I'm glad your religion isn't against liquor," had said Ed.

A flicker passed across the face of Hughie Pemberton. "'The Son of Man cameth eating and drinking,'" he said, "'and they calleth him a glutton and a winebibber.' Barkeep, two more."

It seemed now to Edward that every Indian tribe in Old Mexican, from A for Aztec to Z for Zapotec, must have been represented there in the old railroad station, for such a variety of costumery he had never seen before, nor so many wide sombreros. The locomotives seemed very Mexican, being small and gleaming with gold-bright brasswork, and the small coaches looked to have been recently lacquered in maroon. Don Señor he said, "These train ease name Thee Serpen Eagle. Hew have wan?"

Edward knew *exactly* what the good man meant, and wiggled his hand at the belly band as though he was going to scratch his navel, and the hand came out with one gleaming ten-dollar gold piece, the kind of which they don't hardly make that kind any more, though to his passing-swift astonishment it bore the current year's date: and he handed it over. Don Señor gave him a long, long ticket and, taking a few paces backward, he trotted forward, jumped up and embraced him; and then retreated, waving, the kind of waving in which the hand stays still and palm upright and facing out and the fingers move up and down.

Edward was waved up into the coach by a smiling guard, and settled into a comfortable seat on the *sombra* side. He looked at the crowd in their rainbow serapes and

sashes and bare legs and embroidered dresses. Then he
looked at his ticket. It was headed NUEVO LAREDO, and
then it went on to list such places as *Santiago de
Compostela, Grita de Dolores, San Miguel Allende, Loco
Teodoro, Pulque Dulcon, Guadelupe Cisneiros, Suffragio
Effectivo, Amecameca de Juarez, Cuautla de Moctezuma,
Glida de Pistuquim, Ixtacihuatl, Malinche, Día de los
Muertos,* and GUERRA DE LAS CASTAS (*Frontera con Hon-
duras Britannico*) among any number of other places.
And when he looked up from it in some wonder, the train
had left all sight of station and of city behind and past vision; and was crossing an estuary with many reedy fens
and marshes and the bluest wide river that he had ever
seen—if indeed it was a river. It had to be a river, had to
be the Rio Grande, but in other respects he was puzzled.

The trainman came along now and punched the first
part of his ticket. Said, "It is forbidden to introduce large
animals and debris of any kind into the interior of the
coach, under the Law of the 19th June, 1867."

"I haven't got any large animals, or—" But the guard
pointed to a bird with bronze wattles and white feathers
which looked companionably at Edward. Who began
with, "I never—"

"The nanny-turkey qualify as a large animal," said the
guard, "under the term of the Law of the 19th June,
1867."

Edward said, "But—"

"Well, I have warn you," the guard said, with a shrug.
"Enjoy you visit to Mexico." He walked off down the narrow aisle and dispensed ice-cold drinks, or *refrescos*, to
the passengers, who in return gave him goodies wrapped
in cornshucks and in banana leaves, drinks of pulque,
mescal, and tequila—which he took with salt on the back
of his hand and a bite of a slice of lemon which they
sliced for him. This—as every sophisticated Mexican

knows—is the way that the gringos use in drinking, and he wished to show the gringo guest every possible politeness. By and by an Indio man appeared, smiled faintly apologetically at Edwardo, and put the nanny-turkey, or *totola*, under his arm and went away.

Pretty soon the guard came back and spread out a newspaper on Edward's lap (*Moribund Detective Fatally Pistols Criminal Atrocious*, said one headline. Another said, *Sir Smith Approbates Condition of the Fútbol Mexicano*. And a third informed him that *Religious Faith Is Not Inconsistent with the Ideals of the Revolution*), and on it deposited goodies wrapped in cornshucks and banana leaves, drinks of pulque, mescal, and tequila, slices of lemon, and cold refrescos.

"Well, gee, thanks!" Edward said.

The guard said, "*Cóma, cóma. Después, hablaremos.*"

"Enjoy you visit to Mexico," she said. Very attractive person, with dark rosy cheeks and a faint line of dark hair on her upper lip.

"Love is out of sight," said Edward. And fell to eating. Outside, maybe in a small amusement park, some sail sort of things were being poked with a thin pole by a thin man on a thin horse. A blind singer passed down the aisle strumming a guitar and singing a ballad about the death of Venustiano Carranza, Constitutional Revolutionary President of Mexico, by twenty-seven bullets as he lay sleeping on the floor of the house where he had found refuge, if that is what you want to call it. (Garcia Lorca had found the same kind of refuge in Granada in the house of Bernarda Alba: but the Spaniards, being a little more ladi-da, had taken him outside before they shot him.) The coroner's verdict in re Carranza was suicide.

. . . *que la vida es sueño, y los sueños, sueños son* . . .

Edward, seated at the breakfast table of my hogan near Pickerel Creek, began to chuckle, and I of course asked him what was so funny. "Well, this one afternoon it was really *late*, and Susanna and I had been walking all over the City of Mexico," he began.

"Oh my *God*," said Susanna, laying her coffee cup (or, rather, *his* coffee cup) down, and her hand on her bosom. "He's going to tell that awful story. I'll die."

"I don't think it's an awful story," said Edward. "*I* think it's a very funny story. And we suddenly got very tired. It was the rush hour, we were both too interested in trying out the old guitars in the old guitar shop on Isabel la Católica, if you know it. And the buses were all jammed, and we started flagging down a taxi and we flagged and we flagged but they wouldn't *stop* for us. And then Susanna suddenly tottered over to this one cab that had stopped for a red light and she said something to the driver and the light changed and he drove *off*, he just drove *off*, and she kept on *do*ing it, and so finally I said, 'Susanna, what are you *say*ing to them?'

"And she said, 'Well, they don't want to take us where we want to go for just the regular fare, so I'm offering them twenty pesos.' And *I* said, 'That's all very interesting, but you don't speak Spanish, what are you actually *say*ing to them?' And she said, 'Well, I'm saying, "*Veinte pesos?*"' . . . Oh, my *God!*'"

Susanna, now as red as Edward, said, "It's not that they took me for a whore," she said. "It's that they didn't even think I was worth the twenty pesos—*that*'s what makes me die whenever I hear that awful story. . . ." Every woman, no matter how respectable or liberated, thinks she could always make a living as a whore if worse came to worse, and it must have come as an awful shock to her to realize that she had unwittingly been trying to, and hadn't been able to make it. Though I don't know *why* not. Maybe because it was the rush hour.

Later on, Earth Brother and Edward had been out

there in what Edward at any rate used to call the Sierra Padres. Earth Brother was saying, "It isn't heavy weaponry that makes the good hunter, you can go out with the latest rifles, telescopic sights, wind gauges, and all those hypes, man, and not catch jack-*shit*. Because you're not one with the Earth Scene, and if you want to be one with the Earth Scene, then forget about a bunch of heavy equipment and concentrate on being natural. And of course *that* means, get below the level of sophisticated artificial inorganic consciousness. Get on the nose level, you dig me?"

Edward said, "Well . . . no . . ."

"Break the *smell* spell! You dig me?"

"Uh . . ."

Earth Brother's smile was only slightly impatient, only slightly tinged with scorn. "If you go out there all stinking of tobacco and soap and all *those* hype things, man, Your Brother the Deer is simply going to flee away from you. You may think you're upwind of him, but Your Brother the Deer is *aware on many levels* and he doesn't always need the wind to smell you; if you smell *alien*, Your Brother the Deer isn't going to stick around, see? Like a dog."

"A dog?"

Earth Brother had been squatting with the friendly native guides, with whom he had—as he had said—established rapport as a result of casting off all external and artificial ideas. When they said words in their language, and gestured, *he* said words in their language, and gestured. He trusted them with his money. They took him where no White Man had been. And now, as absolute proof, see, *they were hunting with him!*

"Your Brother the Dog," Earth Brother said, scratching; "now, no doubt you've been disgusted or anyway an-*noy*ed to see Your Brother the Dog roll in shit. But I want to tell you that there is a reason for that, it is *natural* for Your Brother the Dog to roll in shit, it's his original hunting instinct, dig? Your Brother the Dog is *disguising his scent.*"

He said something in the native tongue and gestured, and the Indians said something in the native tongue and gestured. They looked at Earth Brother with a very great interest as he took off his clothes and walked a few paces away.

"Don't tell me," said Edward, also greatly interested, "that you're going to roll in dog shit?"

Earth Brother gave a snort of laughter. So did the Indians. "If I was hunting *dog—*" he said. "But I'm hunting *deer.* Right?"

"Right."

"So when My Brother the Deer *smells* me, I want to smell *right* to him. *Nat*ural to him. Dig? Like a deer also, dig?"

Edward could speak Earth Brother's native language; so he said, now, "Yeah, I dig, man."

"Right on," said Earth Brother. He got down on the ground and rolled around and around, getting right into it and moving his back back and forth, much as a dog does when it rolls. Then he got up, and, smiling confidently, reached for his clothing. And His Brother the Indian nearest to him took a piece of wood and hit him right over the parietal bone. Earth Brother said, "Unkh," and fell over, bleeding.

The Indians quickly tied his hands behind his back with his dirty white socks. One of them turned to Edward and in perfectly good Spanish said, "*Es loco. Pobre loco.* We got to get him to a White Man doctor. Or," he grunted and tugged up Earth Brother's drawers and pants, "who knows what he might do? You see how he rolls in the filth of the armadillo? Sweetheart Virgin of

Guadalupe! Nobody going to go hunting with a crazy man like that."

They did not offer Edward the slightest menace at all, and, when they came to a fork in the path, showed him which one to take in order to get back to the train.

Sweetheart of Sigma Chi, pray for us. Spirit of Seventy-six, pray for us. John Fitzgerald Kennedy, President and Martyr, pray for us. Not my mother, not my brother, but it's me O Lord, standing in the need of prayer.

When next the train stopped, Edward followed the multitudes. The name of the place was Aquequeque de Iturbide, or something of the sort, and lo! the sight to be seen there was a sort of a catacombs, a kind of a tunnel lined with mummies, Estilo Mexicano. The nature of the soil there it seems preserves the defuncts, they didn't plan it that way, and neither had Edward. The entire bunch of passengers got off the train and he got off with them. It was one kick in the head after another for him, raised as he had been in the North American world wherein no one any more than being born at home dies at home. In North America they just go to the hospital for a check-up. That takes a third of the money. They then have surgery. There goes another third. Real soon after the surgery the heart simply stops beating for reasons (the surgeons assure us) having *absolutely nothing to do with the surgery*, perish the thought, as perished the patient, who is next plasticized at a memorial chapel and slid away beneath banks of plastic grass greener than the real thing. And that of course takes care of the last third of the money. And then some.

But here, boy, it was the real nitty-gritty—only, thanks to the funny what-is-it in the soil, corruption and the worm had somehow been given the go-by. Just everybody, well, *shrunk*. Sort of. The clothes of the defuncts were hanging loose, and so were they all. Hang loose,

Man. Woman. Child. Edward had turned away from a child only to find himself face to face with a very dark adult man. One eye had gone dim and the other was still almost bright and was turned up to look at something which Edward could not see, and the mouth was open wider than he could have thought any human mouth could *be:* the face was, as it were, wide wide open with an infinite astonishment far beyond mere awe or terror. And Edward saw that it was the old Conjur Man.

"But how long has he been *here?*" he cried, hearing his voice quavering in his own ears.

"Long, long time," the guide said. "Long, long, long . . ."

Edward said, "He isn't blind any more."

And he turned and walked away and out of there, very very fast.

The little train was still at the station when he came hurrying along, and the locomotive blew its whistle and all the passengers at the windows leaned out and waved and cheered.

THE 13TH BRUMAIRE

Charles Peace I had known many years. Some people there were who would say, "Surely that is not his real name? No. I thought not. It's a little too good to be true." They were right but they were also wrong. His official name was Gregory John Williams, but he hadn't invented "Charles Peace," he had adopted it as a pseudonym sans permission of the original owner, who had been hanged for high crimes about a hundred years ago. *All* of the originals of G.J.'s pseudonyms were murderers—not inappropriate, as he (himself the most peaceable of men) was certainly the leading American critic of both true crime and crime-fiction writing; his columns of reviews and comments and appraisals appeared regularly in leading publications; every other year a volume of collected essays, invariably subtitled *Peradventures in Crime,* appeared under the colophon of Hippogriph Press, and invariably they contained a preface by *the* detective storyist of present-day U.S.A., Roy Keith King.

Charles Peace I had known many years before the night of that quiet, small gathering at the Williams' house over in Sausalito. I had known Roy Keith King for a long while too. Roy Keith King was there that night in Sausalito, too.

All three of him.

It is, I suppose, common knowledge that "Roy Keith King" is the collective nom de plume (and perhaps the collective unconscious) of the so-called Bloor Brothers . . . half-brothers, actually . . . Leroy Bloor Steyne, Samuel S. Bloor, and Ludlow Bloor-Schreck. They had (or had *had*—nobody was quite sure, nor liked to ask which) the same progenitrix, whom they spoke of in quasi-theological tones as "Our Mother," and it was presumably from her that they had inherited the bloodshot, protruding eyes which were the sole visible physical evidence of kinship.

Their method of collaboration was interesting.

Leroy was the idea man. Ideas would come to him from anywhere, from everywhere—a newspaper headline, a dream, a scrap of conversation, a waking vision—and he would jot them down. That was all he would do. That was his genius; *you* would never see the idea in the newspaper headline and *I* would never get the idea from the dream: Leroy *would*. That was his genius. Leroy was a tall, gaunt man, with the perpetually startled and bug-eyed look of the spectral tarsier. He was obliged by reasons of health to eat often but was forbidden by the same compelling reasons to eat heavily. Being in his presence was a curious, some found it an unsettling, experience. You might be face to face with him and talking to him, but somehow, sooner or later, you found that he had drifted—you never actually saw him *move*—to the periphery of your vision, and there he would nibble his diet wafers rather in the manner of a locust munching a leaf. Or a mantis munching a locust. Leroy was the idea man.

Sam wrote up the ideas conceived by Leroy. He could not have gotten an idea to save his life. But the idea given, instantly he saw where it had to go, and he followed it through his typewriter until it fell, exhausted, on the last page of the pile of manuscript. Sam's nerves were not strong, sometimes he would hiccup and twitch and a moan would break from his lips and a tear roll down his cheek. Sam wrote up the ideas conceived by Leroy.

Luddy *rewrote* the mss. placed in his enormous paws by Sam—for, as it happened, Sam's mss. were completely unpublishable: they wandered along deer trails, fell off cliffs, were trapped in bogs, climbed up ropes and were lost to sight: but Luddy knew how to fix them up. Nobody else knew how. Only Luddy. He had never produced an original line in his life, he was purely a book doctor. Give him the manuscript of the book and he, after one, two, at the most three or four readings, invariably saw all of what was wrong with it. And knew how to make it right. Luddy had had a stroke, he also tended excessively to salivate, and needed the aid of the handkerchiefs his wife placed in his pockets. Luddy rewrote the mss. placed in his enormous paws by Sam.

Charley Peace's square brown house stood on stilts along the slope of the hill (or cliff) in Sausalito. It was a late summer evening, and night was long in falling; the views, miraculously free from heavy fog, were incredibly beautiful, with Belvedere Lagoon, its boats and houses, half-revealed and half-concealed in the salmon-colored mists; San Francisco loomed up across the Golden Gate with the white fog couching at its feet and a great red Japanese woodcut sun sinking unbelievably slowly past its shoulders. Grant Kipsmith came and stood beside me with a glass in each hand.

"Thank you, I already have a drink," I said.

He grunted. "I don't know why you wouldn't have," he said. "The two of these are both for me. Save me having to go look at the Weird Brothers quite so often. If I have half a buzz on by tiffin-time—or is it tucker-time?—then I won't mind so much. My God. Rugose, squamous, amorphous; Lovecraft must have known them personally." He took a long pull at his gin and tonic. "I suppose you never knew their mother, did you?"

I, for my part, took another sampling of my ball of malt. Angel Island suddenly came swimming out of the mist. I wished it good luck, wherever, as it made off slowly through the Maxfield Parrish blue of the surrounding waters. The haze filtered down again. Charley Peace had once said to me, "Grant is a hypochondriac, but he's a *sick* hypochondriac. He may even be a paranoiac, but he's a *per*secuted paranoiac." It was my feeling that Grant's feelings as regards the Bloor Brothers were not based entirely on their various nonpleasant personal conditions. "No," I said, sipping. "I never did . . . She was a mystic of some sort, wasn't she?"

Kipsmith made a noise in his nose as he looked at me over the rim of his glass. He swallowed. "A mystic, you call it. Ha. She ran a neat little racket called The Companionship of Christ the Chiropractor." Grant Kipsmith had perhaps made this up, but I was nevertheless both startled and amused. This evidently gratified him. He smiled a grim, brief smile beneath his long, grizzled mustache. "Oh yes. A great frog of a female, with those huge bulging eyes and that great batrachian mouth. I was"—his voice clicked, and he hurriedly took another drink—"I was always haunted by the hideous conviction that if I were to *kiss* her, she would turn into a *wo*man. But I could never, you know"—he waved a vague hand, grimaced—"*bring* myself to." The thought came to me that the original, or Senior Messrs. Bloor, Steyne, and Schreck had brought *them*selves to do so: a woman thrice wed had to have *some*thing to turn men's fancy. But I spoke no word on this.

The huge red sun stayed and stayed and burned and smoldered. San Francisco looked like Carthage—or did I mean Atlantis?—like something from an edition of the Apocalypse illustrated by Hiroshige. It occurred to me that I really had no idea how old Grant Kipsmith was, or when the mother of Ray Keith King had died, or if indeed she had died at all, or where she was or might be if not dead. "They don't usually go out much, socially, do they?" I asked.

Grant mumbled something about *un*socially. Then he almost snarled. "It's a bloody shame," he said, teeth partly bared. "Looks like a damned nice, honest, eager young kid too. But that's the kind, of course, they would prefer. Next would come a tired old hack. Like me. You know what it's all about, don't you?"

The soft, rich, mellow voice of Charley Peace, familiar to millions of radio listeners, was heard right then. "They *may* be on the sundeck, watching the sunset." In a moment his oval face beamed at us from the doorway. "It is beautiful, isn't it? . . . Leonard just arrived. He knew you were to be here and asked when he didn't see you."

It had been some time since I'd last seen Leonard Williams, Charley's younger son. I made a sound of wordless pleasure and moved to go back in. Kipsmith, however, was in the way, he was larger than I, and I had no desire to . . . well, well, Leonard wouldn't melt, there was plenty of time. And Kipsmith's feelings bruised easily. So many writers' do. "Ask him to join us," I suggested.

Grant Kipsmith waved his glass in assent and handed it to Charley. "And ask him to be just kind enough to bring me another. Your taste in gin, Mr. Peace," he said, suddenly becoming gracious, "is as impeccable as it is in music and literature. You know what it's all about, don't you?" he repeated, our host having gone back inside on a gratified murmuring note. And a most melodious twang.

The sun was gone from sight suddenly. Suffused crimson glow, strings of light, towers and turrets, everything as lovely as everything should always be. In fact, I really did not much want to know if I knew what it was all about. I really just wanted to watch the sunset's end and sip good Irish whiskey and wait for Len Williams to come out. "What's that, Grant? Something to do with Edward?"

It *was* something to do with Edward.

It was common knowledge, Grant Kipsmith said that he supposed it was more or less common knowledge, that Roy Keith King had not entirely written the last umpteen or elevendy-six books which had appeared under their conjoint name. Sam Bloor was as nutty as a bag of pralines, he said. Relays of psych doctors were required to keep him outside of coats with twelve-foot cuffs, he said. Ludlow Bloor-Schreck had suffered sympathy pains of high degree. They took turns having breakdowns. Only that Leroy Bloor Steyne kept coming up with ideas, kept them in business, he said.

"Yes, yes," said Grant Kipsmith. "He can't *help* it, of course. It's like peristalsis, it just goes on. The day's events enter his mind at one end, and he passes out ideas at the other. Well, after *all*. Roy Keith King is a fairly good property. Burton Cahne and the other big bumboes

there at Hippo House have no intention of letting it
wither. And Sam and Luddy don't need *less* money because they're sick. Sam never saved a cent and Luddy
went through his own bundle long ago. So the last, I forget the exact number of R.K.K. titles, they've been semi-
ghosted, of course," he said.

Color like a faint wash of blood ebbed from the bays
and the city and the towns. My relations with R.K.K. had
been casual ones, I was not emotionally involved. But it
suddenly seemed that only my emotions were now affected. I felt faintly sorry. I wondered what it must or
might have been like, to have spent twenty years—as Sam
and Luddy had—in literary endeavors consisting exclusively, in Sam's case, writing books to fit another man's
ideas, and, in Luddy's case, *re*writing such books. Or, for
that matter, giving birth to ideas, as Leroy had, not once
and again, but again and again, and again and again and
again, only to see them all worked over by a second man,
and then a third man. It struck me that the R.K.K. collaboration, world-famous as it was and fiscally rewarding as
it had been, was perhaps not the healthiest partnership in
the world. I said something of this to Grant.

He sighed, deeply, tremulously, painfully. "Ah, the hell
with it. It's a mug's game, anyway. My father used to tell
me, the only man who always makes money at the race-
track is the feed dealer. And the older I grow the more I
see, the only man who always makes money at the writing
track is the publisher. *If*, however, you are gauche
enough to tell this to one of them, he assures you with indignation that he loses money on any book you name.
How, then, does he stay in business? Answer: Mass Pro-
duction! Ah, the hell with it. It's cold. Let's go inside. My
bursitis is bothering me."

Sweet Phoebe Williams, with her bright smile, gave
him the other drink as we came in. "Charley's gone up-

stairs to get a few records he thought you'd like to hear," she said. I smiled. I said nothing. I might like to hear them, and then again I might not. Charley had an intensely extensive collection of records, second only, probably, to that of the family of Jean-Philippe de Phonographe, who invented records. Or Leeuwenhoek. Charley had a record of Leeuwenhoek singing a nursery rhyme in Old Low Dutch. He had records of mildly bawdy ballads "privately" performed by Caruso; Rasputin drunkenly chanting Siberian love songs with a Gypsy orchestra; Mustafa, the last surviving eunuch of the Vatican Choir; Melba singing *Aïda;* Melba singing *Waltzing Matilda;* campaign speeches by Harding and Coolidge. . . . Verdad, Charley had a *lot* of records. Some of them he played on his radio programs and some of them he couldn't, and some of them were a lot more interesting than others.

"Where's Leonard?"

"There, I knew you'd ask. We sent him downstairs to get some wine. He has a young lady with him and she's a very *nice* young lady, and so I suppose they won't hurry. But there's lots of time. He has lots of interesting things to tell us."

I left Grant Kipsmith grunting into his gin and went over to where the Bloor Brothers were gathered around the dips and chips like gnus around a waterhole, even Leroy, though I was as sure that a packet of diet wafers was in his pocket as I was sure that a sheaf of fresh hankies was in Ludlow's. I wasn't, however, sure what Sam had in *his—*

"What has it got in its pocketseses?" I asked him, shaking hands all around.

He looked up, not even surprised, and took out a plastic flask. "Just some brandy in case I get one of my anxiety attacks; hello, Dave." He gave a faint gleep, put heavy hand to heavy chest.

Leroy said to him, fondly chiding, "Negatives, negatives. Our Mother used to tell us, 'You must think Joy *in*'—why hello, Dave—'and that which is *un*Joy will vanish of itself.'"

Luddy wiped his chin. "Why, Dave Rhubarb, with a quotation, if I'm not mistaken, from Lord Tolkung's *Rungs* trilogy. The proper response," he chuckled heavily, "that would be, if I'm not in error, 'Baggings hates it forever.' See, reason I *know*," he confided, "my stepson Sonny is a *big* Tolkung fan. Even has his name on the door in High Lappish. He and his brother Buddy, *al*ways talking it around the house. You feeling all right, Sammy? *Sure* you are." He gave Sam's back a curious little knuckling, patted his face. Sam gave a fainter gleep than before, smiled bravely, took the hand and nuzzled it. Carefully, I did not look at Kipsmith. Ludlow had, I was sure, a stepdaughter as well. Her name hadn't even been mentioned to me, but I know I couldn't go wrong.

"How is Sisty?" I asked.

"Sisty is just fine, bless her heartmph." He mopped his mouth.

And, finally, after much pro forma smiles and the realization that the Brothers Bloor *did* have a guest with them who was neither a brother nor a Bloor, and, oh, well: "Say, Dave, you've met Edward, haven't you? Have you met Edward, Dave? Dave, meet Edward. Edward is the new entered apprentice in our lodge, we're doing our best to smooth his rough ashlar. We can trust *you*, Dave, to keep things under your hat. We're sort of hovering over Edward's shoulders, letting him, uh, sort of, uh, work along with us"—he gathered an ocular consensus, nodded—"on the new R.K.K. book—"

"What's it called?" I interrupted. The right thing. My

zeal was all to hear about the new R.K.K. book. Scarcely had I paid any heed that Edward constituted a sort of sub rosa fourth Bloor brother, oom beroofen. *Definitely* the right thing. Sam even took his hand away from his chest. Leroy smiled faintly and with a single finger smoothed his big mustache. Luddy drooled benevolently.

Leroy said, reaching for a heavy-duty chip and plunging it into the poi, "We call it *The Third Side of the Mirror.*" He nibbled and licked.

Charley Peace had just joined us. "*That* sounds intriguing." He had a box of the old phonograph cylinders. It might be anything from Schumann-Heink's "*Stille Nacht, Heilige Nacht!*" to "Cohen on the Telephone." "That sounds *very* intriguing." He gave a slight anticipatory breath. The brothers exchanged flickers. Sam spoke.

"Well, Cha-har-ley, we could hardly refuse you-hou-hou, excuse me, Charley, you know how my nerves, engaged in a new pra-ha-ject, anybody else invited me rye-hight now, stayed at hoe-home, I'm allrye-hight, Luddy." He stifled a gleep, waved his hand, went on. "Crime is committed, fingerprints taken, *nice* clear set, only thing *is*, you see"—his smile was half-shy, half-sly . . . his smile was reflected on his brothers' faces . . . Roy Keith King, it came to me, was a sort of three-sided mirror in self.

A door opened somewhere, feet and voices sounded, bottles clinked. Grant Kipsmith, who had been morosely studying an album of Mozarabic masses, said, with something like optimism in his voice, "Must be Len and the wine."

"—only thing *is*, you see," Sam Bloor went on, somewhat more loudly and rapidly, for he had observed, as I had, Charley's glance begin to stray, "when they check out the *prints*, they learn, uh, they learn, uh, well, for *one* thing, the files list *three men* on file as having *those same identical prints*—and all three of *them* are in *jail!*"

There was a short silence. We were all looking at Charley, and it was suddenly obvious to all of us—including, after a second, Charley—that he had not gotten a word of this last part. He smiled, he canted his head, he said, "That sounds very in*tri*guing . . . will you just excuse me one moment?" He hastened over to greet his son and to relieve him of the wine. The smiles of the Bloor Bros. were a bit faded, a bit set. *Sigh* Once more into the breech—

"—the implication is," I said, "that all three had been in jail at the time—"

"—*at* the *time*—" said Luddy.

"—the same time that the *crime*—" said Sam.

"—as the crime was com*mit*ted; yes!" said Ludlow.

They looked at me. Their large protuberant eyes glistened. They waited. I said, Well, *well*. I said, One such coincidence would have been difficult *enough*. I said *Wow*. . . .

"*Wow!*" This wow wasn't me saying it. It was the new young man. He was a very young young man, with hair a distinctive shade of red, and he looked as though he were just in receipt of his first kiss. The next thing for me was to give the signal for young Edward to tell how great it was, being an entered apprentice (or new ghost) under the world-famed Roy Keith King imprimatur. But just then Charley came back and he had an open bottle and he had glasses and he balsamed the collective Bloor hurt with a soothing line of winesmanship, the burthen of which was that he was only a small naïf burgandizer but he hoped that they would be amused by his presumption. I got away.

Grant Kipsmith inclined his head toward the brothers and raised his eyebrows and opened his mouth. I lifted a forefinger and continued on my way.

Len Williams' young lady was indeed a very nice

young lady. I smiled an avuncular smile, with Ptolemaic echoes, but I do not think that either of them even saw me. Phoebe saw me, though, and she lightly rested a hand on his nigh shoulder. "This is my son the sheriff," she said. He gave half a turn and his eyes half-focused.

"Dave," he said. "Hel*lo*. Cindy, this is Dave Rhubarb."

Cindy had already made what used to be called a three-point landing, and, seeing her, head-on and attending to my presence, I more than admired his good taste, I envied it. She had black hair, a lush figure, and a beautiful skin totally untainted by greeny-blue eyepaint or whitey-gray lipstick. "Is this another of Leonard's little jokes? Or are you really named Dave Rhubarb?" she asked. "Of course, I'm happy to meet you in either case."

"I'm happy that you're happy. But why should you doubt that I'm really named Dave Rhubarb? Do you doubt that Leonard's father is really named Charles Peace?"

In a fine mock dismay that was mighty fine and not a bit overdone, she said, "Oh dear. I just don't know these famous noms de plume, or is it noms des plume*s*? Until last year I never read *any*thing that wasn't assigned to me in school, and I really haven't caught up with modern literature yet."

I looked up to find myself, or, rather, ourselves, almost totally surrounded by Bloors. Leroy, Sam, and Luddy may have been far out, but not so as to be oblivious to Cindy; they might make a collective crack-up next week, but this week they were still with it enough to decide that they wanted to be where she was. As who could blame them? Charley Peace introduced them—adding, "I think you may know them better as Roy Keith King."

It was immediately obvious that here was one famous nom de plume, anyway, which she certainly knew. "Oh my goodness!" she exclaimed, and she even flushed a lit-

tle. Leroy smiled from ear to ear, his mustache com-
pressed under his nose and his yellow teeth gleaming.
Sam giggled and hiccuped. And Luddy, with a com-
pressed smirk that thrust his mouth out and puckered his
chin, teetered on his heels. This was making up for Charley's little lapsus earlier, all right.

Who, next putting his arm around Leonard, said to the
three half-brothers, "And this is my son the sheriff."

It took a little while to sink in. In fact, it was probably
not until Cindy, taking her friend's arm, said, "Did you
know that Lenny is a deputy sheriff now? He really is.
Are you going to put him in a book?" that any of them
felt inclined to examine the statement at all.

"Well, it's true. In a way," said Leonard. "It's part of
my master's program in criminology. For my M.A., I
mean. I'm on the staff of the sheriff's office down in Byrne
County, and they've given me the same status as the other
staff people. Of course, it's really just another police force,
county instead of city or state . . . I don't ride a horse
or wear a badge or anything. *Say!*" He suddenly observed
an idea in his path, and caught himself up short before
he ran over it. "I've been a writer's son long enough to
know enough not to make this I've-got-a-great-idea-for-
you-I'd-write-it-myself-if-I-had-the-time scene—" All the
writers there either smiled wearily or nodded sadly or
both, or (if their names happened to be Grant Kipsmith)
gave a few angry grunts.

"*But*, since there *are* several crime writers here, and
while the matter hasn't been classified as secret any more
than it's been made public yet—"

Charley said, "Len, drop the other shoe, please."

Cindy jiggled his arm, we all pretended not to notice
the simultaneous jiggling of her oh my *God*, her lovely
bosom, no: we all smiled indulgently at Len, and Len
went on, "Well, you know, sometimes police natter and

gabble over the teletype, you know, and I happened to see this particular sequence, it ended abruptly and nothing more's been said on the subject, so, uh—"

"*Len*-ny!"

Jiggle/Jiggle.

He grinned apologetically. "Evidently someone somewhere has, or thought he had, reason to believe that at least three men and maybe even *four*, with three in jail already—that they all seem to have the same fingerprints. . . ."

There was silence. Boy, was there silence.

"Thought some of you crime writers might be interested," said Lenny.

There was a longer silence. Broken by Charley Peace's mellow voice. "Well!" he said, cheerfully. "*That* certainly sounds intriguing!"

LEMURIA REVISITED

If one finds oneself in a Bloom-like situation, one can but bloom, right? *Kennst du das land?* Where the lemon blows? What are you doing *here*, then? Downstairs in the jakes, Edward, Red Edward. Older now. He writes, but not on the walls here. Sometimes he thinks: might as well for all the good. Upstairs in the Arcade. On one side the coffee shop and restaurant, on the other side the deli, the art print shop and foundry. In the coffee shop, Undine, companion of so many nights but now no more forever. UNLESS. Big eyes and big eyeglasses. Big boobs but not big boobglasses. A lack of consistency there, Undine. Had tried virtue but won no vir, had allowed herself to be seduced into abandon but found no ring in that mirkwood, was now gone up to virtue again, locked the barn door and announced that the key would come only wrapped in

a marriage certificate, so: lots of luck, Undine. You can't
fuck worth a fiddlehead fern, but you deserve a break. I
forget just why.

"'And there in the snow the ptarmigan couches in
cold,'" he muttered, jacknifing himself and clutching up
his clothes. "'O white upon white,' Jaysus, it's frostbitten
I am entirely," as the cold seat kissed his not-so-cold ass;
"'in the height of the high Himalay.'" Him? Her? He
subsided with a sigh. Isaac says such things have no place
in books. Find no place in *his* books, see you. And do *they*
sell? Don't ask. Like knishes used to, on Second Avenue.
Some things are sacred, Isaac feels. Oh, not God, of
course. Instead of not mentioning the Ineffable Name, he
wants not to see mentioned any of the Effing names.
And/or Essing names. Don't venerate, don't copulate,
don't eliminate. In one's books, that is. Still: a nice man,
Isaac. And every man hath his own madness.

Edward had heard about old Second Avenue. One of
Edward's grandfathers had followed the Old Religion.
Jacob Adler, pray for us. Boris Tomashevsky, pray for us.
Mother of the Muse of Maurice Schwartz, Spirit of Gold-
faden, pray for us. Edward sighed, stirred.

Saw himself in fantasy promising on the morrow to
lead Undine down the cigaretbutt and spittleflecked aisle
of the office at City Hall, lay procathedral of the not always unfriendly sons of saint pathrick. Lay indeed. There
must be an easier way of lay. Saw himself drawing all his
money out of the bank and a whileder fantasy that was
than any which had preceded it: all *what* money under-
line *what*, and exclamation point! like the peak of the
stale whipped cream on a charlotte russe. Once, he remembered, the impermissible grandfather had bought
him that archaic confection. Rare visit back East to see
Daddy; trans.: Mommy wanted Money. Mommy Wanted
More Money. Then Daddy died and so did the Daddy-

side Grandpa, and after that it was all strictly the lapsed
Little Brown Church in the Vale side of the family. Until
Mom's remarriage had brought *Earl* in as father, "Earl,"
whom the Malachy *and* the Snyder sides with rare agreement and rare good sense had both despised: "Earl," the
jack-leg-est jackass and drunken bum to end all such, and
who had outlasted Mom by one year. And as to the de-
tails of how Edward, Redward Edward, Edward Rufus,
had cozened what was left of his own jack out of *Earl* and
then hit the yellow brick road, behold, are they not written in the Book of the Wars of the Lord?

Not on your tintype.

Minheer and Minhag America, pray for us. They were
determined to let Undine make an honest man of him:
and more. And, ah, the sweet scent (if only in their own
fancies) of Ivory Baker Priest and Katherine O'Shay Gra-
ham and Francine I. Neff. Dorothy Andrews Slater. And
company. Luring him into alleys and hitting him on the
head. Repeatedly repeatedly. He could feel the blows.
Selling him brass rings, the rogues of the upper arcade,
but no cigars. Mutual funds whose closed ends would
stay closed or whose open ends would never open for
him. And then at length when whoozy and barely any
bread left, lo, and the owner and manager of the art print
shop, the former of which had been milking the place forever and ever and the latter of which had gone into the
Mafia deeper than the Maricot Deep for pony-playing
money at six for five, taking everything from his, Edward's, palsied fingers for engraved wedding annulments
and telling him the hour made no never mind that that's
what they were in business for, boy. Some people they
would let go floodle, but we known her since she was a
little girl and you we know like you was our own son, so
let the fires blaze upon the hearth and the lead melt in
the lino buckets of our bucket shop.

Well sir and memsir, time enough to let the sweet waters of oblivion wash away this estained scene, at its best a cheap echo and imitation of Bloom. What did Isaac think of Bloom. Never asked, had Rufus Edward. However, had never asked Isaac anything and gone away refused. Maybe your books sell better, Ike, because they are "cleaner," and maybe because you got there not only with the fustest and mostest but bestest maybe. Irregardless. Ir. Kir. Kiriath Chadasha. Carthage. Garth. Girth. Gash. Gush. Cush. *Delendo est blanco*. Boom bloom blam. But we are not you, so bear with us, sweet Isaac A, for the sake of anything you like.

With a hasty flush and turning his hands into icicles at the tap and a vision of himself frozen stiff down there forever with one foreleg upraised at the knee and wondering if this was maybe what happened to all the mothering mammoths found so posed and frozed there in Siberia. What? With their tums full of *but*tercups? Well. Do *you*. Have a *better* idea? Of what *did*? Happen to them? Who knows what kind of landlords they had in Siberia in them days? Even the best of landlords is a landlord. OR. Maybe The Them, the hyperintelligent Atlantean Lemurian UFO Aliens from Outer Space had popped the mamms into the quick freeze for lunch. For *late*r. And forgot to come back. *Or*, and here is a chilling thought, suppose they have simply yet to *come* back? What are they going to *do* when they find that someone has already eaten, as it were, their porridge all up? *Uh*-oh.

"You haven't been crying, have you?" asked Undine hopefully (Edward, Redward Edward, would have you carefully observe this correct usage of the much-abused word *hopefully*), a sense of wonder and her never very great abbondanza of good sense submerged *just* like Atlantis. Spirit of Edgar Cayce. Rise again. Mount unto the cabin. Sleeping Prophet, awake.

"Have I been *what?*" he asked, jaw dropping, just like in the old books, farthest from his *mind*, "crying," what next, would she bite her lip?

"Your face is all red," she said. There. *There!* By God she did it she did it she did it she *did* do it She BIT HER LIP! "Oh, Edward," she said.

He did his bloody best for her. "Leave me alone," he muttered roughly, and walked away with rapid strides. It was almost as good as a marriage for her. Better, maybe. Hell, yes. Sooner or later marriage would pall, even before it petered. But for this memory there would be never a disillusionment; already her mind was enshrouding it like a pure rock-candy stalactite. The tough part of it was that now he'd have to stay away from the arcade for long enough to let it all set, let it harden, and take final form there in the misty caverns of her mind. And this was too bad because he rather liked the arcade, rather liked its prohabitants, every one of them an archetype of clear shining dishonesty, and maybe far above all liked the atypical coffee house and its continental breakfasts which were honest to gormengast as near to a continental breakfast as you could *get*, on the North American continent anyway; almost he could see taste and smell right now the clean sweet butter and the crisp roll and the good honest coffee: ah well. He might have married the cook who at least knew her place, but marry Undine who did not, no this he never could. He smiled a sickly smile at Ernst of the Vienna Deli, dear old phlegmy protonazi Ernst, who sold German beer made in Germantown, Pa., but added an aura of authenticity to the transaction by charging for it on the Pittsburgh-plus pro-rata system just as though it had come from *gemütlich alt' Umlaut* where they made the cunning little VWs and the tootsy little valves for the gas chambers; although to be sure, or unsure, they might never have gotten around to Edward,

who was after all only one-quarter, ahem. Only maybe
they would might.

Visions of an interethnic joke danced like sugarplums
in his head. Saddly addled head. Bran or brand-new widower sobbing bitterly. Wildly, then, if you like. Comfort-
ing friend (Bildad the Shuite in the original version no
doubt) saying, Never mind, don't carry on so, eventually
you'll remarry. With a wild scream of absolute agony the
bereaved demands, But what am I going to do to*night?*
Undine had not been the fulfillment of his boyhood
dreams (as Christ knows he hadn't been hers re girlhood
and maidenhood, to say nowt of maidenhead), but he
had, he *had*, you know, put a lot of effort into her and she
had become familiar, nothing glamorous about that, no,
he had grown accustomed to more than her face.

And now he was going to have to start all bloody over
again. The excitement of the chase, take it away—Forty
years ago, Father, said the old maid in the John O'Samara
novel; but I like to think about it—the point here was that
he, Edward, foxfire-red Edward, *did*n't particularly like to
think about it. One of the good things about the era as
had just come to an end was that he hadn't *had* to think
about it. Need had been nullified by gratification, therefore need had bred no fancies. "Why don't you get married?" people (some people) asked. Laying it on the same
level as, "Why don't you get your hair cut?" On which
same level maybe it should be laid out consistently. Get
married every month or every two months. Whenever it
got too long. Would work out cheaper, too. Wouldn't stay
cheaper, though.

No of course a woman. No of course it wouldn't have
worked out. If a woman would drop the blade in the slot
before even breakfast like that (this) and without their
being married, can you imagine what cute tricks and
lovely surprises she'd feel free to pull and damned well

would pull *af*ter marriage? It wasn't right, leave alone it
wasn't wise of her, it wasn't *right* of her. He had after all
deserved better than that of her, he reflected, the warmth
of self-righteousness and self-pity rising in him. But he
was unable to think halfway straight about the matter, its
past or present or future, not on an empty stomach. Look
look, his legs were shaking, had just then wobbled. Weak
with hunger as well as shock. He needed some food in his
stomach. He needed, to begin with, about three nicely
browned slices of rye toast, which he surely wasn't going
to get nowhere a-tall, not even if he bought the Hotel
Grand Babylon cash down for gold, he wasn't. Nor two
eggs scrambled lightly in a bit of unsalted butter, he
wasn't. And as for a cup of English breakfast tea: forget
it. However, as this was an emergency—

A coffee royale was in order, in order for him to think
straight. But was there any point, Edward thought, in trying to think straight? Wasn't it all straight enough without having to have any further thought about it? In that
case maybe a coffee royal (café royale, coffee royal, take
your goddamn pick and shut the hell up) was in order not
to have to think straight about it. In order not to have to
think about it. Or about anything else. Was he making
too much of it? Would it be paying a decent tribute to
her memory if he thought less or even little about it?
Where the fuck was a *bar?* Or even a greasy *spoon* for a
cup of plain blah but *cof*fee or of Lipton's. Who needed
all the eye was just now meeting in window after window
when all it sought was coffee, tea, or booze? Who *need* ed
nylon hose, flowers, imported herring-sauce mix, automobile mats on special sale, greeting cards for a sister-in-
law's birthday, didie dolls, towel sets, or any of the rest of
the rubbish which kept meeting his eye when all he
wanted was a bar or a restaurant or even a little old
woman with a charcoal brazier and a chaldron. What was

he *doing, here?* How far had he *walk*ed? Was this, wherever it was, one of those rotten *"home"* neighborhoods where the bars had family-plan bowling alleys (for planned families) in them and didn't open till the collarstud agencies had closed? Why in the hell couldn't his heedless stumbles have led him into a socially deprived section of the city where the greengroceries didn't come wrapped in plastic surrogate condoms and the socially deprived shopper was able to save the diff between U.S. Choice and U.S. Standard and spend it in a friendly neighborhood bar of which there was usually at least one in between every other store which wasn't. The restaurants around *here* of course would (a) open even later than the bars and (b) would be so damn dim that only by following the huge white flapping menu of the "Hostess" (Usherette would be a better name) was it possible not to be lost forever without unraveling a ball of string: guzzled by a minotaur, may the Ghost of Grandmother Mary Malachy have mercy on us—

Not that the menu would have more than two choices of anything for all its come-on size. Certainly there were no lunchrooms in sight, but if his famine-feeble legs would only hold out he would for sure eventually reach some sort of franchised establishment, probably called BIM'S or ZAP'S and featuring such delectable goodi-staples as:

Three and half-pound Country-killed Ground Rib-tickle BIMburger with Imported-style relish, genuine nonorganic French Fries curled by French curling-iron heated over charcoal-style fire (Ketchup 75¢ extra per order): $12.95

OR

Four-foot-long ZAPfurter with Swedish pineapple chunkies on Neapolitan-style "Hero" roll with spe-

cially vapor-softened crust and Free Courtesy Paper
ZAPkin: $11.98

And just then at that moment a freshly minted angel
was dropped down from Heaven so lightly that he only
hit the pavement with the slightest of slightly audible
plops, and this angel was made in the form of a white-
haired man of late middle age and Fenian antecedents
with a beautiful and inimitable Imitation Strawberry Ice
Cream Cone Pink complexion such as is attainable only
through many years of internal treatment with bar whiskey at a level temperature and away from bright lights.
This angel had on his face a look slightly strained and
slightly expectant. "I knew you was going to ask me
that," he said, nodding unsurprised his (pray pardon, ladies and gentlemen) hoary head. Edward the Red, not
aware of having asked him anything at all on a vocal
level, felt it was not for him to quibble. "'Al,' I says ta
myself," the angel said, not stopping for an instant his pur-
poseful or you might say relentless tread, Edward following along beside, "'this kid looks like he needs a drink.'"
And for the moment neither said more word.

He/Edward had afterwards a faint confused impres-
sion that he had been led along and through a shady,
musty hall terminating at a closed door which had a wee
window in it and that his vergil had knocked twice and
then thrice and upon the wee window's being opened had
uttered certain ritualistic words, such as "Sean sent me" or
"*Benny hot meer geshickt;*" but he recoils from taking his
oath upon the matter, feeling that there are some things
for which the world, but anon, sir, anon. He is however
certain that behind a long article of ceremonial furniture
there stood a man with the looks of one marked by years
of exposure to and experience with every manner mode or
method of human vice and suffering or illness or illusion,

such looks being seen from time to time upon the faces
and/or countenances of Buddhist bonzes, Jewish phar-
macists, and Irish bartenders.

"Al," said the guide through the Dark Halls of Hell,
"This kid here needs sumpthin a drink and some
breakfass. Give him a hot cup a coffee with a ball a malt
in it and then give him a glass a orange juice with a ball a
malt in it and then I think he could use a roar egg beat up
with a ball a malt in it."

Such was the older man's detachment from the Worlds
of Maya, Formlessness, and Form, that it was not until
the pink-faced angel dropped on the long altar in front of
him a small wadded number of elderly dollar bills that he
was able to reattach himself and prepare the viaticums as
ordered. "You seen Al yet this mawning?" he asked. "I
ain't *seen* Al yet this mawning," said the other. "Him and
Al was here pretty late lass night. Wad a you," he asked,
turning slightly to Edward, "a noddist or a professor or a
writer or sumpthing?"

Edward nodded. The other two exchanged the looks of
those whose lowest suspicions are confirmed but who
from compassion forbear to curse the deaf or place a
stumbling block before the blind.

Not long after the coffee royale and the orange royale
had been followed down the Golden Road to Samarkand
by the egg royale, damsels appeared with dulcimers, followed by minstrel boys returned from war, followed by
Edward producing two ten-dollar bills and the curious
words (which he could not recall ever having heard let
alone said, before), namely *Oysters all around,* he was
blest copiously by several old ladies all of whom were
named Agnes, and had his sleeve plucked by a young
man with a leatheroid portfolio under one arm and a pal-
lid sheen of sweat upon his face who begged the favor of
a quiet word with him in a quiet corner; which Edward

felt in no way inclined to deny, and, in fact, executed several veronicas on the way thither as well as demonstrating the principle and practice of levitation.

"I understand that you're a professor of writing at an art college," the young man said, causing to materialize before them two glasses whose provenance Edward was unable to determine upon immediate thought, but which he ascertained (by the simple method of sampling both, and would one man in one thousand have hit upon this simple method, which, amplifying the genius of simplicity, recalled Columbus' trick with the salt and the egg? No.) contained some ice and soda water with two balls of malt in them; "and I would appreciate your kindness when you realize that I've just obtained a position as Area Representative of the Blessed Virgin of the Month Club—"

Edward said, "—Ah—"

—and the young man said, agitating Redward Edward's coatsleeve, said, with great haste and infinite reproach, "Now don't misunderstand me, say, what do you take me for, don't I know that you are of an opposite persuasion—"

"I am?" Edward was surprised and intrigued at this way of putting his three-generational absence of any denominational affiliation whatsoever. "You do? Would you happen to remember who it was that persuaded me?"

"—and Mr. Miles Sheeley, our District Supervisor, he's an old friend of my mother's brother, Uncle Vincent, he give me this list of good Catholic families kindly provided by the Archdiocese, and Jesus, Mary, and Joseph, didn't he have to pay an arm and a leg for it, 'contributions' they call it, my grandmother, rest her soul, she used to say, 'Our Lord in His tomb wasn't watched for free,' he said to me, I mean Mr. Miles Sheeley, our District Superintendent, not Our Lord or Uncle Vincent, my mother's brother, he said, 'Stick to this list, Bobby, and you may make some money or you may make a lot of money or you

may make no money at all, but the worst that can happen
to you is that you make no money at all: but if you go *off*
that list God only knows what might happen to you and
we may never even get the portfolio back that you haven't
paid for yet, but whatEVer you do, Bobby,' he said,
I mean Mr. Miles Sheeley, our District Superintendent of
the Blessed Virgin of the Month Club, because before
that I was with the Society for the Propagation of Fidelity
Insurance Company and Mr. John J. Hearn, *he* was the
District Superintendent, I was in the mail room, so this is
my first opportunity in direct-approach canvassing and
Mr. Miles Sheeley—"

"—your District Superintendent," said Edward, buzzing
a bit about the occipital bones.

"You *know* him?" the young man asked, surprised.
And, not waiting for an answer, he went on, "And he said
to me, 'So whatEVer you do, stay away from the Jews,
Bobby, they'll break your heart, you can talk yourself
blue in the face but they'll never sign the contract even if
you have the map of Jerusalem printed on it in living
color, and the Proddasints are just as bad, believe me,' so
don't think that I had in mind to persuade you to *sign*
anything, Professor, but as this is the sort of in your field,
I mean Art and Lidderachure," and here he allowed his
portfolio to open and discharge and disembogue an
amount of illustrated printed matter, "and this being my
first opportunity in direct-approach canvassing, now for
the current month until the fifteenth we are featuring the
Blessed Virgin of Pompeii and after that it goes onto the
Blessed Virgin of Cracow and after that the Blessed Virgin of Guadalupe in the month following, with the holy
pitcher in laminated plastic frame and the illustrated brochure each one with the imprimatur and the octave and
the Holy Mass and the plenary indulgence and the lay
apostolate badge plus the raffle for the free tourist-class

boat ticket in connection with the Blue Legion's pilgrimage to Our Lady of Fatima when we, that is, the Blessed Virgin of Fatima, when we get to her, participation in this specially arranged raffle being limited to paid-up members of the BVM of the Month Club, and I wondered if you'd be kind enough to appraise my approach and observe my technique, seeing that this is somewhat in your line, if you wouldn't mind, Professor." And he wiped his face and scanned the face of Edward. Who assured him that nothing could or would give him any greater pleasure, and as they were somehow by this time and by now standing in the front of a sedate yellow brick apartment house they entered the lobby and went upstairs. The young man wiped his face again and consulted his list and dubiously rang the bell. The door was opened by a woman who was not exactly old and was certainly not very young, with pink hair, clad in a kimonoid garment of the same color, and upon the Area Representative's informing her that he had been advised by the Archdiocese to call upon her, invited them to enter into her apartment, although it might not have perhaps been fully certain to a third observer (had one been present) that she fully understood and appreciated every nuance of what was being said to her: she herself stated that she had been up very late the night before.

"My friend isn't here right now," she said; "she had to go to New *Brun*swick before her brother-in-law got back, because, well, oh, you don't want to know all about that, do you understand about the *money*, because I'm just sick and tired with all these *checks*, if I wanted rubber I'd move to Akron—"

"Checks aren't necessary," the young man said, "and it's thirty-five dollars a year, payable in advance, that is, well, uh, *no*: payable in installments of three dollars each,

but only thirty-five dollars if paid in full in advance either
in cash or—"

The pink lady, apologizing for a slight yawn, said that
she was glad they understood and that thirty-five dollars
cash was just fine and in advance, and she held out her
hand; that is, she held out the hand which she was not at
the moment using to hold her wraparound. "I'm not sure
I've got that much," the Area Representative said, a slight
frown on his face. "Mr. Sheeley said we sort of pick it up
as we go along, and—"

"Let me see what I've got," Redward Edward said,
"seeing that this is your first opportunity in direct approach—"

"His *first*," the young lady said, indulgently, with something very like, almost, a simper, as Edward emptied his
back pocket; "well, isn't that *cute*. Well, listen, everybody
has to start sometime, and believe me, I was a lot younger
than he is."

"If you've got two fives I've got a ten," Edward said.

"I have two twos and a half a dollar and what is this,
two dimes or—"

"Never mind, just lay it down here, now let's see: Six
ones and a twenty—"

"Give me the twenty and you take the ten and then I'll
only need one of the fives and you take back the two twos
and I'll take back the six ones and you keep the change
here."

Edward said, "Well, okay, if you're sure it won't put
you out." The young man ("Bobbie") shook his head and
the lady in the kimono took the money from him and
where, exactly, she *put* it, Edward was neither then nor
thenafter quite sure, because she continued holding her
garment wrapped around with one hand and with the
other she took the Area Rep. by one of *his* hands.

"Come on, honey," she said.

The young man half-turned back to Edward, as he ("Bobbie") and she were leaving the room, and said to her, "He's supposed to observe my approach and appraise my technique—"

"Well, he isn't going to observe your technique *here*," the lady said, firmly. "He can either wait until we're through or maybe my friend will be back from New Brunswick by then. And be*sides: What* technique? You're cute, you know that?" she said, guiding him through the door.

"Yeah, but Mr. Miles Sheeley—"

"What, *that* old—" but the door closed upon her tones of mild surprise and definite disparagement.

Edward smoked a scented cigarette of which there was a box upon the piecrust table, and was observing with keen interest a large painting over the mantel of the fake fireplace, which was either *Aristotle Contemplating the Bust of Homer*, or *The Horse Fair*: he was not quite sure which: when the door burst open. "You can just pick up your sweet little tootsies and get the hell *out* of here," said the pink lady of the place, who was clearly in a snit. "*I* don't know what kind of apartment house you may think this *is*," she said, in a state of some fury, "but I can tell you right now that this is a re*spect*able, well-be*haved* apartment house. You came *in* that door and through the front door downstairs, didn't you?"

"Yes," Edward said, "but what *hap*pened?"

"I'll *tell* you what *hap*pened. I just said to him in a perfectly friendly and decent manner, 'Come back any time you want to get your balls off again, honey,' and he just gave me this *look?* and he made this weird *noise?* and he said, 'Oh my God!' and *then* he went out the *wind*ow, like someone shot him out of a *gun, out* of the window and down the *fire* escape, all I *need*, for Christ's sake, because this is a *de*cent and re*spect*able and well-be*haved* apart-

ment house: and if *you*, think it *isn't*, you can go take a
good hot *shit* for yourself: now get your goddamned
briefcase you rusty-headed son of a bitch and get the hell
out of here and *next* time you can just go up to Spanish
*Har*lem and—"

She shoved him out and closed the door behind him.
Quietly.

Edward, after a few moments in bewilderment and
then in thought, began to whistle in a well-behaved and
respectable manner and looked all around the environs of
the respectable and well-behaved apartment house (and,
indeed, to tell the truth, it was doing nothing untoward
whatsoever) and looked all around the neighborhood and
called out, "Area Representative!" and "Bobby! Bobby?"
and even, once, "Mr. Miles *Shee*ley wants you." There
was no response.

He came to think quite seriously of returning to the bat
cave and laying the portfolio on Al₁ or Al₂, but—he realized—coming to rest on a bench in a small park—he had
no idea in the world where that was. Or *he* was. Except
that he was on a bench in a small park. But he had no
idea where *that* was. It seemed empty, except for a
woman with her hair in a sierra madre of curlers who was
pushing a baby carriage at one end of the park and a man
strolling along from the other end. After the man had
strolled through and back again and was coming by once
more and Edward had finally realized that this was only
one man and not three and that he had been and was still
looking at Edward all the time (who really felt by now
too *tired*, what with one thing or another, either to sell his
life dearly in defense of virtue or to submit to whatever
indignities might be all the current mode), the man sat
down beside him: and it was evident that there was after
all no peril. This man's clothes were very clean and very
closely pressed and of very good quality and very worn

about the edges if you looked very closely: and he had the faded sandy look of a long-retired Anglo-Saxon athlete.

"Not insurance," the man said, looking at Edward. Who said, "No."

"Not stocks and bonds or mutual funds, either."

"Right again. No."

The man slid a bit closer and regarded Edward with an air of keen interest overlaid with wariness. "Books? No. Not books. Mm. You haven't got the *look* of a Britannica man, not even a new one. Real estate. Hmm. Uh-uh. Well, fellow, I have to admit that you beat the heck out of me. Usually I can size up a guy with a portfolio like that right away. But . . . Hey. Don't tell me. Wait a *minute*. Have you got privately printed *dir*ty books in there?"

Edward felt very sandy inside the eyelids, but he threw off fatigue and drew himself up. Said, "I resent that, *very much*. As a matter of fact this portfolio contains the contents of an Area Representative of the Blessed Virgin of the Month Club."

The retired pole-vaulter (Class of '36) looked at him with incredulity. Scorn. Contained (but still visible) amusement. And then he asked, very very quickly and very very low-voiced and *very* very intently, "Does it *pay?*"

Surprised, less at the question and its manner than at his own state of vincible ignorance, Edward said, "Gee . . . I really don't know."

Mr. Decathlon repeated and increased the Scorn Look. "'Don't really know,'" he mocked. "I suppose you haven't even *tried*. Got a yellow streak in you a mile wide, hey. Quit before you've even started. I used to see kids like you back when I was trying to help them get started selling the *Saturday Evening Post*, some dog would bite'm in the rear end or maybe a drunken bum'd kick'm

downstairs, and they'd turn *yellow*. I'd say t'them, 'What?
You want to be a quitter? Is that what you want to be?'
Get'm blubbering, first battle already won. Let's see,
now—" Without permission and with practiced hands he
snapped open the portfolio and immediately located and
drew forth what seemed to be some sheets of instructions
or directions. He read them with intent, having put on a
pair of gold-rimmed nose-pinchers which greatly changed
his appearance: he looked, in fact, so much like a high
school principal that Edward had an almost irresistible
temptation to just punch him in the nose and then run
like hell: a temptation he resisted because Mr. Thirty-
Yard-Dash of 1935 might easily run him down and then
subject him to a wide variety of YMCA-type tortures.

"Dash is my name," said Mr. Dash, giving Red Edward
a keen look and his right hand. "Brentwood Dash, just
call me Brent, TY was just an old college-days nickname,
not that I ever finished, the Depression caught up with
me and I had to look lively and hustle, rustle, and scratch,
I can tell you. Don't suppose that there's anything that
can be legally sold which I haven't sold it. Challenge,
challenge! That's what I respond to: *challenge*, yes sir.
I've sold tangibles and I've sold *in*-tangibles and I've sold
things which baffle description, classification, and cate-
gory. Now, just to give you one example or instance, not
so long ago I was operating on a charter-at-large to initi-
ate into the higher degrees by the Grand Lodge Oriente
of Cartagena in any English-speaking area wherein the
Grand Lodge Oriente of Cartagena didn't otherwise oper-
ate; and naturally for my efforts I was entitled to charge
processing fees, initiation fees, engrossing fees, and so on.
*Noth*ing to do with the other Masonic bodies in the
United States, York Rite so-called Blue Lodge or Scottish
Rite or Royal Arch eckt eckt: *noth*ing to do with them.

But do you think that *they* saw it that way? Think *they*'d leave me alone? Haw!

"'Conspiracy,' no sir, there's no 'conspiracy' on the part of the Blue Lodges and the Scottish Rite Masons to take over the Government of the United States: Blue Lodge and Scottish Rite Masonry *is* the Government of the United States, young man, and you better *know* it. If the time ever comes when you ever want to feel that you can try to get away with murder, then take my advice: pick something *easy*, where there's at least *some* chance of getting away with it: kill a policeman or commit something trivial, like *treason*. But never, young man, and I do mean NEVER! never try to issue any so-called clandestine, irregular, or unofficially recognized Masonic degrees in the United States of America."

And he shook his head so vigorously that his nosepinchers flew off and he rescued them with a lunge. "Unless, of course, you're a nigger," he added. "They don't *care* about *them* and *their* degrees. . . ."

Edward had listened with great interest, but, unless touching the end of his sharp and ruddy nose with the tip of his index finger was a response, response he had none.

Mr. Brent Dash returned to his portfolio. "Now . . . admit this does interest me . . . mmm . . . mmmm . . . uh-huh—" He scanned, he muttered, twisted his mouth into a small and taut smile. "Oh just listen to this, now, will you, ahah, 'Failure to maintain payments will result in cancelation,' ahahah, why of course, why: isn't that the way the Roman Catholic Church *always* controls them? Fear. That's how. *Fear.* Well. Now. I've sold Methodist, Lutheran, and Presbyterian insurance, as well as nondenominational Protestant policies for the Christian American Mechanics and Brotherhood, *as* well as, you know, my work on behalf of the interdenominational Holy Land Family Pilgrimage Tours, but somehow or other I *never* got around to offering the Virgin Mary on a monthly subscription basis, as it were. Challenge. I *rise* to challenges, young man. You don't. Difference between us. You see. So. Tell you what. A hundred dollars. Taken?"

Edward had become increasingly aware that the Road to Samarkand had not only gone off the Gold Standard but had taken a detour which had landed him in some place which was the moral equivalent of Queens. "Oh, uh, no," he said, looking around in uncertainty, "I, ah, can't, ah, have to, ah . . ."

Mr. Brent Dash inclined his head to one side and tipped Edward a slight, tight smile. "Oh," he said. "I've done business with you people before. Never accept the first offer, hey? Not even for your own brother. *Okay*. Hundred and fifty, can't go higher than that, element of uncertainty, new and untried territory, *but*. Brentwood 'TY' Dash loves challenge. *Revels* in it. *So*. A *hun*-dred. And *fif*-ty. *Dol*-lars. Cash down. Deal? Young fellow, you got yourself a deal."

He started to slide the portfolio over to his side of the bench. Edward, shaking his head, started to slide it back. "I can't *do* that," he said, sincerely. "*I'm* not the one—"

Mr. Dash held the portfolio in a grip of iron. College wrestling, 1934–35. "What do you mean You Can't. *Course* you can. Who *is* the one? Your manager or supervisor? That what you're worried about? Don't. There is *no* problem connected with our little deal which won't vanish like snow in the springtime soon as I walk into his office with five hundred dollars' worth of sales, I mean, *this* case, orders, *mini*mum. Memberships, then. Same difference. My first day: you bet. Of course," he said, cagily, "that won't be all mine, or even most of it. You know what the commission is. But I don't like to take advantage of your youth or inexperience, although I know that when Mr. Miles Sheeley and I get our wise old heads together he isn't going to expect *me* to offer my years of experience on the same basis as let us say another. SO." He reached two fingers into what must have been the last living watchpocket in North America, and produced a number of bills, folded very small. *"Tell you what I'm going to do,"* he pronounced the ritual words.

Edward, underwhelmed, heard more than Mr. Dash's voice echoing in his brain chamber: to wit, he heard also the voice of the young man with the sweat-sheened face and the portfolio; wondered *why* he had left the mailroom of the Society for the Propagation of Fidelity Insurance Company, *why* the intervention of his Uncle Vincent had been necessary to obtain the subsequent position with the Blessed Virgin of the Month Club, and *where* he had learned his incredible dexterity with the bill-switch game.

"Two hundred dollars, and that's it." And with that Mr. Dash gave the portfolio a sudden twitch which whisked it out of Edward's hand. Who said, "You're sure, now, that you're going to *square* this with Mr. Miles Sheeley?"

Mr. Dash looked at him with reproach and in amazement. "Young man," he said, "isn't it enough that I'm in the black books of the Masonic Grand Lodges of fifty states, the District of Columbia, and the Canal Zone, *plus* the Northern and Southern Jurisdictions of the Ancient and Accepted Scottish Rite: do you think I want the entire Roman Catholic Church *and* the Jesuits Order *and* the Inquisition after me? *Take the money."*

Edward took. He sighed, but it was a small sigh. "If you've got a piece of paper I'll give you a receipt," he said.

"Just what I was going to suggest," was Mr. Dash's crisp comment. "Here's paper and here's the gold-plated Individual Enterprise Boyd Rhaeburn Prize Pen which I got when I was selling for Sheaffer back in fifty-six. Don't forget to date it."

*To advancing to BVM of the M. Club Area Repre-
sentative for therapeutic massage.* . . . . . $ 25.00

(Edward wrote)

*For appraisal and observation of method and tech-
nique.* $175.00

       Total $200.00

Mr. Dash, commenting that different religions did
things differently, but, after all, we were all going to the
Same Place, rose to his feet, wished Edward good luck,
and, with a crisp nod, strode off to the exit/entrance of
the park. Edward, feeling just then that words of prayer
might not be out of order, murmured, "Blessed Virgin of
the Month, have mercy on us. . . ."

Large bronze bridle bells tinkled.

A beam of sunlight fell just then upon a signpost reading SAMARKAND. Five and twenty score Bactrian camels
padded softly out from between the public lavatories and
the tennis court, defiling along the asphalt path. They
were laden, fore and aft, with oliphants' teeth, precious
bales of cardamom and carpet wool, cases of Carstairs
and Seven-Up, Nephi, Moxie, essence of cajaput and oint-
ment of spikenard, Sapolio, scented soap, shagreen and
Shredded Wheat, and many many bundles labeled MU-
HAMMAD SPEAKS. The smell of charcoal fires faded fast.
Two by two, rolling and swaying, the camels passed the
sign reading SGT. FRANCES X. FOGARTY MEMORIAL PARK.

Sakers sounded.

Mounted on the Godolphin barb, Redward Edward followed close behind.

IN WHICH THE LODGE IS TILED

The year that Edward finished his master project on the Secret Languages of Brazil and began his lesser-known but equally important inquiry into the curious and significant practice of gold eating in the Levant, there occurred a diversion which occupied him for two months. It began with a preparation for a Sequestered Convocation of one of those Orders which, since the extinction of the Holy Roman Empire and the consequent dispersion of the Great Giaours from their headquarters in Courland, have never met publicly.

Rufus Edward was then in his thirtieth year.

He was reclining at almost full length in his tub (it was that the tub was long, it was not that he was short) and drinking a glass of sweet white wine and Sybil was waiting to wash his back for him—waiting quietly, as he did not care to be interrupted at either activity. However, as he set the glass down carefully in the soapdish (Sybil held the soap—Pear's—in her hand), she said, "I saw Stratton today."

"Did you? Which Stratton was that?" He spoke as if multitudes of Strattons prowled the streets below.

The gaslight hissed very quietly. R. Edward said that electricity glared. *And,* the fact is, electricity *does* glare. "*Dr.* Stratton. Professor Llewellyn Ap-Gomer Stratton."

"Oh, that poop." He reached his long and ruddy hand toward the glass. Sipped.

"Why do you call him a poop?"

He smiled. Asked, "Wouldn't you care to join me?"

"*You* answer *my* question *first.*"

He sighed. "I'll tell you why I call him a poop. Last week, on that afternoon of intolerable heat, I turned into a dispensary to take something alexipharmacal against the sunstroke—"

"—and came back half-crocked; yes, I remember."

He thought momentarily (he said) of drowning her, but decided that the gesture would be inexcusably wasteful. And continued: "Hardly had I slid into my seat and given my order when *Stratton,* whom I had not noticed to be there, else I would have driven my camels to another oasis, *any* other oasis, slid in alongside me and turned those protruding and dolorous eyes on me and cleared his eyebrows and raised his throat, or perhaps it was the other way around, you know Stratton's way, and in the hopes of sidetracking him from whatever prize piece of boredom he was set on inflicting—"

"Vain hope."

"And effort vain . . . I said, entirely on the spur of the moment, 'Isn't it odd that so many speak Spanish and so few speak Esthonian?' "

"You would," said Sybil. "*Only* you would. And then what happened?"

He shrugged his speckled shoulders, causing ripples to spread far and wide. "Then nothing happened, which was what I'd hoped for, then my drink came and I drank it, then there was a sort of cough, no, not a dry one, a nasty phlegmy one, and *then* Professor Llewellyn Ap-Gomer Stratton proceeded to explain to me that it wasn't at *all* odd, and just *why* it happened that so many people spoke Spanish and so few spoke Esthonian . . . an address which lasted thirty-five minutes by my ice cube; and I couldn't escape unless by climbing over him—which, had I been equipped with alpenstock and spurs (Oh, I know they use other things nowadays, but never mind), I should certainly have attempted. And damned well succeeded, too, is there any more malvasia?"

She asked if he were ready to have his back scrubbed,

he asked if there were any reason why he couldn't have both, plus her, and playfully threatened to pull her in with him: then the phone rang. "Damn," he said. And, "I am supposed to be somewhere else in one hour." And, picking up the instrument, "*Yes?*"

There was a long silence, during which Sybil rubbed steam off the pier glass and looked at herself. She had struck quite a number of poses before she heard him say, "Very well," and saw the watery reflection of his arm as he put down the telephone and picked up the glass. "Please fill this at once and then proceed to wash my back, and therein fail not. Move, vainest of women, *move.*"

Edward drank the white malmsey moodily as she plied the Pear's and the washcloth. "This should be a lesson to you," he said. "'Let us not open Satan's mouth, lest he accuse us.' . . . That will do." He stood up and got out of the tub.

"What happened?"

"That was Stratton." He mopped his flanks.

In the next room she glanced at the clothes laid out for him and said, "You haven't got an undershirt. Wait—"

But he wouldn't wait. He said that he knew it. He picked up his shorts. An uneasy expression settled on her pleasant face. "I feel suddenly odd. You know what I mean. Shall I scry for you?"

He fastened the shorts, snap, snap, snap, and sat on the edge of the bed and began on his socks. "That is not the precise verb which I had in mind, but there really isn't time for either."

She looked around nervously. "There *is*, there *is*. For scrying, I mean. Don't laugh." And, while he finished his dressing and peeped into a kit bag he took from a cabinet, she poured the contents of an ink bottle into the glass he had drunk the wine from, and, seating herself at a table, looked intently into the gradually calming surface of the liquid, murmuring to herself.

"I won't be back before midnight. And I'll have eaten. Believe me, there is nothing— What do you see, Sybil?" he asked.

She shook her head, blinked, ran her plump fingers through her black straight hair. "There, it's gone. Something about a dog and something about a moon that was inside out—I saw that one *twice*—and there was something really *nasty* which I couldn't quite make out, and that means you shouldn't go." She looked at him with a face of such self-conscious deceit and such curiosity as to his reaction, mixed, that he burst out laughing.

"Just for that," R. Edward said, "I shall kiss you."

Black-haired Sybil took the kiss from red-haired Edward and gave him one or two herself and put her arms around him. "Well, I made that up, about it meaning you shouldn't go," she admitted, "because *I* don't know *what* it means: but I wish you wouldn't go, you are going, aren't you? *Be* careful."

"I'll be back about one A.M.," he said.

He did not see her again for two months.

"Well, this is really very kind of you, Knight Edward," said Dr. Stratton, in the cab. He, too, had a kit bag between his feet. "In a way, I have to thank you twice, you know."

"I didn't."

The night had begun to drizzle. Things gleamed. "Yes, yes. It was just two years ago, or approximately so, more or less, that is, you know, about two years ago less a few days. I'd just published my paper on," he gave a modest cough, "those Malabar Black Mass objects which *you* know about, and so that is *one* reason, *one* reason," he tittered, "why I recollect the date so well. It was just about,

ohhhh," here he rolled his eyes, deep in thought, then: tri-
umph! "Two years ago!"

In the demidarkness Redward Edward yawned and
yawned.

"It was at Commissioner Sanderson's that I observed
you were wearing the Golden Pin, and—"

"Damn! I must have forgotten to take it off! Yes, *I*
remember now. Damn."

And so the poop Stratton babbled on: how at first he
had thought nothing of it, how next he had thought something of it, and what that was, and what he did about it,
and what *that* was, and more . . . much . . . much . . .
more . . . Redward Edward yawned again. "Ahah, mmm-
hmmm, and so poor Marsh agreed to nominate me a Ser-
vitor and so of course he was to lead me on in tonight at
the Convocation; then they called up to say how ill he
was and had even so very thoughtfully suggested *you:* it
is, I need not say," he said, "very kind on your part to
agree," a-babble babble babble. The cab turned, and
turned once more, the streets and sidewalks gleamed, up
ahead, though still some blocks away, the battlements
and serried chimneypots of the Palace of the Prince of the
Holy Poverty swung briefly into view.

Then everything ceased to gleam, and, although Edward was sure that the cab had turned at least once more
before stopping, everything was dark, dark, dark. Once
indeed there had been a brief, dim light, and a voice
which refused to become identified said, "What! Red Edward? . . . of him I should not have thought it. . . ."
RedEd desired very much to turn and to confront the
voice, but for a reason he could not bring to mind he was
staring very hard at something on the floor of the cab and
so could not, could not turn his head. Later, he thought it
must have been Stratton's kit bag, or something which
had been in it: but of the kit bag, its contents, the cab,

and, for that matter, of Stratton himself, there was now no sign.

The old man with the crooked shoulder and the empty blue eyes (eyes which never looked into other eyes but which saw quite clearly enough all the same) sucked in his breath sharply when he saw Edward at his door. Alarmed he may have been. Upset, perhaps. But the sound he made was merely one of his many mannerisms. "Yez is hurt," he said.

"I'm not," said Ed. He pushed at the door and it gave way, although not enthusiastically. The old man bobbed his head and bobbed it again sucking in his breath. He wore an ancient sweater and tangles of grizzled hair protruded from it here and there. The room smelled strongly of grain and old men and of the many pigeons whose voices softly stroked the air. "Yez is dirty," his hand gestured but did not touch, "all on that side."

"I did slip and fall. But I am not hurt. What do you mean by it, you dirty old devil?" He moved forward as the man with the crooked shoulder moved backward, old man shaking his head and saying what was no doubt in his own mind intended for, "Oh, no" but which came out, "*Aww* . . ."

A sharp suckle of air . . .

"*Naw* . . ."

Then there was the wall behind him, or, rather, the row of cages in which the doves cooed; reaching these, he began to sidle along them shaking his wicked old head. "Naw . . . Naw . . . I wouldn't do nothing to yez. Yawda know that. Whatser matter? Huh? Huh? Boss? Huh?"

Edward reached one finger out which did not quite touch the filthy and ravely sweater. "I rode in a cab tonight. Someone was with me. He wasn't there when I woke up, and I suspect he's been kidnaped, just as I suspect the cab was not a real cab, and I *know*—I don't suspect, I *know*—the agent used was mandragore. First I went blind, and then, after it was too late, I smelled it. So—"

They had reached the corner of the room and a table, clotted with filthy rags, filthier rags, and incredibly filthy crusted bottles and jars, barred the road to Cathay and the way thither.

"*Awww*," said the man with the twisted shoulder. He began to sink down, supporting his descent with back-thrust hands. He sucked in his breath. "*Naww*," he declared. Then, half on his back, he held his hands up and out. How many decades he must have used this reflective and defensive stance, how many protective crowds it must have drawn, how many attacks (and how many well-justified) it must have saved him, would-be attackers retreating in alarm or (equally effective and hence equally welcome) disgust—

"*Naww*," he repeated, his eyes staring at the middle of the air. "*Naww. . . .*"

"Benty, it was mandragore, and nobody but you, incredible as it is, nobody but *you*, you vile old dog-robber, nobody in the *world* knows how to make mandragore any more but you. Therefore, you must know about it. And," he reached up one of the foul bottles (hand-blown and God knows how old), sniffed briefly at it, grimaced, held it poised over old Benty—who cringed and drew himself into the fetal position, "will tell me. Now."

Benty awed and nawed and continued to contract in upon himself until it looked not unlikely that he might be sucked up, into, and through his own nasty navel. E. Red let fall a single drop. It was thick and came out slowly. Benty shrieked as though it had been red-hot acid. A single vacant blue eye he exposed. "Awww, have a haht," he said. "Yez don' know what that can do to the skin."

"Wash it clean, I suppose. Get *up*, Benty. I have already considered drowning one person so far tonight, and you—"

A rictus of fear followed, followed by a perceptible rising of the old dirty man's skin into gooseflesh. Who began forthwith to babble. "Listen, hahd *I* know who it was for? Man comes a me, he says some poor old Chinamun is sick, needsa dawg t'eat, *you* know them old Chinamen, they get this da zease, *I* dunno whutch a call it, they gotta have some nice dawg meat t'eat, n when ay yeat it, it gives zum like re *leaf*. Yez is heard a that. So he ass me, would I make up some *man*dy. Uh right. But I din, I mean, I din *know*. Eyah's no law against makin mandy. Mandy is *good*. A little bit uh vit, it's lie kit puts new *life* in ta yez. A little bit maw, so its puts ya ta sleep fra while. But it don't hurt, it don't *hahm* nobody. *Aww*."

"*Naww.* . . . !"

What man?

Who was the man?

What did the man look like?

Benty's shaggy body shook with simulated fear and then with dry sobs such as would not have deceived a macrocephalic idiot. But answer the questions he would not.

At least, not until Edward, Edward Redward, the antique bottle still in his hand, moved to open one of the pigeon's cages to which he stood nearest. Harmless mandragore may have been, in the final analysis, and perhaps it was only the close and stinking air: but he knew he could not stay long in this filthy little room. He turned away and unhooked the latch. The doves burbled. He held the bottle (blown, by the shape, the telltale shape of it, long long before the invention of that aptly named machine, the Jersey Devil)—he held the bottle, tilted it.

"Listen. Listen. Listen." Benty was next to him, all pretense gone. His eyes still looked vacant, looked elsewhere,

but that was the habit of a lifetime. "I can't *tell* yez nothing. Yunna stan me. Listen. Do yez wanna buy a *coin?* a
nole coin? Nobody expect me ta *keep* it. Somebody *pay*
me t'elp im ketch a dog nice n quiet, fee don' pay me in
regalar money, *he* can't blame me fie sell it. Right?"

Edward put out his hand. His right hand. He put his
left hand in his pocket. Something gleamed as had the
streets gleamed several years earlier that night, changed
hands.

"At's right. At's right. Nobody can blame yez if yez
sells a *coin.* I got enough troubles. I doe need no maw.
But *you*—you ane got nothin a worry about. Mandy wone
hurtcha. It's not like none a these *drugs,* ya know: chloro-
form, dope, ether: *them* things. Naw.

"Mandragore is *good* for you."

Adelbert de Muschwitz, Prince-Principal of the Noble
Order of Knights Sworn to Holy Poverty in Defense of
Lusatia, had in point of actual fact, never been in Lusatia.
His poverty may have been holy, but it was also nominal.
His predecessors had on many occasions fought Saracens,
Swedes, Turks, Finns, Poles, Greeks, Russians, Protes-
tants, Popes . . . had declined to fight Napoleon. Who, in
consideration of the then Prince-Principal's having agreed
to surrender the Order's last strong (but not very) hold, a
tiny island off the Coast of Dalmatia, allowed them to
withdraw in full panoply of arms and banners. The former consisted of twoscore crossbows and ten arquebuses.
On certain ceremonial occasions these were still mus-
tered. The Order's once vast lands in Saxony, Moldavia,
and Courland had all gone long ago, but the Prince-Principal before last had made prudent investments in less ex-
otic but more stable countries. The present Prince of the
Holy Poverty had been less prudent. However, he was
still recognized as a Sovereign by several nations of a traditional or indifferent bent, he enjoyed the trappings of

the position. His expense account was almost adequate, and he was a man of imposing mien and fond of mirrors, of which his Hall of Audience held many.

They held few audiences.

He murmured a greeting in Late Medieval Latin, and Edward Redward returned it according to the formula. "You'll excuse my not wearing the ruff and the muff and the swords and the trowel and the apron, since this is an Informal, Ser Knight," the P.-P. said. A strong odor of expensive cologne emanated from his well-kept flesh; it was one of his major minor extravagances, and he excused it to the Order's Almoner on the grounds that its basic ingredients prevented plague.

"Since this is an Informal," said Edward, "I beg leave to ask if you'll excuse the 'Ser Knight.'"

The Prince of the Holy Poverty, who had been admiring a new fawn-colored cravat in a mirror, stroked his neat goatee, murmured, absently, "Certainly, certainly . . . er . . . excuse him from what? Oh. Oh, I see." Gradually he removed his gaze from his own reflection, turned it on his visitor. "Always glad to see you, Edward. What's on your mind?" Absently, he drew from the pocket of his shantung silk coat (ordered by mail from a Hong Kong tailor, who being himself a Squire-Paladin of the Holy Poverty, gladly provided it at a discount) a periodical printed in very large and very small type on green paper; murmured to himself, "The third race, the third race, who looks good in the . . ." Raised his eyes, met those of his audient, and begged his pardon. "So what *is* on your mind, Edward," he asked. And before the guest could answer, the host, his mind wandering again, said, "Say, by the way, who *does* own Lusatia these days, nowadays? I mean, which brand of the paynim are we theoretically sworn to redeem it from? The sorbs? The Serbs? The Saxons? The Slovaks? The Litvaks? Reason I ask, you know all these things, some fellow was in here just the other day, said he had a scheme to *actually* redeem Lusatia from the paynim—the Saracens?—I *hope* not—babble, babble, babble; so I said 'Pax vobiscum,' and then of course he had to go."

Faintly interested, despite his own impatience, Edward asked who this person was. The Prince-Principal preened his nose in the mirror, made as though to pick up his scratch sheet again, at length shrugged. "Who can remember?" he asked. "Dutton? Sutton? Hutton, Hatton, Stratton . . . something like that. A real poop . . . Hey. What's that you've got there, Edward? It looks like . . . It is . . . a golden groat. Say, a funny thing happened at the Convocation, maybe you didn't notice, but the Grand Logothete couldn't find *his* golden goat, I mean *groat*, I mean . . . say, Edward, what does 'groat' mean?—turned red as a beet, funniest damn thing you ever saw. . . . Or did you see it? Say, come to think of it, I didn't see you there.

"What are you looking at me like that for? Something wrong?"

The Prince-Principal of the Noble Order of Knights Sworn to Holy Poverty in Defense of Lusatia glanced anxiously into a mirror.

DELICATESSEN was painted in faded, faded, ornate letters on the store window, and a battered metal sign advertised a well-known soft drink. Edward had never been in the place before, but the instant he entered he recognized it as an archetype. Such places are always owned by men named Hans or Ernest and have splintery wooden floors which are swept an average of once every quarter of an hour. They smell very strongly of vinegar and have very little on display in the way of wares—on top of the glass display case, a large pickle jar, usually almost empty, inside the case a small piece of cheese, a small end of roast beef and a small end of ham, perhaps one knack-wurst, a pint of salad, and some rye bread. In that part of the establishment referred to by Ernest or Hans as *The Back,* is the beer, the soft drinks, the stove on which the coffee is made *To Go.* One winces at the small resources on or out of which Ernie is obliged to sustain life, one goes on wincing for ten, twenty, thirty years, wondering if Ernie is ever going to be able to make enough money to afford a *large* piece of roast beef, an *entire* ham, or a *whole* rye bread. And then one day Ernie isn't there any more and one learns that he has retired and moved to Florida where, in partnership with his brother-in-law, a retired plumbing contractor from New Brunswick or Queens, he now owns and operates three motels, a liquor license, a restaurant, and an all-night grocery. Never again will one hear Ernie's inimitible conversation, to wit:

"What can I do for you?

"How's the family?

"What else?"

The odor of vinegar was very sharp. The man behind the counter had scant hair around his head and abundant flesh around his jaws. "You are the Grand Logothete," said Edward. This time, so sharp and so strong was the odor of vinegar that he never smelled the mandragore at all, even after he went blind and before he lost consciousness. He did, however, hear, as he lay on the splintery floor in *The Back,* a strange voice out front asking, "Say, where's Fritz?" and a second strange voice replying, "Fritz retired. *What can I do for you?*"

Back in the brownstone which was Edward the Red's home or at least his headquarters or *pied-à-terre* when in East America, Sybil was scrying again. In her nervousness she had dropped the bottle of cuttlefish ink which, costly though it was, she preferred to employ for the process; and was obliged to make use of a strong solution of potassium permanganate; fortunately it was a *strong* solution, and she could see everything fairly clearly, but she was always uneasy about using the Stanley Steamer herself, and at that hour of the morning the trains were slow. Herman was closing up the store as she got there and started to explain this to her, but she, not stopping, held out one hand with the two middle fingers clenched around the thumb and the index and little fingers straight out: he said nothing more. Redward Edward she could not find, but, in *The Back*, between a stack of cases of Hoffman's Pale Dry empties and a stack of Trommer's Malt, on the splintery floor, she found a golden pin.

Herman was gone as she left. Nobody would steal a showcase, and its entire contents were hardly worth a hex.

There was nothing about a dog in the infinitely deep pool she gazed into, this time, but there were still the two moons turned inside out, there was still something instantly nasty, and there was an additional and utterly indefinable Something Else. But there was no hint of his, Rufus Edward's, his whereabouts. She had already invited Oliver the Midget.

Oliver asked, "Whom do you suspect?"

Sybil said, "The last person he spoke to before he left was Dr. Stratton. Professor Llewellyn Ap-Gomer Stratton, the poop. That one."

Oliver nodded, swung his brightly polished little shoes to and fro. "How about you?" he asked. "You all right? You need, oh, *mon*ey, or anything like that?"

She denied it with a shake of her head. Began to cry. Stopped. "I just know that something's wrong and I want to find out what, that's all. I want to *know*—Oliver. Oliver."

He patted her in several places. "Have no fear," he said. "Oliver Small is here."

She snuffled, wiped her nose, eyes, cheeks; smiled. "And I can always scry for you."

He pursed his rosy little lips. "An interesting term. Wonder what its etymology can be. From *descry*, perhaps?"

"Oliver! Don't just sit there wondering! Get—"

"—moving. Right." He slipped down and stood up.

"I'm sorry, honey. I didn't mean it that way. Just—"

He smiled his total forgiveness, waved, was gone. She found some of his words repeating themselves to her: *Have no fear, Oliver Small is here.*

Fritz Snyder, sometime Grand Logothete of the Poor Knights (to use yet another version of The Order's name) wiped his face. "I tell you it was just a mistake," he said. The man sitting opposite said nothing.

"I was assured that mandragore—they assure me that it is mandragore that is the best: obsolete as medicine, yes, but for *this* purpose . . . and they tell me that only this one crazy or half-crazy old man, he is the only one who still knows how to make it—" He wiped his face. The silence across from him continued. "But be*cause* he is half-crazy, they tell me, for a stranger he won't do it, not unless you break into his craziness. I ask, 'How break in?' They tell me, 'For example, offer him gold.' So. It happens that I have the one old gold piece, I find it in my Uncle Otto's trunk when he dies, just a little one. For one two-dollar gold piece, does it pay to bother the Government? So I keep it." The face opposite said nothing, but it moved. The other man spoke more rapidly. "It was just a mistake. I forgot I put the golden groat in one pocket and the two-dollar gold piece in the other, and so I give the old crazy *man* the golden groat and when I—when *we* find it in Redward's pocket I know I didn't make no mistake about him."

The figure opposite stirred in the shadows.

"Fortunately," it said.
And added, "For you."
The Grand Logothete shivered.

PARTIAL COMFORT

Whose love is given over-well
Shall look on Helen's face in Hell,
Whilst they whose love is thin and wise
May view John Knox in Paradise.

—*Dorothy Parker*

Someday my son, as yet barely five, may astonish and
entertain his grandchildren by recounting how he once as
a child heard a sound which even now has become almost
as obsolete as that of the post-boy's horn: the ring of the
gong as the waiter or steward goes from car to car
through the train of cars (as our fathers' mothers called
them) announcing that a meal is being served in the dining car. By that time it will have become as archaic a
sound and gesture—the very notion itself, for that matter,
of railroads (if indeed they will still exist at all) as something which moved people from one place to another—as
archaic as what? canalboats? dirigibles? (Once, though
then older than my son is now, I saw either the *Graf
Zeppelin* or the *Hindenburg* passing overhead, not a
mere oblong far up and far away, but low, low, very low,
great and magnificent and evil, passing through the air
with the deliberate speed and all the malevolence and
majesty of a great shark which has recently dined well.)
Perhaps, no: almost certainly, some sound-tape enthusiast
or railroad buff has already recorded the steward's or

waiter's gong; and that's well, for who knows how now the hot-corn man used to chant his cry of roasting ears?

Who cares? I know, I know. Few care.

He came through the shamefully dingy car sounding his gong, his hair and jacket quite white, about the only neat sight which the railroad had so far on that whole trip provided us; my boy looked up, his mouth very slightly open, his brow very slightly frowning, his glance just a bit sideways, all the way he did when faced with a new thought or wonder. I looked up because I was hungry. I wasn't thinking then of the increasing obsolescence of the passenger train, wickedly helped on by swine railroad officials who blamed their increasing loss of human traffic on the airplanes or buses—had been thinking in part of what was being left behind by the dwindling day and the growing dusk and distance from New York, thinking of the woman to whom I had once been married (Cornelia, mother to my son, one, count him, one: a jewel, though not a Gracchus) and to whom I was next day going to relinquish for the time being the company of that conjoint child; had been thinking, too, of the woman whom I might, just after all might marry (Ruth, mother of no man's son)—to be sure a railroad conductor or brakeman was in most ways a less conventionally attractive sight than an airline hostess, though each one surly and sullen in his own individually rotten way, not supplied with plastic curves and plastic smiles—

My eyes waited a moment for a nameless something, then met the eyes of the waiter (or steward) as he struck his small gong and made his small announcement and our eyes seemed to lock for just a moment longer than I could think of any reason for. Then he passed on; a vast and ancient woman in a fur coat (she needed it right now, although for several hours of the trip she could have grown orchids in the baggage rack: God rest you, railroad gen-

tlemen, may you spend eternity rattling from nowhere to
nowhere in one of the trains of cars which your brute
cupidity has helped to ruin and to wreck . . . Azriel Ben
Hur, he used to say, "The present is a cross-section of
eternity" . . . Indra's Net?), she got to her feet and
started in the direction of the hot victuals, pausing to turn
and smile at Sim and ask if he weren't hungry, before
clutching her Pannonian sables (or whatever they were
calling muskrats the year the coat was made) to her volu-
minous throat and staggering straight and game ahead
without waiting for an answer. Then I decided that I had
been staring at the herald with the gong because he
looked familiar and he had been staring at me only because I had been staring at him.

Question: Why did he look familiar?

Answer: Why not?

Q.: Where would I have met a dining-car waiter before?

A.: What's the matter, you were never in a dining car
before?

An exchange perhaps unworthy of Aristotle, but at
least it did provide an answer of sorts, and the more I
thought the more I was persuaded (though not with
quite, I trust, the degree of *loving* Persuasion used by
James the First in urging some male contemporary to accept a piece of fat preferment, meanwhile doubtless
pinching his cheeks and feeling him up the ass and nat-
tering about prudence and popery and all of that; do you
think they all licked honey even in a Silver Age?—still, if
your Annointed King and Principal Talent Scout and
Chiefmost Employer was a faggot, you could at least feel
safe about bringing your wife to his cocktail parties—if
you *had* a wife)—the more I was persuaded that Occam's
razor had shorn the right hair and that I remembered the
waiter quite simply from having met him across the board

in the, or at any rate in a, dining car. "What was that man doing, Papa?" asked Sim, finally coming enough out of his Sense of Wonder to ask a question. "Calling us in to supper," I said. And, observing a sort of general exodus taking place in the wake of the vast lady, as though word had somehow gotten around in the evening dews and damps that there might be a shortage of manna, I asked, damned fool that I was, still after five years of fatherhood not having sufficiently assimilated the lesson that if you want a kid to do something that you want done, you *tell* him, I asked, "Would you like to have supper on the railroad train?" Big alternative: Was the New York Central going to stop at Troy or Rochester or whatever region in between for a hearty snack in case he *did*n't feel like liking to? Chenango County, maybe, where the voice of some soundly Republican Appleknocker was until just before the then-recent Reapportionment the equal of any number of thousands of Catholic, Jewish, or Nonsectarian Infidel votes for the State Legislature. He didn't want to.

"I don't want to have supper on the train, Papa. I want to go to the bathroom."

If he had not only not wanted to eat I might have left him in the moldering seat by the window, but before that could be done he needed help in getting the door of the WC open and then he needed help with his fly and then he was half-fascinated and half-fearful of the close-stool, or crapper, and no wonder, with half of the latest Canadian cold front rushing up and threatening to suck him through after it was flushed—and what five-year-old in his right mind would want to get blown out into Chenango *County* or wherever. "I don't need anything to eat because Uncle Wilcox let me have part of his steak sandwich," he said, while having his hands forceably "washed" under the trickle of water allowed by the New York Central, which was of course obliged to have its

water supplied in goatskin bags carried on the heads of
native bearers from the Oasis of Bhou-al-Bhleb. "I'll just
stay in here and make another pish and then I'll go back
to my chair again and look out the window." The hell he
would, he wanted to stay in there and work the treadle on
the commode if you prefer that word, and he might not
only hold up if not indeed burst half the bladders on the
train but he might get locked in as well, and he was—I
could see by the calculating scance of his sideways glance
—about halfway ready to stick his hand down in the
hopes of finding Something Out There in the fresh, clean,
open air of the Goiter Belt. Not being a Christian Scien-
tist, I couldn't leave him there alone.

"Nix," I said. "You are coming out with me and if you
don't want to eat, you don't have to, or I'll whack you
one." His mind cut through the tangled syntax to the
meaning like a keen-edged sword, and out we *went.* "I
hope you thanked Uncle Wilcox for letting you have part
of his steak sandwich," I said, and, adding irony to sar-
casm, "Did he let you have part of his drink as well?"

"Yes," the kid said. "But only sips. He said that bar
whiskey was bad for children. He would, he said it
would—" Here he hesitated, remembering: thank God, unlike his mother (marvelous woman in a million other ways,
only not for me) he was not an *um*filler; when he couldn't
find the word to say, he didn't say it. "—corrupt my palate," he finished.

With that the pinball got through to Home Zero or
whatever it is or was called, and, with almost audible
clicks and clacks, everything began to fall into place. It
was the waiter/steward's white hair which had put me
off. It hadn't been white when I had last seen him. After
all, it was a good bit over twenty years ago and he was
middle-aged then; he was entitled to have had his hair go
white in the meanwhile. Suppose it had been an airline

stewardess instead. What do you suppose the chances would be of her being on the same run after even twenty years? Even ten? I am Black but still employable, O ye daughters of Jerusalem . . . or, unless you were traveling via El Al, likelier of Kansas City. Anyway, that was the answer, because that was the last time I had traveled by train between New York and Chicago, and that was also the first time I had met either Wilcox Robinson or Sarah Mendoza G. He was wearing the uniform of a naval ensign and I don't remember what she was wearing. Never was one for being a clothes horse, Sarah wasn't. Always had all her zippers zipped, and all of that, but, as though to illustrate or exemplify the old saw or sutra about Women don't dress for Men, they dress for other Women, she (Sarah) never dressed. As it were.

At any rate, although I then heard an old man with a Roquefort nose grumble that dining-car service still wasn't back to what it had been before the War, it was not as worse as I subsequently lived to see it, even if only once more on this particular train . . . But no, that is not the rate, that is the rut. Unlike the wicked railroads, I cannot deduct what amount to campaign expenses off my taxes; argal. At any rate, then, there I was in the dining car, that long ago *there*, my first long trip or voyage as a civilian, and I was pleased when she sat down at the same table. Someone my own age. That pleased me as much as anything did; I had not yet heard that anyone over thirty was the enemy of everyone under thirty, but . . . Ah well. Ethnically, I could not docket her.

At any rate, she sat at my table, and I was pleased, but having been conditioned to believe that everyone *had* to be ethnically docketable, I was mildly puzzled by the fact that she was (a) dark, (b) blue-eyed, and (c) had a nose which, oh, just a bit, turned up at the end. Today I would say that she was "a handsome woman," but *a good-look-*

ing girl was my then inner-directed description. She made
me a polite smile. I returned it, and, being shy, said nothing, but thought how I might by and by find an opportunity to say something. Then this tall and young and,
forgive again the impoverishment of my vocabulary—
"good-looking"—ensign U.S.N. came sauntering down
the aisle, bosom full of fruit salad—including, I noted,
with a mixture of resentful respect and respectful re-
sentment, the Purple Heart—and stopped. At our table/
goddamn him, I thought. Recollected that I was no longer
in the U.S.N.R. myself and hence might fling into his
strong white teeth any retort I cared to make . . . or
dared to . . . without fear of Captain's Mast or Court
Martial . . . except of course that he would or anyway
could almost certainly have thrown me right on my ass,
"decked" me as we used to put it. I forgot all about not
being able to tell if the young lady was an Azerbaijanian
or a Lemko, a Kashub or a Basque, and just concentrated
on hating the tall and handsome young ensign—a senti-
ment which, I observed with a dull glow of hatred suddenly directed almost entirely against myself, she did not
share.

"Tell me," he asked her suddenly, lounging so far back
in his chair that a bound of the Central's well-kept rolling
stock over a gap in its equally well-kept rails almost
caused him to fall ass over teakettle; "Tell me," he said,
righting himself, unperturbed, and looking at her with
what seemed a very genuine puzzlement and concern,
"How did a nice girl like you get into a dining car like
this?"

She shrugged. "Oh . . . I don't know . . . luck, I
guess."

I was greatly shocked and perhaps equally greatly
distressed. (Those were other times, other manners, you
must remember.) To *think* that an officer and gentleman,

even "a gentleman by Act of Congress" as we enlisted men used to say, feeling the hate and the envy which the Scheduled Castes feel for a Brahman—to think that one would *dare* address a variation on a line from a dirty joke to a perfectly strange young lady! And, what was either almost as bad or far worse, to think that she, a perfectly respectable-looking young lady, would reply to this insult with the same joke's punch line! It could not—neither one had so much as laughed, or even cracked a smile—but it could not, it just could not be a coincidence. No. No. It was a deliberate exchange. There was only one admissible explanation.

They were sophisticated.

And as I sat there, trying, as though I had eyes like a mule (it suddenly occurs to me to wonder . . . is it, after all, *true* about mules? . . . it isn't true about Chinese women . . .), to keep one eye on the menu and the other on this suddenly admirable young pair—for "couple" one could not call them—the young ensign suddenly and very solemnly popped, that is the only possible verb, he popped a skullcap out of nowhere and placed it on his head. And continued looking at her without a change of countenance.

And she, without a change of countenance, looking at him, asked, "Are you a rabbi?"

"Only for lay purposes." As jokes go, it was, I suppose, not much. But it was then and there too much for me. I burst out laughing. Unfortunately I had chosen that moment to take a sip of water, I knew it was going to go down the wrong pipe, but I didn't care where it went as long as I didn't spew it out, as I was desperately afraid I was going to. It was thus, clutching the table with one hand and waving the other distractedly, my face burning and my chest paining, that I decided to forgive him. Fortunately, considering how very much he has enlivened my life.

He looked at me with sympathy and concern. "It's the water," he said. "It will do it to you every time. Obviously you are one of those unfortunate people whose systems can't stand water, just simply cannot *tol*erate it, and yet you will drink it. You say to yourself, Oh, just one sip won't hurt me. Everyone else is drinking water, you say. And yet you see the results. No one can help you unless you make the effort to help yourself. Allow me to order you a little mixture which I call a Rebel Yell. The Central serves a modest but adequate Coca-Cola, to which one adds several drams of whiskey purely for purposes of diminishing the otherwise excessive sweetness of the Coke: plus a slice of lemon, to ward off the dreaded scurvy." He held up his hand for the waiter. "I will have one with you so that you needn't feel you're all alone in this hour of crisis and of change." I was not capable of a reply.

The young lady, who had been looking at him with a trace of admiration, said that she thought she would like one herself. But he shook his head. "No, no," he said, firmly. "*My* tastes are already formed. But you should not at your age drink bar whiskey. It corrupts the palate." She protested, but he stood firm. She might have a gin and tonic instead, he said. She shrugged. The official, that naval official instinct and ability to order others around was now (so it seemed) being demonstrated upon civilians too. I resented and I wondered and I marveled.

The waiter now appeared and before the young officer could give orders for drink, said, amicably, but firmly, "No sidearms in the dining car, Lieutenant. You know that." Now, addressing an ensign as "Lieutenant" might be ascribed to either ignorance or tactfulness, but the other part of the waiter's remarks ruled out ignorance.

Here I must attempt to research time-eroded memory, but as best I can recollect, the Officer of the Day on or at any naval ship or station was always distinguishable from other officers because he (1) carried a revolver in a holster, and (2) he kept his hat on. He also . . . I'm sure I do remember seeing it . . . ate in the enlisted men's mess. Maybe that was part of his duty for the Day, seeing that our food was up to par. Therefore the waiter's reference to "sidearms" was simultaneously a reference to keeping the head covered. He had clearly had a lot of experience with Navy, in order to be so well acquainted with its great and glorious traditions, as inflexible as the ancient early adolescent custom that unless anyone who broke wind immediately whistled, knocked on wood, and cried "Peanuts!" it was the privilege, if not indeed the duty, of his circumjacent compeers to punch him in the arm.

The ensign merely raised his brows a trifle and said, "I am sure that you don't mean to be disrespectful to my religion."

The waiter took a second look at the skullcap. It was velvet, of so dark a blue as to be almost black, and it had gold vines and little leaves embroidered over it. If the U.S. Navy had actually issued skullcaps to its officers, this was the kind of skullcap it would have issued. The waiter took a second look at the ensign. "You're not an Ede, by any chance, are you, sir?" he asked. Or should I spell, "Eed" or maybe even "Ead"?

"I don't know why not. . . ." The ensign's face expressed a vast, but vastly suppressed, astonishment.

The waiter's brown face at once seemed to cease to be respectfully and semipaternally critical, and became instead at once not merely relaxed, not only almost genial, but—how am I to put it?—egalitarian? Perhaps. "Well, that is certainly different, then," he said. No mention of *sir*. "I might even be Jewish, myself, you know—"

"Certainly," said the ensign, who was certainly not. "*Are* you?"

"No, but I might be. Rabbi Mathias' synagogue is near my house, and I see them all the time, going upstairs there, the Black Jews, I mean." If my ears had been prickable I would have pricked them up (can ears be pricked *down?*—an interesting conjecture, though one possibly fraught with peril for the human soul) at this mention of the mysterious and melaninous Rabbi Mathias, Disciple of Aaron, Minister of Moses, Vicar of Solomon, Lord High Religious Legate of the Sons and Daughters of Menelik Spreading into the Diaspora out of Ethiopia and Kush . . . I have followed, spasmodically, his rabbinical (as it were) career for over thirty years now: and I find him every bit as mysterious (and of course melaninous) as when I began. "We belong ourselves to the Macedonian Memorial A.M.E. Zion Church back there," the waiter said.

"'In my father's house are many mansions; if it were not so, I would have told you.'" "*Aymen,*" said the waiter, then, having sufficiently played at verbal pattycake with the White Folks and/or Ofay Bastards, he got down to business. "Can I bring you people anything?"

And so here we all *were* again. Twenty years at least had passed. Kings of the Earth had been murdered like mongrel dogs, dynasties had been obliterated, islands had risen, smoking, out of the sea, and other islands had in turn (or out of turn) subsided like Atlantis and Lemuria (or, if you prefer, Gondwanaland), Gallant Agrarian Reformers had reverted to the status of Yellow Perils once again whereas formerly perfidious Nippon had ceased to be anything of the sort (in California, nowadays, everybody was very, very fond of the Issei, Nisei, and Sansei; in California, nowadays, lots of people were complaining

about how overbearing "some of the Chinese" had become . . . the British lease on Hong Kong would expire,
after all, with the expiring century: and then where
would they all go?), strange and not-so-nice and not-so-lit-
tle foreign wars had proliferated like cancers; children
had been begotten in lust and in love and carelessly and
with careful planning and had waxed great and themselves begotten and born, countries familiarly fixed upon
the map for decades had disappeared, and countries with
names as alien as Hittite inscriptions and with outlines
strange as runes had taken their place—

And all the while, for more than four lustrums, this
same waiter had traveled back and forth, back and forth,
in dining cars between New York and Chicago, Chicago
and New York. New York and Chicago themselves had
changed more than he had. We were, to be sure, not *all*
here. Sarah Mendoza G. had—before, during, and after—
not only become and ceased to be Sarah Mendoza G.
several-other-surnames, and was now as she for long had
been a resident of the picturesque mountain townlet of
New Brighthelmstone, New Jersey: was probably back
there now at this very moment, carefully putting an apple
log on her fireplace fire: *I know she wants to have written
but I'm not sure that she wants to write:* had written,
whether wanting to or not. Wilcox Robertson was, for the
moment at least, in his warm and treasure-crammed
apartment overlooking what he semi-fondly referred to as
Pigeon Shit Park; for the moment at least neither taking
presumably scientific measurements of the protuberant
buttocks of the female Hottentotten *in situ,* nor following (for presumably professional purposes) a thousand
parasangs—give or take a hundred parasangs—of the route
of Marco Polo or Ibn Battuta or Friar Odoric: and,
enwreathed, enwreathed in expensive if possibly as-yet-
unpaid-for pipe-tobacco smoke and the fumes of the best

Scotch whisky, with doubtless a volume of theology in one hand and a pretty woman's foot in the other, was (with his third mind) conjuring up notions for books yet to write in order, not merely to sell, but also in order to write off the costs of his latest trips as Business and Professional Expenses—

"My friend and fellow citizen, when Negroes sold for six hundred dollars, of which at least three hundred dollars was to the profit of their fellow Negroes on the Slave Coast and Hinterland, when gold was sixteen dollars an ounce and placemen were few and the Chief Magistrate of the Republic blacked his own boots and taxes were of the excise variety alone and used for such laudable pus, I mean purpose, as building a National Road across the Alleghenies with now and then the construction of a frigate to go and chastise some camel-thief of a barbary bashaw—" Pause for lifting glass and long rolling round-in-the-mouth taste, appreciative sigh, "—*one* thing. But now, politics, dis*gust*ing business, aside: to tax everyone in everything, Negroes included, and even including the once by definition untaxable Indians, in order to support *hordes* of placemen and bashaws and camel-thieves: so all that I have to say on submission to such taxation is just that. Frigate."

—and Sim, who was here now, had not even been thought of then, not conceived in any sense of the word, and his mother (voluptuous though alas so uneven-tempered Cornelia) a mere member of the pre-kindergarten set—

So we were not altogether here now as we had been all there then (except of course Sim, who could not have been there a-tall). It was not exactly the same knot or nexus in Indra's Net. But it was a reminiscent reflection of it. I decided not to bother asking the waiter if he could possibly remember the incident. I decided to ask him in-

stead for a small steak and salad and light on the journal-
box dressing, and a Canadian whiskey . . . this last having become for reasons obscure and complex but in some
way connected with the Hoboken Terminal from which
left the only trains still serving (at least in the stud sense)
New Brighthelmstone, New Jersey, my Standard Train
Drink.

"We are going to the Kaan," said the young woman in
the dining car, dwelling on the last word, which, indeed,
she did not spell.

"C-a-h-n?" I asked, getting some breath back at last.
"The Cahn, head of Clan Cahn? Cahn of the Isles?" She
smiled slightly an indulgence of my attempt to evade
what was clearly to her the Major Trump: that She Knew
Something which I did not. "Or do you mean you are
going to the K-h-a-n, a khanserail or caravanserai, an
Anatolian or Bactrian establishment for the refection of
travelers?" Her smile altered just a trifle, but she gave her
head a small shake, firm to the end . . . or almost. One,
or, to be exact, two more words, intended perhaps to en-
lighten but likelier the more to mystify me. She said?
"The shy kaan."

Once again I tried her on her (so I thought) her own
terms. "C-o-n? A bashful Celt?" She smiled that same
smile. She smiled it as she would smile it a hundred thousand times more. *I* know *Some*thing *You* Don't Know.
The explanation could hardly have been of more simplicity and of less consequence. She and he were going to a
Convention of Science Fiction fans, to be holden in the
City of Chicago. That was it. And that was all of it.

But by now, of course, you may have guessed all, the
All, of all in All. It is I who am myself, I who am Azriel as
well. I am Wilcox, I am Harpsichord, I am Smith, I am
Sim, I am the waiter and the steward on the train, I am

Mathias, I am Edward, I am Everyman. I am the stag on a hundred hills. I am the slayer. And I am the slain.

James E. Berzelius Smith, alias Needle Nose, alias the Great Bezoar, alias Ghod the Alchymist, and several sundry other such numinous names, was then as now, world without end, amen, editor of Magazine *Scientifiction*—pronounced by him and by his friends and followers: Sci-EN-ti-fiction—pronounced by his nonfollowers and foes as, Scientific Shun. My Lord J.B. had yet to retire to his great retreat and world headquarters at Castle Fen in the Isle of Wen from which even now he not only edits The Magazine but directs the far-flung (though some say not far enough) activities of The Great Grammatica (Inc.). Therein and therein only is taught (though not of course for nothing: "That which has no price has no value—" JEBS) the Teaching of the Pax of the Perfect Paradigm and the Deeds of the Divine Diagram: it has been calculated that, one way or another, it in the long run costs a Diplomate in Diagrammed Grammatica twelve thousand dollars to go on up to the Great Grid and make the Big Breakthrough into Level Eleven—maybe the biggest bargain since Jesus Bar Miriam was sold for thirty pieces of silver to the Romans, who, God wot, have been selling him ever since; on the other hand, maybe *not*—since this is said to be the same sum the Average Man or Woman has to pay in order, by the Rules of the A.M.A., to die of cancer: whereas on Level Eleven there is no disease, no defeat, no impotency—

But this too all lay in the Urn, as yet unhatched, for it would be another five years before the publication of *Diagrammed Grammatica*.

James E. Berzelius Smith, then, editor of Magazine *Scientifiction*, and a man of many whims of iron, all subject to change at semioccasional intervals, to the heavy sorrow of writers in Missouri or California, who, not hav-

ing had a drink with him lately, were still turning out stories based on (say) psychocybernetics at a time when
Berz had already flung himself, heart, soul, and Magazine, into (say) Problems of Space Cramp—but Wilcox
Robertson had *al*ways had a drink with him lately. Often
he had had a drink with him the night before, and, so
soon as the bars had closed and he had poured Berz onto
the 3 A.M. Waffle Iron to Troutsburgh, would go home
and turn out a story based on the latest whim, turn in for
an hour's sleep, and turn out again in time to serve early
mass at St. Cornelius the Cappadocian's . . . for Wilcox
was a strong Anglo, or Cantabrian—to use his own preferred term—Catholic; and was later to utter many a
moan about the Protestantization, as he considered it, of
the Church of Rome.

The movement of Jebs Smith to the Isle of Wen, and,
indeed, his growing involvement with Grammatica, may
not have unfavorably affected the general management of
Magazine *Scientifiction;* but it seriously affected the
day-to-day lives of five or ten writers who had been in the
habit of dropping into Jebs's office with ideas in their
heads and departing with advance checks in their pockets
—the idea, meanwhile, having like as not been turned in-
side-out, stood on its head, dyed, trimmed, nose-bobbed,
and shoved feet first up its own anal orifice; until at last
Ghod the Alchymist had recreated it in his own image—
now the poor lads (and at the very least one poor lass,
Sarah Mendoza G.) were obliged to *write* the stories *first,*
before they could hope to see a penny of advance money
. . . of course they eventually had to write them again,
and sometimes again and again and again. Different people reacted differently. Gunther Bloor stopped writing altogether, in order to pay his bills was obliged to sell his
stamp collection, made so much money on the deal that
he became a professional philatelist. Fenrys Wolfe had a

nervous breakdown, from which he was rescued by dia-
grammatic systemization, grew so convinced that This
was *It* that he became himself a Smith Franchised Sys-
temizer (S.F.S.) and eventually not only the first of the
Upper Companionate but *the* first to make the Big Breakthrough onto Level Eleven. Sarah Mendoza G. solved this
and other problems of being a writer by becoming an editor: from The Old Stone House, New Brighthelmstone,
New Jersey, emerged the first of the so successful *Stf.
Quarterlies,* which have never failed to appear at least
three times a year. But Wilcox Robertson, whom the consensus predicted would not, could not, survive the change
in circumstances—Wilcox had made what was perhaps
the smoothest switch of all: taking the moneys for his
novel *Changeling Cassiopeia*—which, by a fortuitous
"error" (i.e. finagling) in the bookkeeping department of
Winthrop and Wesson, had been withheld from him until,
equally fortuitously, hard-cover as well as magazine publication had been achieved and paid for: this preventing
either his boozing up a single cent of it or its seizure in
any part by creditors (it was Edward who, sending Wilco
a ten-dollar bill along with the brief note, *Buy whiskey,*
had received the sad reply, *Sorry to tell you the ten-spot
was all pissed away on groceries*)—Wilcox had taken
every goddamn *penny* and hopped aboard a tramp
steamer two steps ahead of the creditors, whom he eventually paid in the widest conceivable variety of piasters,
duros, zlotys, drachmas, shillings, and sundry other curious currencies—Straits Settlements dollars and Pon-
dicherry rupees not excluded—and, having missed the
boat one stopover in Famagusta, retired to a pre-Turkish
house in the Troödos Mountains with a case of native
rum, a case of native brandy, a keg of native wine, a Mal-
tese mistress, reams and reams of mottled paper, the
complete works of Dr. Pusey, the Cambridge Medieval

Histories, and the oldest functioning typewriter in the Autocephalic Archdiocese of Cyprus: thus and there produced the first of his fabulously successful historical travel novels, *A Bauble for Berengaria.*

—Although, to be sure, there were and still are those who attribute Sarah's change of (as it were) format to the presence in a rotting canalboat on the nether outskirts of New Brighthelmstone of the gray but game figure of Dr. Sc. Spacke-Sprocket, retired thither to recover from a deep metaphysical ennui occasioned from overlong occupation of the chair of philosophy in the College of West-Jersey (*never* omit the hyphen; worse than eating with pigs).

"Scratch was the best thing that ever happened to her," Pike Thompson insisted, using the nickname which The Guid Doctor not unnaturally preferred to Scrymgeour. Sarah of course used neither; she called him Scry. "I'm going scrying," she used to say, putting on the high boots requisite for a safe journey along the moldering and boggy barm of the old canal to the C.B. *Petunia Frisbee* (not its real name). "Scratch," Pike went on, "was only completely ineffectual as far as his own profession was concerned." Pike said, rubbing his Martian forehead in a well-remembered gesture. This statement of his was, as we were all later to realize, very far from the entire truth: but when we all did learn it, it was too late. Certainly the Guid Doctor was capable of utterly effectual if utterly sly action when a group of moneymen proposed to reactivate the canal by pumping it dry, lining it with concrete, and devoting it 100 per cent to motorboat use: he wrote up a so-called *Defense* of the notion and, under the title of *Let the People Play*, planted it as a nonymous "editorial" in a biweekly of notorious party-lining inclinations: which of course killed the swine scheme but *dead*, to the total rout and confusion of its hyperpatriot promoters. "If it hadn't

been for Scratch," Pike said, "she would probably
never've gotten on the ball and really *done* something
about *Stf. Quarterly*," said Pike. "She'd probably have
gone back to tending bar at the Dimity House, or married
a mink rancher . . . both, to be sure, honorable estates:
but, still." Instead of which she now had *P*osition, *P*res-
tige, and even *P*ower of a sort. As well as *P*ecunia, though
not one hell of a lot. Was it not Dr. Sc. Spacke-Sprocket
who first had had the genius idea of printing and distrib-
uting the *Quarterly* as a book and not as a magazine?
Matter of doubt if this had brought it any much more
money, but the difference it made as far as the other *P*s
were concerned was enormous, and let none underes-
timate La Mendoza: it never was money she made for
first. Never, never.

But the one who had suffered the most (Edward said)
when Berz Smith became, successively, increasingly difficult to beard in his den in New York, and Laird of
Wen, was Stuart Steinberg. Stu's talents, though bright
enough in their own ways, had no depth of root. He
required constant supplies of attention and of money and
of what he called "feedback," and when these ceased (or,
at any rate, ceased to be steady) he crumbled and dis-
solved. He had always feared the potent and maleficent
They. And now They came down upon him; They took
away his two cars and They took away his house in Tuck-
ahoe and They took away his daughter by his first marriage; and then his second wife—undoubtedly prompted
by They—left him, left him openly and notoriously, left
him loudly and scornfully; and, what was worst of very
all, left him for Nathaniel "Nose" Naseby, the most despi-
cable man in publishing. James E. Berzelius Smith had
foes, but Naseby had no friends. It was not merely that he
was a crook, not merely that he was a cutthroat, a liar,
rogue, blackleg, pirate, plagiarizer, holder-back of money

due, and book cooker. He was simply *nasty*, both posi-
tively and negatively. He had no hair, no brow, no chin—
nothing but Nose. That is, he did have, also, both body
and mouth odor, but he mostly had the Nose, and the
Nose (the heritage of far too many generations of in-
terbreeding between what Scratch once referred to as
"Boston Untouchables"), the Nose was huge, the Nose
had blebs and bristles and warts and red veins and blue
veins and pimples and pustules and crusts and crannies
and crags, and he talked through it in a voice which was
nasal and snottled. He and Sandra ex-Steinberg, and *she*
was a *dish*, were seated at the bar at the QuebCon (you
will recollect that there had earlier been a ChiCon),
Naseby with his Nose in her beautiful cleavage, when
word was brought to them that Stu had locked himself in
the pissoir of a small bistro in Old Town and there with a
single-edged razor had slashed vertically and effectually
both of his wrists and had started on his throat before
falling down forever on the piss-soaked and bloody floor.

I had last left Uncle Wilcox in open communion with a
gentleman from the Infernal Revenue, a little Mr. Blyberg. Wilco was calm, quite calm, helping himself to
ample pinches of Fribourg and Treyer's Latakia snuff,
then twelve shillings the quarter-ounce (inasmuch as
Freybourg and Treyer, who have been in business since
the reign of Queen Anne, do not export, the question has
sometimes been asked: How does he *get* the stuff?—the
suggestion that it is brought to him by the last practicing
Bow Street Runner, must, I fear, be discountenanced).
Mr. Blyberg, used to investigating and exposing the pec-
ulations of plush-cutters, was not. "*Mis*-ta Robertson," he
said, "now let's be *reez* na bull. I redja book, this slatist
one, *A Cake Fuh Muhree Anta Net*. Bewdy full. Lovely.
In fack, Tie red dit *twice*. Whudda yuh thinka *that*. But,
Afta rawl. *Mis*-ta Robertson. *It* sawl about *France!* It sawl

about thuh French Revva *Lu* Shun! *You* claim, you put
inya claim faw rexpenses connected witha writing of ya
book—t'three t'thousan t'three hunnut dollars! faw ra trip
ta *Tahiti!* Now *Mis*-ta Robertson! What, I yask ya reez na
blee, what has Ta*hi*ti got tuh do wit'th thuh French
Revva *Lu* Shun?"

Wilcox sneezed with enormous contentment into one of
his genuine cambric handkerchiefs, the making of which
had entailed searching out an ancient Mrs. Ambercrom-
bie, who must have been the very Last of the Needle-
women, and all but goosing her with an electric cattle
prod in order to divert her attention from the TV set and
back to the gussets and seams. After pleasurably and deli-
cately mopping a single tear which had made its way
down his by now heavy and bearded cheek, he stuffed the
linen up his sleeve with a flourish, and, with another,
tapped small Mr. Blyberg upon the latter's knee.

"There you have it," he said. "You have put your finger
upon the kernel in the nut. 'What does *A Cake for Marie
Antoinette* have to do with Tahiti?' A professional and
trained historian, gray and webby from long years in the
Bodleian or the Vatican Archives or the *Bibliothèque Na-
tionale*, could indeed scarcely have phrased it better.
Well. I see that there is no keeping anything from *you*,
Mr. Blyberg, and therefore I Will Tell You." He slid forward an inch or two. Mr. Blyberg's expression was an intent mixture of pleasure and forboding. He drew back his
head a notch as though ready for reproof and simultaneously dropped his jaw a notch as though ready to snap
up goodies. Wilcox, in a revery of reflection, three-
quarters closed his eyes. "Where shall we begin . . . ?"
he murmured. "Shall we commence with the French occupation of Tahiti under that King Louis-Philippe, whose
father, Philippe *Égalité*, denounced to the Convention his
cousin Marie-Antoinette, only to follow her eventually to

the same fell fate under the murderous blade of the guillotine . . . ? Eh . . . ?" Mr. Blyberg inclined his head to one side, pursed his lips and raised his eyebrows in judicial consideration. "–and from that point work backward? *Or!*"–his face altered, his eyes opened wide–"shall we instead commence with that Jean François De Galaup, Comte de la Pérouse, great and immortal navigator, whose quest for the Nor'west Passage, commissioned in the reign of Louis XVI, husband to Marie-Antoinette, led him from the whale-tormented seas of the Alaskan Coasts to the vast spaces of the Austral Oceans whence rose as though from the depths in the faint rose dawn the infinitely welcome contours of the Friendly Islands. And if so, what was his fate and that of his brave squadron? Was it to perish upon the cruel reefs of Vanikoro?" An expression of grief distorted his face. Mr. Blyberg's lower lip trembled a trifle. "Oh, but surely, surely," Wilcox went on, as though imploring, "at least a *few* of the ships' boats must have survived to make their way to a Polynesian island, and there beneath the breadfruit trees amid the scent of the bougainvillia and the frangipani the sunburnt sailors would have found more than mere *wel*come in the slim brown arms of the exquisite native girls, whose slender and hospitable hips and small yet proud and high young breasts," his voice never faltered.

Mr. Blyberg nodded and nodded and nodded. Clearly, investigating the books of Krazy Kut Kool Kaps had been nothing like this. "*Ravish me with a kiss,*" his expression seemed to say.

I remembered an earlier Wilco, one intermediary between the limber young light in the navy uniform and the Henry VIII figure of two decades and some years later, a Wilco still unreconciled to increasing ponderosity, emerging from the steam and mists of the athletic club where he had dragged Edward and me as reluctant guests, drops of hot dew trickling down a beard still all free of gray. "Why does it have to be," he said, not so much inquiring as declaring, "that women, I mean unmarried women, whether unmarried *de jure* or *de facto*, why does it have to be that women, such women, if copiously screwed, are almost always copiously screwed up?"

Edward asked, "You think that there is something to be said for conventional morality? You must, you inquire only about *women*. Is it that you yourself do believe in the double standard, or that you believe only some sort of quirk or kink, operating on other levels as well, can or will bring women to break the taboos which have operated to keep them out of the public domain?"

There was a querulous grunt from the fogs behind Wilcox, Edward's fiery pubic hair the only bright spot, now that he had begun to towel his head, in the grayness round about us. "Why all this introspection and philosophy, young men?" asked someone. "Believe me, the simple way is the best way: if you can get laid, get *laid*, and thank God that you don't have to jerk off onto a bunch of *eggs*, like *fish*, for Cry sake."

Wilco wiped water out of his eyes. "Another thing . . . If the double standard is all wrong, as our generation so piously believes, then why has nature placed in the female body a sign to indicate virginity, and not in the male body?"

I said that I had thought about it and once discussed it with Theo Thornton. "He said that perhaps it had once had some positive survival value and that its negative survival value wasn't great enough for nature to dispense with it."

Drops flew as Wilcox shook his head. "What survival value? Gibberish. As for nature, nature is the robe of God." This was the first indication I had had of that growing inclination which was eventually to lead Wilcox, first to the font, and thence to membership in the Third Order of Saint Austin, or Glastonbury Brothers, to fasts and vigils and retreats and serving as acolyte at early masses in high, chill churches heated only by incense burners, to thoughts of priesthood and monasticism, and very probably to that incredible trek across the length and breadth of the Nether Orient with stops at every place which possessed a Syriac or Anglican church (or else a toddy shop).*

Where are the steams and fumes of that sweatbath? Where are the years of yesterday? the days of yesteryear? The death of Ivan Ilych? Does he not die daily? And are we redeemed? I scribble and scrabble and paw among the dusts, sometimes scratching something with a stick which none bother read. "Why don't you like what I write?" poor pimply postpubert Charley Landerman, half-drunk on crud whiskey mixed in soda pop and half on his own success, if that was the word, in actually selling his sex-substitute space fantasies to *real magazines;* poor Charley had asked Stuart Steinberg that at the first pro for professional con for convention he poor C had gotten to attend, god among gods he had thought. "Because you write shit," said Stu, a few several years still away from his own doom in the semipublic crapper in Quebec. No doubt Charley didn't suffer any more than you or I would if jammed up the anus with a red-hot poker like which Angevin king of England. Rory Kelley told me once. Leave it to the Irish to know. What's the matter, they aren't entitled?

Well, and if what I have been writing is shit also, how come I cannot even go easily to stool but must be painfully costive and bloody, not once and again. "Still starving for art in the pulps?"—the well-known sneer. Terror

* See *In the Tracks of Saint Thomas,* by Wilcox P. G. R. Robertson.

and shouting and fire upon the ramparts. The last Indian attack upon New York City. Having captured the fleet of ferryboats the maddened Redskins pour their fire upon the weakest and least defended spot of the municipal wall opposite West Thirty-eighth Street where the Tammany Milifia now pays the price of excluding Negroes from the ranks of the powder monkeys and pitcher mollies. Summoned from his shop, kosher butcher Asser Leavi assumes command of the eleven-pound gun and drives the Canarsies into the reddened waters of the Hudson whilst the Iroquois pause to loot Tiffany's—a fatal error which guarantees forever control of the Hudson Valley by the White, or, at any rate, the non-Red, Man. Only my son Sim, one small candle, a tiny taper, offers his pure firefly-sized light to guide me in through deepening darkness. Lord with me abide. Weighted down with masks, I dare not stalk naked and alone. Brave youth cry not out against me.

Consider the case of a certain friend of mine and of Edward, who, tired unto loathing with his own world of overstuffed furniture and overadvertised whiskey, drugs, long automobiles, money-grabbing, and the unfaithful flesh of pale-blond women, turned in joy and heartpounding enthusiasm to helping a group of young Blacks build a braver and newer world—to find that they defined it in terms of overstuffed furniture and overadvertised whiskey, drugs, long automobiles, money-grabbing, and the unfaithful flesh of pale-blond women, including, just as incredibly quick as they incredibly could and did, the unfaithful flesh of his very own pale-blond woman. Ever the Christians eat their god.

And by what thin threads had sweet and not so damned old Scry Sprocket been kept to life, which of us had come even far toward guessing? until poor Sarah, knowing in certain terms that he was troubled and that he was sick, but yielding to his urging that she anyway go and attend the world convention with its drinks and its parties, its editors and its agents and its adulations and its autographs, had gone and had dallied and lingered and enjoyed and then returned to find him dead in his bed in the canalboat, a faint smile on his dusty face and a cobweb already spun over the left lens of his spectacles, because the desire to live had not been strong enough in him to rise up and venture forth for food and medicine: my father, my father, the chariots of Israel, and the horsemen thereof.

A woman with green eyes, something I had often encountered in fiction, but never (so suddenly it occurred to me) never in bed, had smiled upon me in a coffee house in the old middle West Village, and though she had almost at once wandered out into the night before I could collect my scattered members for the chase . . .

. . . still, thither I had returned hopefully night after night for a week, two weeks, never seeing her there and learning only unhelpful shreds and thrums of witting, such as that she was alleged to be a Great and Good Friend of a railroad brakeman with talents as a poet, that she had a brother about whom nothing else was known, that this and this that. And then one night another smile in the same coffee house from another woman, nothing in the least like the first one, like (instead) (and in shape) all the Thurber Women you had ever seen, and yet withal this both young and pretty, damnedest combo since Victoria Woodhull and Commodore Vanderbilt—no: damneder, because them two were two and not one. Cornelia.

Weighted down with masks, dare I stalk naked and alone? How can I when I observe with terror and with disbelief that in little less than six or seven years (afraid to calculate lest it come even closer [. . . turns no more his head/because he knows a frightful fiend/doth close behind him tread]) I shall be fifty years old. How can this be? *Half* a *cen*tury? The swift seasons have rolled (and *roll*ed and rolled), but where are the statelier chambers I had bid my soul build? From Dr. Romano's unwinking gaze at my asking this aloud, I assumed, too rightly in a trice I soon learned, that he had never heard of the nautilus as either a poem *or* a goddamn mollusk; when I put it to him thus, he countered, "Why are you always trying to put me down?" Is it *my* fault (I ask) that clinical psychologists can't write prescriptions even in states where chiropractors can? Or that nineteenth-century New England poets are no longer taught in our grammar schools . . .

Cornelia, or, Slowly the Sinewy Ivy Strangles the Sheltering Wall. A Novel in Two Volumes. By a Gentlewoman. So it doesn't strangle. Topples. All *right*, then. *Clutch*es. Now you're happy? I took her to Chinese restaurants and I took her to Armenian, Indonesian, Australasian, Franco-Swedish, Bosnian-and-Herzogovinian restaurants, I treated her to museums of Modern art and museums of Classical art and museums of Baroque and Rococo art and American Indian and of Outer Mongolian Art. I bought tickets for two to woodwind and percussion concerts and electronic insaneophonic concerts and the Grand Ballet de Montenegro, and what I couldn't think of to spend time and money and attention on her for her pleasure, she, I assure you, could. And whenever I suggested going to my apartment, she had to change her underwear: to her apartment, her landlady wouldn't allow visitors except between 1:00 and 1:15 P.M., with the doors open and the shades raised. Hotels? Bless you, there wasn't a hotel between the Battery and the Adirondack State Forest Reserve where she wouldn't go, so long as it had a bar or a restaurant or even a lounge where she could rest her feet. But the force of gravity kept her from going one story higher. And more than one skipped date was accounted for as anything from cyclical indisposition to fires in the B.M.T.—when, actually, as I learned not so damned long later, she was posing in skin and hairnet for a maker of what were not yet entitled (and never should have been) "underground movies"—or so she said he said. And thus it was, during one such wait and wait and wait, that I realized that I loved her, and when at last she appeared and gave me a sunny smile and asked if she could order something expensive from the pastry bar, I said, "Yes, yes, yes, I love you, I love you, Cornelia, come uptown with me," and she said, attention divided between me, the whipped-cream goody, and her reflection in the dark glasses of an enormous Spade, "All right," she said. "All right."

The girl with the green eyes I never saw again.

What song the sirens sang, who cares? Who gives a shit?

A year or two later she told me that, such was her chagrin to think that after she had in effect yielded me the full freedom of all her luscious limbs and instead of hurling her and me into a taxi I actually took us uptown on the subway, so almost she hadn't gone through with it. But only almost. Pale in the dim light she paused in the doorway after the ritual first visit by permission to the bathroom and I arose from single bed and went over and took her in my arms. "Cornelia. Cornelia. Cornelia."

"All right," she said. "All right."

Next day I suggested she stay. She shook her head. "I have to change my underwear," she said.

At that time I was writing mostly short stories. I wrote when the spirit moved me, and it moved me in curious ways and in waves and cycles and epicycles. It would be nice to think that it was love, love, love, and love alone which moved her at last, underwear and all, from her tiny room upstairs from the Kiev Bakery on what Bhoob Busby called East Filth Street and up and over into my three chambers in an antique apartment house abaft the ass-end of the largest unfinished cathedral in the world—moved by the spirit? moved by The Spirit, Wilco Robertson one day arose and called upon the Bishop and then and there offered himself as a candidate for the Priesthood. Did the Bishop say, "This is my beloved servant, Wilcox, in whom I am well pleased?" No, the Bishop didn't. What the Bishop did say was, "I will have my secretary make an appointment with the Diocesan Psychologist for a screening session." Wilco was moved by The Spirit not to go. "That man wouldn't have passed Our Lord," he said to me afterwards, half in gloom and half in wonder. And who knows, half in relief—

—but I'm afraid the thing that did the trick was Cornelia's discovery that nobody was going to wake her up at seven in the morning or ask her to retire before midnight or indeed to keep any other stated schedule. Wind in the willows, bow down your harps. Would we marry? We would.

We called up our mothers to inform them. "You're kidding!" hers cried. "Well . . . you're a big boy now . . ." said mine.

"So she's making an honest woman of you," said Wilco. And Edward? He smiled. Goddamn him. He smiled. He only smiled. Edward smiled.

But by now you have of course guessed all, the All of all in All, It is I who am Edward, I who am Azriel, I am Wilcox, I am Smith, I am Sim, and I am Susanna and Sarah, too; I am the steward upon the train, I am Mathias and I am myself. I am the stag on a hundred hills; I am the slayer and the slain.

Afterword for The Redward Edward Papers

The piece which you have just read (I hope that you have anyway read it and have not been indulging in selective skipping) is perhaps the oddest, as well as the longest, to appear in this volume. So perhaps it deserves some special attention by way of Afterword. I cannot

point to any particular flash of inspiration. After thirty-
odd years as a professional writer (and they have been
very odd years indeed), I no longer can recall in every
case just what the original inspiration was for every story
I have written. *"Where do you get your ideas from?"* A
gentleman once asked me this in such flattering tones that
I gave him, free, a five-minute discourse explaining where
I get my ideas from (more succinctly: from everywhere).
And he next asked, *"Yes, but where did you get the idea
for 'A Canticle for Leibowitz'?"*—a good story, and one
which, as it happens, I did not write, as it had already
been written by Mr. Walter Miller, Jr. It is no use, then,
asking where I got the idea for *The Redward Edward
Papers.* Oblivion hath blindly scattered her poppy. I will
say that several parts of it are drawn from the life. My
own life, that is. But you would be unwise to draw particular inferences from particular passages. There is a river
in Macedon and a river in Wales, as Falstaff reminds us:
but Theocritus I think it was who pointed out that no
man ever bathes twice in the same river. Be it where it
may.

If it be the same river.

When this was first written, my then-agent wrote to me
of a certain character, "-------- is Fletcher Pratt, isn't he?"
And perhaps still thinks that -------- *is* Fletcher Pratt. The
fact is that -------- is *not* Fletcher Pratt. I had never met
Fletcher Pratt, we had never been in touch with each
other at any time, I had to be sure heard of him and to be
sure I had read him: that was all. Absolutely all. More to
my knowledge of him than this, there hardly was. How,
then, to explain the fact that someone who had known
him personally was ready to believe that he appears in
this story as a character? You may call it, if you like, Coincidence. You may, if you like instead, say that something had filtered into my mind from the Universal

Aether. Or the Akashic Records. Similar similarities have been known to happen. Ask any writer.

The Mexican railroad in the story may indeed be based on an actual railroad which I had ridden in Mexico, and it may indeed be based upon some dreams of railroads which I have had, and which have nothing to do with Mexico. Randall Garrett has said, elsewhere, "We write ourselves into our stories." True. And often we write our dreams, our visions, our fancies, our hopes (lost and found) (and forlorn) as well. And often indeed we write that which we do not know at all. For instance—

Many years ago I sat down and wrote a certain story entitled "Now Let Us Sleep." It appeared in *Venture*, the science fiction magazine of that name. Simultaneously (do you understand what I am telling you? *Simultaneously!*) there appeared in *Fantastic Universe* magazine a story the title of which I do not recall and which was written by Mr. Tom Shaara. The theme (it was a fairly unusual theme) was identical. And, not only that, it contained eight identical scenes! I had never met Mr. Tom Shaara. I had never been in touch with him. I knew nothing, really, about him, other than that we were both writers. He did not know of my story and I did not know of his story, and yet it might be said that in effect we had each and both written the same story!

This is how it sometimes happens. Luckily, seldom.

If, therefore, on reading *The Redward Edward Papers*, you may think that you recognize some person or some scene, I can think of no better reply to you than that of Oliver Cromwell to the Scottish Independents: *"I beseech you, brethren, in the bowels of Christ, consider that you may be mistaken."*

Afterword to Entire Book

Amy Lowell, who wrote poetry, also—once—wrote a letter to George Antheil, who wrote music. *"Do not think that to be different and queer is necessarily to show originality,"* she cautioned him. *"Do not be afraid of the old any more than you are of the new. Be yourself! The bizarre may be enormously original, or it may be simply the weakness of a personality not strong enough to find its own idiom . . ."*

I am not a musicologer and cannot say if Antheil heeded her advice, or, if any, how much. Still, it rings a bit oddly in the ear—this, from a woman who, in an age when it was daring for a woman to smoke cigarettes, smoked cigars! (They were, however, on the lines of cigarillos, not, as legends say, great huge torpedoes.) But it is an interesting turn or twist on what one might think would be the likelier text: *The conventional,* she might have said instead, *may be enormously useful, or it may be* (and here I pick up Miss Lowell's very words) *simply the weakness of a personality not strong enough to find its own idiom.* This is more, I think, what one would have expected her to say. It is as true as what she did say. Why did she—whose poetry was after all not all that conventional in its own early day—why *did* she say it, *that*, then? Because, I suppose, George Antheil was chiefly known then, as I suppose he is chiefly known now, as the composer of what is sometimes called "experimental" music.

At what point a style ceases to be an experiment, it is perhaps hard to say.

"Be yourself!" she, Amy Lowell, said to him, George Antheil. Advice given by many to many, and still usually good advice. Here is José Ortega y Gasset: *"Heroism is the will to be oneself. We come into this world to play a part for which neither script nor role has been established. It is for us to compose and act out the drama of our existence. No one else can or should do this for us."* Here I pause. Am I about to begin a discourse on The Writer as Hero? I had better not. Besides, the stage is after all not exactly empty. Others there are who speak and move about on it. A certain amount of co-ordination is at least necessary. A writer may invent his own language and write in it to the exclusion of any other: but unless he provides a translation we will know nothing of the story, even though we may be much moved by the majestic cadences of the invented idiom. If, that is, it has majestic cadences. And if one is moved by such. There may still be audiences who drop into raptures at the sound of the dramatic verse of Racine, Molière: permit me, however, to doubt it.

Permit me, furthermore, to doubt the absolute correctness of the statement of Don José Ortega, a philosopher whom I hold in general respect, as, in general, I do all philosophers (including, and why not? holders of that very interesting degree, Ph.C., meaning, and I kid you not, *Philosopher of Chiropractic*). Is it not very often indeed that we are asked, demanded, to play a part or parts for which both script and role have been established? Is this not exactly what every religious, every political, every social and economic rule and school—is this not just what each one demands of us? And yet I do not wish to discard Don Ortega's statement *in toto*, no. I would go on to his third sentence, inserting . . . somewhere . . . the one word *nevertheless;* as it might be, *"It is for us* nevertheless *to compose and act out the drama of our existence . . ."* And, hark, the echo answers, the echo of his first sentence: *"Heroism is the will to be oneself . . ."* and close upon it are the words of Vincent Sheean, saying, *"We have come to see the hero as a man simply trying to become what he conceives himself to be."*

Now, not every man is a hero, not every man is a writer, not every writer is a man. Taking into account the annoying and nowadays perplexing overpreciseness, sexually, of many of the nouns and pronouns of the English language, let us substitute *writer* for *hero.* And look at some of those sentences once again. Here is one person called The Writer, in a world which usually expects from The Writer, in that one's Writing, a pattern and a part and a role conformed to; is it not so? Sometimes The Writer is satisfied, is indeed happy to oblige. Sometimes The Writer is unhappy at being unable to; sometimes The Writer is happy not to. Sometimes, fairly rarely, The Writer is able from the start, or almost so, to create for that Writer a different part, pattern, role—and succeed. Such a one, in our time, was Ernest Hemingway; he succeeded, in his role of Innovator, almost immediately. Ironically, and, I am afraid, undoubtedly,* his Innovation was based upon the Innovation of Gertrude Stein: who did not at all succeed at once. She laid it on thick, she laid it on far too thick, so that so thick are the Writings in which she most tried to compose and act out her own drama that they remain obscured, closed—Then came Hemingway, snatched from the treasure pile just enough dragon gold to light his own audacious way. Awestruck,—after a first moment or two of astonishment,—surprise, we fol-

---

* I am aware that here I poke my augurial staff into the nest of literary wasps . . . "hornets," rather, I hasten to say. *Fiat justifia, ruant coeli.*

lowed him. Once again the dragon was alone in her too-enchanted cave, and long she pondered. Perhaps some echo reached her there, perhaps the very words of another woman, also a Writer: *Do not be afraid of the old any more than you are of the new.* And then she wrote: *The Autobiography of Alice B. Toklas,* and then she wrote: *Everybody's Autobiography:* and if anyone has read Gertrude (as distinct from having read *of* Gertrude), the chances are that these are what one has read: distinctive, enchanting, yet not so distinctive that the enchantment fails.

Amy Lowell, Ernest Hemingway, Gertrude Stein, in no case is The Writer hid behind The Writing. Each was a personality in her and his own way and day; it is true, is it not, that the personalities are known to millions who do not know The Writings: Amy in her *pince-nez* there on the stone fence smoking her segar, Ernest with his rifle and his beard and his dead animal, Gertrude with her mannish haircut as massive as a monument, and unmistakable behind her is sweet Alice with her horrid mustache. Giants in the earth. Giants in the earth. Gone, gone, the old familiar faces.

Onward.

Here is Edmund Wilson, he says that Evelyn Waugh's *Put Out More Flags* ". . . *is not a piece of propaganda, it is the satisfying expression of an artist, whose personal pattern of feeling no formula will ever fit, whether political, social, or moral.*"

Has The Writer, The Artist, then, the right to personal expressions of feelings without regard to current formulas of political, social, moral feeling? Absolutely. Certainly. Need you ask? Do you wish a touchstone? This is it. Apply it to any society—Roman Catholic Ireland, State Lutheran Iceland, Communist China (*anti*Communist

China, for that matter), Secular Protestant America;
Wherever.

Onward.

Has The Writer also the right to personal expression in
writing without regard to current *literary* formulas?
Again: yes. Of course. And if the publisher and or the
public does not like it, The Writer may publish it himself,
herself, oneself, or guard it in a cave: or both: or maybe
try something else, if a something else can be found. It is
certainly very odd how many baroque little tyrannies in
the past functioned also as patrons of the arts, as com-
pared to our own Great Republic. James Thurber has
preserved for us the comment of the Dean of the College
of Liberal Arts at the University of Ohio the year the
State Legislature passed his school by without a penny
and paused to bestow great bounty (in the form of great
barns) upon the College of Agriculture: *"Millions for ma-
nure, and not one cent for literature."* Magnificent lament.
The Writer, The Artist: one ignores this imbalance at
one's peril. The only kind of property, be it remembered,
whose title is extinguished by mere passage of time, is
property in art and invention.

Those who have grown gray at the tablet and the style
will not need to be told. For others: there is still room to
pause, to go elsewhere; *"the wheels are to turn and the
dry fields burn,"* sang Sydney Lanier. He consumed himself in his singing as he was himself consumed in a known
fixed measure of time.

—a known fixed measure of time. Most of us can only
conjecture.

*"It was not by gentle sweetness and self-abnegation
that order was brought out of chaos; it was by strict
method, by stern discipline, by rigid attention to detail,
by ceaseless labour, by the fixed determination of an in-*
I 23 *domitable will."* Thus did Lytton Strachey write about

Florence Nightingale; thus might any of us write about Lytton Strachey. If any Writer who does not achieve instant success through sloppy ease (some do) is not willing to accommodate to such a discipline, then that one had better go to the Middle West and open a paint factory, writing—if one *must* write—for a hobby, in spare time. And if this, or its equivalent, is not available, be prepared, O my brothers and my sisters, to suffer and to die.

We must in any event suffer and die. The question is not, Are we to suffer and die? The question is, Having suffered and having died, what have we left behind us? If my Reader is also a Writer and if my Reader's ideal answer to this last question is something along the lines of, "A nice, sizable estate in blue-chip stocks and tax-exempt bonds," my Reader may skip my last paragraph, coming round the bend fast; it is by Sybille Bedford, and it is found in a tribute to *Titania*, as Parmenia Migel called Isak (born Karen) Dinesen, in her biography; Tania is described as one of

> . . . *that small band of independent writers who dared to write as they please, and as they must, little, early, late; the grand and lonely ones who had the courage and the genius to keep—at their cost—to their vision and eccentric disciplines . . . without regard to fashion, the mainstream and the time, not because they were dilletantes but because they were artists.*